M000190340

A DIFFERENT WAY TO DIE

ALSO BY ROBERT LANE

A DIFFERENT WAY TO DIE

A JAKE TRAVIS NOVEL

ROBERT LANE

Copyright © 2021 Robert Lane

All rights reserved.

ISBN: 978-1-7322945-3-0

Mason Alley Publishing, Saint Pete Beach, Florida

All rights reserved. No part of this book may be reproduced, scanned, or distributed in any print or electronic form without the author's permission.

This is a work of fiction. While some incidents of this story may appear to be true and factual, their relation to each other, and implications derived from their occurrences, is strictly the product of the author's imagination. Names, characters, places, and incidents either are the product of the author's imagination or are used fictitiously. Any resemblance to actual persons (living or dead), localities, companies, organizations, and events is entirely coincidental.

Cover design by James T. Egin, Bookfly Design

"Look well into thyself; there is a source of strength which will always spring up . . ."

—Marcus Aurelius

A DIFFERENT WAY TO DIE

1

Twenty-four years ago

The detective with bushy hair stood at the shore letting his eyes slide over the motionless water. He'd always been a man more comfortable with the void than with clutter.

He and his younger partner were at Midnight Cove, a mangrove-ringed inlet on the west coast of Florida. A solitary buoy in the water marked the spot where a majestic boat had floated. Fire ate the boat, and water swallowed the fire. The man who lived on the boat, and the man's boat, now belonged to the sea.

"Such a tragedy," the detective with the bushy hair said in a ministerial voice.

"You got that right," his younger partner said. "She was a 1958 Chris-Craft Constellation. Forty-two feet of wood and beam. They don't make them like that anymore."

The bushy-haired man considered his partner. He couldn't decide if the insensitivities bred by the job had stained the man, or if he inexcusably failed to grasp the situation. Oddly, and to his mild surprise, he didn't care.

"They do not," he said after a pause. "Now it's just another entry into Davy Jones's locker."

"What's a Monkee got to do with it?"

"It's a mythical sailor graveyard," the man with the bushy hair said. "Not 'Daydream Believer.'"

"Says who?"

"I think Daniel Defoe was the first to pen it."

"Danny who?"

"Defoe. He wrote *Robinson Crusoe*."

"Jesus, Harold. The shit you know. Lemme ask you—I heard you got a double major in philosophy and English, that true?"

"It is."

"The hell you wearing a badge for?"

"Lem*me* ask you something. How did he get to the shore?"

"He had a dinghy, but it went up in flames as well. Between the fire and the tide—it was hauling ass at one and a half knots —the whole kit and caboodle is halfway to Cancún by now. Only thing that stayed home were the dual Chrysler engines. The dive team says they went straight down. Why are you staring at the shore?"

"Looks like an easy swim," the detective with the bushy hair said.

"And then what? His car's still there. Woman next boat over said the vic—what was his name again?"

"Christopher Callaghan. Twenty-two years old."

"Right. She said double eleven was a loner. Took his dinghy to his car and back to the boat."

"What if Christopher decided to go for a night swim and leave his car?"

The younger detective let out a harrumph. "No one saw a creature climb out of the black lagoon and hail a cab. Besides, why torch your own boat? His canoe wasn't even insured. If there's no insurance fraud, then it was an accident."

"I might check it out anyway."

"Knock yourself out, champ. We located the next of kin, his mother. You want to come? It's always a gold-medal moment."

Had you been able to see the detective with the bushy hair's eyes, their inherent sadness would have shocked you. But he always wore sunglasses, even on a cloudy day. They were his Plexiglas shield.

"Wouldn't miss it for the world," he said.

As they approached the front door of Elaine Callaghan's house, he took those sunglasses off. He folded them and placed them deliberately in the inside pocket of his suit. He rang the doorbell. He took a step forward, not backward.

Elaine Callaghan crumbled before he stepped over the threshold. But the detective with the bushy hair was ready. He caught her and held her tight. He rocked her gently and whispered words we do not know while his partner shifted his weight from one foot to another, and Elaine Callaghan wailed the sound of a mortally wounded animal.

2

Yankee Conrad IV sat in a restaurant on Beach Drive in downtown Saint Petersburg, Florida. He draped one graceful leg over the other. His bow tie was robin's-egg blue, his suit Tom Wolfe white, his pants disturbingly wrinkle-free. An exceptionally tall and erect man, his head perched over the lunchtime crowd like a conductor searching for the horn section of his orchestra. He exuded an unpretentious and natural gravitas, as if his comportment had accompanied him at birth. Despite the Florida summer air that burned with fever, I would have preferred to be outside under an umbrella, but Yankee Conrad had made the reservation and so we sat inside where it was cool and dark and comfortable.

We discussed a recent trip I'd taken on his behalf to Switzerland, although I doubted that was the reason he had extended the luncheon invitation. I inquired if Elizabeth Walker's affairs needed further attention—my trip over the pond had been to tie up loose ends regarding her estate. He indicated that her file was closed and then took a sip of coffee. Someday, someone would calmly sit across from another person and—as a prelude to a sip of coffee—indicate my file was closed.

I knew little about the man. My sole trip to his office had been consumed with our discussion regarding the estate of Elizabeth Walker. I did recall his snarly secretary. We put people in slots, and for some puzzling reason, I couldn't categorize her. Such relationships are condemned to purgatory unless serendipitously clarified. So it would be with Ms. Snarly.

"Recruitment is always a delicate operation," he replied after I asked him how his businesses were doing. His eyes crested the rim of his coffee mug.

"Recruitment?"

"I'd like you to revisit an old case. A missing person."

The waiter dropped off our food, disrupting the flow of conversation. Yankee Conrad, without even a glance at the menu, had ordered pompano, the daily catch. He had explained in detail how he wished it to be prepared. I'd felt a tad common ordering a cheeseburger, but my five-mile predawn run had been followed by a thirty-minute date with my punching bag. I'd been working on my vertical roundhouse kick, and failed again at striking the red X. You never know when a well-placed vertical roundhouse kick will come in handy.

"How long?" I asked after the waiter left.

"Pardon?"

"How long has she/he been missing?"

"He. Twenty-four years."

"What happened to the last two decades?"

He dabbed his mouth with the white cloth napkin, folded it —perhaps neater than he'd found it—and placed it to the right of his plate.

"He perished in a boat fire. His remains were never found, although that was not surprising. His boat was moored in a bay, and there was an unusually strong outgoing tide that night."

"No teeth? Bones?"

"Nothing. The police investigated. But with no body, no

known enemies, no apparent conflicts, we were left with little to investigate."

"We?"

"I was involved."

"In what manner?"

"He was my nephew. The police kept me apprised."

"I'm sorry for your loss."

"Thank you. We were quite close."

When we'd first met, Yankee Conrad displayed encompassing knowledge of my past, although his source remained a mystery. He impressed me as a well-connected man of exemplary character. A good man to have in your corner. And like a vertical roundhouse kick, you never know when such a man will come in handy.

His entry into my life was well timed.

My partner, Garrett Demarcus, and I had performed contract work for our former commanding officer, Colonel Janssen, starting a year after our discharge from the army. But the moral ambiguities of my work had disfigured my naive intentions. I'd grown weary of toting a gun and had fallen victim to the unintended consequences such a weapon is prone to produce. I made the decision, for Garrett and myself, to disengage from Janssen. But while working at the church's thrift store and serving as the de facto property manager at Harbor House—a shelter facility that my neighbor Morgan and I operate—kept me busy, they left a hole. Yankee Conrad had asked if he could call me from time to time. I'd said yes. A wise bellman, upon noticing my forlornness in leaving his grand hotel, had once told me, "If you never check out, you can never check in."

"Why now?" I asked.

His chest rose and fell, although he was such a thin man it was more like a letter envelope expanding and contracting. "Christopher's mother, my sister Elaine, and I were content to accept that Christopher had perished in the flames. A few days ago, my sister received this."

He reached into a wizened leather satchel and placed a medallion on the table.

"May I?"

"I had it dusted for prints. There were none."

I pushed my plate to the side and picked up the medallion. The waiter came by and asked if we left room for dessert, a tired line that he gave his best shot. Yankee Conrad politely dismissed the question and handed the waiter a credit card.

The medallion was tarnished copper with a thin leather strap looped through a hole at the top. Inscribed on the flat surface was *Saint Christina be my Guide.*

"The female saint of mariners," I said, turning it in my hand, feeling its texture with my fingertips.

"It belonged to Christopher. A gift from me, actually. His initials are on the back. Along with the medallion was a proposition that in exchange for five hundred thousand dollars, we will be told what really happened to him. But the money comes first."

I handed him the medallion. "And we don't negotiate with blackmailers."

"We do not."

"You suspect foul play?"

"I suspect a sham."

"But?"

"One cannot be sure."

"He gave the medallion away," I said. "And someone's trying to cash in on it. They have no information, but you don't know that, so you pay."

"That is the likely scenario, although I would urge you to start with no expectations or prejudices."

"It does me, nor your wallet, any good to sweep things

under the rug and then pay me to find the dirt. What doubts have you been harboring?"

His flat look held neither condemnation nor approval. He sucked in his cheeks, further collapsing his skeletal face.

"My sister is not well. Her mind has become unmoored, and I am fearful that she is drifting away at an accelerating pace."

"I'm sorry, as well, to hear that," I said, wondering in what manner that addressed my question.

"We were, unlike her son and I, never close."

"And yet?"

"If my sister's memory is to be of any assistance, then time is a factor. But more importantly, I wish to protect her from those who may seek to use her weakness for monetary gain."

"Your doubts?" I said, circling back to my original question.

The waiter presented the settled bill along with Yankee Conrad's credit card. He thanked us for the opportunity to allow him to serve us—always a nice line and, in this instance, delivered with uncommon sincerity. As Yankee Conrad, with matched politeness, informed the waiter that we appreciated his time, my eyes wandered. A poised older couple had taken a table next to us, and the woman ordered a glass of red wine. Few people drink red wine with lunch. What grand hotels had she checked in and out of? What lessons could she impart to me?

"They never found the body," Yankee Conrad said, reining in my wanderlust thoughts. "I know of no reason for him to have faked his death, nor anyone who would have wanted to cause him harm. Perhaps I was not as thorough as I should have been."

"And if it's a hoax?" I said.

"Then you've done your job. But I need to be certain. There is a detective who worked the case. He will be your first stop."

"What about your sister?"

"I will notify her to expect you."

"His father?"

He hesitated, but then, as if aware of his gap, said, "I lost track of him years ago. Elaine and he divorced while Christopher was still in school. He worked, at least during that tenure, for a government intelligence agency."

"What are the particulars of the demand?"

"A wire transfer to an offshore account. After that, information to follow. While it has been some years, I am most eager to wrap this up. I assume you can grant this matter your undivided attention."

"Front and center."

He gave me contact information, and we headed outside. He faced me before we parted in separate directions.

"I urge you to start with a clean slate. And Mr. Travis?"

I'd given up having him address me by my first name.

"Yes?" I said, for he'd caught me somewhat distracted. I'd gotten stuck on his earlier comment that his initial investigation was not as thorough as it should have been. Above all, Yankee Conrad exuded thoroughness.

"I ask you to always act in my family's best interest. To treat all information with utmost confidentiality."

"You have my word."

Those were easy words to say, but hard words to keep.

3

Harold Hendren, the detective who had investigated the case nearly a quarter of a century ago, lived a mile inland from my house.

We agreed to meet for drinks at Hurricane's rooftop overlooking the Gulf of Mexico. I arrived first and secured a table in the shade. The late afternoon sky struggled to hold its colors as the sun slipped behind dark clouds with slanting battleship-gray curtains of rain far out on the Gulf. Below me, beach walkers waded in the salty warm water. A guitar player strummed a tune that was blurred by the bar's own speakers. Like a needle that kept dropping at the beginning of the same album over and over, the bar had been circulating a seventies playlist since the day it opened.

A floppy man with a wrinkled shirt hanging over cargo shorts spotted me from the top of the steps. I raised my finger and he nodded. He stopped by the bar to collect a beer, laughed with the biblically bearded bartender, and then joined me at the table. We introduced ourselves, and I thanked him for taking the time to meet with me.

"No inconvenience at all." Hendren tilted his head toward

the Gulf. "The voice of the sea speaks to the soul. I understand the victim's family is engaging you?"

I'd given him the details on the phone.

"That's correct," I said.

Hendren still had every strand of hair from the day he flashed a smile for his high school graduation picture. If he'd ever had a hairbrush, he'd either lost it or forgotten what end to use. He kept his sunglasses on, shielding his thoughts from the world, or the world from his thoughts—your pick.

"Do you remember the case?" I asked him.

He grunted. "You remember the ones you lost more than the ones you won. Understand?"

"I do."

"You ex-law?"

"Ex-army."

He arched his thick eyebrows. "You do this type of work before?"

"What type is that?"

He bobbed his head. "I hear you. Christopher Callaghan. Yeah, I remember. He lived on a Chris-Craft. Double CCs all around. Gorgeous old boat. But she flamed out like dry sticks soaked in kerosene. A fast tide mopped the deck."

"The official verdict?"

"Death by fire. It was cold that night. The boat had a generator for a heater. Consensus was that a bad wire sparked a fire. Next boat over saw it erupt in flames."

"The guy in the next boat over, how far away was he?"

"She. Name was—I don't have it. One of those words that you don't think of being a name, but it works, you know? Her boat was moored about a hundred yards north. She called the fire department. Course, it wasn't their jurisdiction. The call gets routed to the Coast Guard—not their playground, either —and finally to the Pinellas Sheriff's Department. Problem is, response time on sea is not exactly like barreling down 275.

By the time their boat got out there, there was nothing to get to."

"But you were called in."

"We were. The vic listed a house as his address. The woman in the nearby boat—Sundown, that was her name. Funny how memory works. Sundown said there was a man who lived aboard, and he kept his car on the shore. The car was still there."

"Any other boats anchored in the vicinity?"

He scratched the rim of his nostril. "Just those two. She told us that night they waved from across the water."

I asked him about potential romantic involvement.

He nodded. "We checked. She had a boyfriend. We didn't sense anything between Sundown and Mr. Callaghan. She claimed they were just casual friends. That she would occasionally putter over to his boat and vice versa, but not that often."

"Did you question her boyfriend?"

Hendren landed a disapproving look. "He wasn't there that night. Rock-solid alibi. Turns out he had more than one bunkmate."

"Did Sundown know about that?"

He squinted his eyes at me. "You're taxing my mind. I don't recall if I thought it necessary to share that with her. That wasn't the way I played."

Hendren explained how he and his partner had little to investigate. There was no building. No fingerprints. They broke the news to Elaine, Yankee Conrad's sister.

"She took it hard," he said. He took a swig of beer, his sunglassed face wandering over the Gulf. "I remember holding her just to keep her from falling down. He was her only child. Parents divorced. I mean it was never a part of the job anyone enjoyed, but it had to be done, and you were no good if you didn't have the guts to do it. But man oh man." He shook his head. "She just wailed. A terrible, caterwauling sound."

He took off his shades and rested his sullen eyes on mine. He seemed a man immensely comfortable with himself.

"I majored in philosophy in college," he said. "I thought it would be good to be in the thick of it, not just ponder it all. I got what I had coming."

He paused, creating a silence best left to itself.

"We checked out his car," he said, his voice perking up. "It was locked, and there was a path to a stake where he tied his dinghy. So nothing there, right? But I hiked the shore and found another set of tracks. They were coming out of the water —get it? No tracks going in, just out."

"Whoever made them could have gone in someplace else."

"Could, but I never found any tracks going just into the water, only out. The tide was running two and a half feet that day. So the tracks I saw had to be made during the period of the fire."

"Where did they lead to?"

"Nowhere, man. Just like the song."

"Your theory?"

He shrugged. "Theory dreary, that's all I got after mulling it over for years. Take your pick; someone was waiting for Mr. Callaghan on his boat. They killed him, torched the boat, jumped overboard, and swam to shore where a car picked him up."

"Or?"

He sucked in his left cheek."I know where you're going. He blazes his boat, slips into the water, and swims to shore."

"His boat wasn't insured."

"Bingo. It only fits if there was money motivation. But we couldn't find any motivation. Not many people knew him. Those who did liked him well enough."

I asked him about Chris's social security number and charge cards.

"Oh, the man's dead in that sense. We checked every few

years. He's gone." He dipped his head at my bottle. "Want another?"

"I got it."

I went to the bar and ordered two beers. A gust of cool wind swept in from the edge of a storm sliding to the south. It brushed me with a desperate eagerness. When I returned to the table, Hendren had his wallet out.

"It's on me," I clarified.

"I appreciate that. But I've got something I want to show you."

He fidgeted and brought out a scrap piece of paper. "The woman, Sundown, who lived on the boat next to him? This was her boat's registration number. Although now, looking at it, I can't tell whether that's an eight or a nine. I don't know if you can even find her. But I always felt she was holding something back."

"How so?"

He took a sip of cold beer and then placed the bottle on the cardboard coaster.

"There are two things that the recipient of bad news goes through. First is shock, and then grief. Sundown did the shock part fine, but the grief? When we told her we feared he burned to death and went down with the ship, her reaction lacked authenticity."

"You mentioned that they weren't particularly close."

"Correct. So it made it hard to judge her. But what I'm saying is she was confused on how to act. Maybe it was just me, but I can't deny what I felt."

He handed me the piece of paper. It contained a series of numbers, the boat's registration that would have been placed on both sides of the bow.

"It's nice here," he said. "I lost my wife two years ago today." His lips turned down, and his face took on a sadness that encompassed every philosophy he had ever known. "One day she just dropped. Brain aneurism. Day before? We thought about walking on the beach, but she was busy, wanted to buy presents for a grandkid's birthday, even though it was still two weeks away. We never took that last walk. Never knew it was our last chance."

"I'm sorry for your loss." I'd been saying that a lot recently.

He puffed out his cheeks. "I've made peace with it. Had she known it was her last day?—I think she would have been glad to have spent it shopping for a grandchild's birthday present. You married?"

"I am."

"Kids?"

"One. Little girl."

We were quiet for a few beats, the conversation at a crossroads. He asked that I keep him in the loop. We headed for the stairs, taking the winding metal steps down the three levels to the ground. He turned to me when we realized our cars were in opposite directions.

"There was a stiff breeze that night," he said. "Perfect time to incinerate a boat."

"If you had to put money down?"

"Hard to believe the flames spread so fast that he couldn't get above board. Problem is, the entire murder scene ceased to exist. We're not just talking no body, we're talking no scene. *That* is one perfect murder."

4

The tourist sailboat *Magic* slid by the end of my dock on Boca Ciega Bay off Pass-a-Grille Beach. Its billowed canvas inhaled the wind, and the sun glittered the water like silver coins. A woman stood on the aft deck, her long dress flowing in the breeze. She held her head high, her hair shielding her face. Lightning flashed from the east, threading the sky with electricity. The paint-by-number scene was the same every summer night, but the flowing dress, the windswept hair, the face I would never see—those marked the day.

Kathleen, my wife, sat next to me on our screened porch, proofing an article she'd been laboring on—something about the role of Southern literature during the civil rights movement, Hadley III, our cat, stared at a gecko on the other side of the screen, and Joy, our daughter, rocked in the corner in her bucket swing playing with colored beads. On the other side of the screen, Morgan grilled asparagus. I took a sip of whiskey and sat straighter in the chair, gathering the moment in my arms, alert to any intruder encroaching upon my peaceable kingdom.

Kathleen plopped her papers on the glass table that the

summer humidity smudged every day, challenging my obsession to keep things ordered and neat.

"If I have to discuss *Mockingbird* one more time, I might implode," she said. Kathleen—Dr. Rowe to her students— taught English at a college a few miles from our house.

"I thought that was high school material."

"No longer. For our purposes it's outdated social conscience that romanticizes the status quo of the time. Who's your first stop?"

I'd filled everyone in on my conversations, although neither Joy nor Hadley III showed any interest.

"I'm visiting Elaine, Christopher's mother." I shot a glance at Morgan. "Like to tag along?"

"Be happy to," he said, rotating the asparagus.

"She suffers from dementia," I added.

"How far down the happy river is she?" Kathleen said.

"Her brother indicated she's in the rapids."

She yawned. "Maybe that's better than a lazy trip."

Morgan plated the asparagus aside sea trout that I'd caught off the end of the dock when the tide was running out to the Gulf at five thirty that morning. I reached over and poured more red wine into Morgan's glass. I started to do the same to Kathleen's.

"I'm good," she said.

I continued my pour. "Now you're better."

"We're supposed to be drinking less, remember?"

"How do you feel about that?"

She took a healthy sip. "Not particularly committed."

Morgan said, "Just because she has dementia doesn't negate her as a reliable witness of past events."

"True," Kathleen said. "She could easily recall events from twenty years ago more accurately than last week's schedule. Don't be in a hurry to judge her."

"I won't."

In a peachy southern drawl, which she occasionally paraded out, she said, "Darlin', you were *born* in a hurry."

I put some fish on the floor. Hadley III scrunched her paws under her and, like the furry grand dame she was, nibbled it with no sense of urgency. The mellow B side of Dusty Springfield's *Dusty . . . Definitely* dropped on the turntable of the 1962 floor-model Magnavox. The album was not released in the United States until Dusty's death, thirty-one years after she cut the record. I thought of going thirty-one years without access to such a soulful rendition of songs and then wondered why anyone would want to murder Christopher Callaghan. And while I had every reason to believe that he'd perished as an innocent victim of a boat fire, I could not shake Detective Harold Hendren's remark: the perfect murder. No crime scene. No body.

Perfection, revisited decades later, renders a fuller appreciation of the original act.

5

Elaine Callaghan, Conrad Yankee's sister, lived in a graciously maintained old-money house a few blocks north of downtown Saint Petersburg. A street where the homes vied to out-majestic each other with their wide front porches, gated yards, and second-floor balconies from which to peer down upon the pedestrian world. I parked on the shaded brick street, as another car was in her driveway.

A pleasant woman who filled the threshold answered the door. She greeted us and introduced herself as Angie, Elaine's live-in companion. She had curly dark hair, and her face was smooth and golden brown.

"Welcome, Mr. Travis. Mr. Conrad said you'd be payin' us a visit."

"Please call me Jake."

"That'll be fine, Mr. Travis."

Morgan thrust out his hand. "Mr. Morgan."

She shook his hand. "Ms. Angie." She paused and then wrapped thick fingers of her other hand around Morgan's. "The soul of the ocean is in your eyes. The salt of the sea is in your blood."

Wonderful. Yankee Conrad's sister suffered from dementia, and it appeared as if her live-in help rode the sidecar.

"I grew up on a sailboat," Morgan admitted.

"That is why you keep the moon so close to you."

Morgan reached inside his shirt with his free hand. He withdrew a moon talisman around his neck. It never left his body. "It was a gift from my mother."

"Come. Allow me to introduce you to Ms. Elaine."

The two of them padded off, leaving me to wonder if Voodoo Angie had gotten lucky or somehow she'd seen the moon talisman through Morgan's shirt. I followed them into a house that reflected a life that had largely exhausted itself. Neatly arranged furniture faced each other like lonely girls at a dance, their unindented pillows vying and begging for attention. A tambour-style mantel clock measured the distance from what used to be. An odor hung in the air, time layered the walls like wallpaper. The odor—there was something else, but I couldn't place it. I'll come back to it later. A bookcase of meticulously aligned books anchored one wall, not a single book out of formation, daring to draw attention to itself. Soundless pictures cluttered polished end tables.

Not all pictures are soundless—only the ones that contain the dead.

The pictures were of Christopher, posed like a virtual Adonis, with his mother in exotic places. Mountains. Beaches. A rooftop bar set against a magenta sky. Other pictures were of the two of them with other people, wine bottles cluttering the tables and exuberant smiles cluttering their faces. More than mother and son, they looked like good friends. They were both attractive—that breed of photogenic people that thrilled every camera pointed in their direction. There appeared to be little age difference between them. At least for one-four-hundredths of a second, life was good.

We exited the rear door onto a covered patio. The smoky

beat of music curved from a speaker on a wrought-iron table. A woman was hunched over a patch of flowers. She put down a trowel, stood, shed her gardening gloves, and strolled over to us.

"Ms. Elaine," Angie said. "This is Mr. Travis and Mr. Morgan. Remember your brother told us about them? They are here to celebrate the life of Christopher."

Her strawberry-blonde hair, although not long, was tied behind her neck. She wore purple shorts, a gaping white shirt, and sandals. Elaine Callaghan expected you to look at her, and you could not help but oblige. And while age had yet to vandalize her body, cruelly feasting upon her mind first, her well-tended eyes gave her away. Despite stenciled eyebrows and fake eyelashes, her vanity desk effort could not hide her limpid gaze.

"Which one of you is the sleuth Yankee hired?" she asked. She cocked her head and trailed a finger up her neck and behind her ear, sensualized by her own touch.

I raised my hand.

"Are you good?" she demanded of me.

"Pardon?"

"Are you good at what you do? It seemed simple enough."

"I am."

"Then you will find my Christopher. His birthday is in three months. It would be nice if he were home for it."

"I will do my best, Ms. Callaghan, to find out what happened that night."

"That is not your job. My brother gave you his medallion. That proves he is alive. You are to find him and bring him back."

"Yes, ma'am."

"Don't patronize me. Do you think my son is dead?"

"I don't assume—"

"The answer is no. If you do not start with that presumption, then Yankee is wasting his dollars on you." She flashed her eyes to Morgan and then turned to Angie. "Perhaps some short-bread cookies would be nice for our company."

Angie lumbered into the house, and Elaine stepped closer to Morgan. She placed her hand on his chest above his open collar, and then brought it up the right side of his neck, stopping there.

"I haven't seen you for a while," she said.

Morgan cut me a look and then shifted his eyes confidently back to Elaine.

"We've never met, Ms. Callaghan."

"Pity." She lowered her hand and fondled his moon talisman. "There's still time, isn't there?"

I was eager to discover if she could be any help or if she and Angie were both too far down Kathleen's happy river—not to mention weirdly captivated with Morgan and his moon talisman—to be of any help.

"I have a few questions I'd like to ask you."

She stepped away from Morgan. "I'm sure you do. Please, have a seat." As I pulled back a chair at a round table, she added, "Mr. Travis?"

"Yes?"

Her eyes jumped to life. She flashed them between Morgan and me. "I'm just foolin' with you boys," she said. "You two look like shriveled roosters in a henhouse. I'm sure Yankee told you I was suffering from dementia, or perhaps he coined a more appropriate word—after all, we live in such a sensitive era. One must never let the great Yankee Conrad down. You haven't worked for him long, have you?"

"I'm not sure I work for—"

"You do, you haven't, and you'll learn. He's using you. You can count on that."

"I don't—"

"My brother never imagined a life with the word 'fun' in it.

22

He is cursed with the heaviness of each passing moment. The solemnity of the seconds."

I considered asking what I would learn, or be used for, but dismissed her comments. Over shortbread cookies that dissolved in my mouth, she told us how the police had knocked on her door and how a tall detective with hair to die for had supported her while his pinch-faced partner stood stupidly off to the side. How she and Christopher, her only child, had traveled the world: Bangkok, London, Paris, Key West. "For two weeks every September we went to Portland Maine and ate cold-water lobster, drank even colder beer, and sailed Casco Bay, the damp breeze cooling our flushed faces." How Christopher's friends would join them and Elaine would pick up the checks. She spoke as if her life was a chapterless book.

"How long had your son lived on the boat?" I asked.

"The *Ms. Buckeye*. That was her name. One of our great-grandfathers—they get confusing after a while, all these people who are larger in death than they were in life—ran a freighter out of Cleveland before moving to Tampa. I don't know the date. Yankee always keeps track of that stuff as if he's Moses recording the holy words. As if nothing could be more important than so-and-so moved to Tampa in 1893—heaven forbid, not 1894. As if the measure of a person is her knowledge of her ancestors. For our purposes, he moved during what became known as the Gilded Age, although tell that to a Black sharecropper in Alabama.

"The Chris-Craft that Christopher lived on was bought nearly half a century later by my uncle, from the Cleveland bloodline, so there you go. *Ms. Buckeye*. If you learn one thing about my family, Mr. Travis, it is we are hopelessly stuck in Fitzgerald's boat. Especially Yankee. He thinks you can poke your finger in the air and touch yesterday."

"I find it works the other way," I said.

"Excuse me?"

"Yesterday pokes you."

She rolled her tongue over her lower lip, her eyes begging mine, but for what, I pretended not to know.

"How long did your son live on the *Ms. Buckeye*?" Morgan asked.

She looked at Morgan. "Have you ever run your hand over varnished mahogany?"

"I have."

"Mr. Morgan was raised on a sailboat," Angie interjected. She'd taken a seat behind us.

"Then you know," Elaine said to Morgan. "It's like caressing a satisfied lover." She flicked her eyes at me. "No poking about it at all." She focused again on Morgan. "Christopher lived on the *Ms. Buckeye* for a little over a year. He hadn't an enemy in the world. How long did you live on your boat?"

"Decades," Morgan said.

"And how would you describe such a life?"

"Enchanting."

Elaine reached across the table and touched him with a slim and delicate finger that showed no sign of recently being captive inside a purple-flowered gardening glove.

"Yes," she said, keeping her hand on Morgan's. "Enchanting. That *is* life, is it not?"

"And before he lived on the boat?" I asked.

"Why do you ask?" she snapped, irked that I'd interrupted her séance with Morgan. "He lived here, of course. This is his home. Would you like to see his room?"

She didn't wait for an answer but rose, shoulders back and her chest forward as if expecting someone to snap a picture of her. She waltzed into the front of her house, Morgan and I waltzing after her. We climbed the circular front steps, a worn flowered carpet runner in the middle with tarnished brass carpet rods. Elaine traced the wood banister with the tip of her finger as we followed her down a wide upstairs hall. Pictures of Elaine, Christopher, and his friends decorated the wall. They stood with arms tangled around each other like wild vines. We entered a front bedroom that faced the street. The view was partially blocked by an oak tree that owned the front yard.

The room looked like a dried flower, long past its glory but refusing to fall. A poster of Sinéad O'Connor's cover of the Prince song "Nothing Compares 2 U" hung over a bed that was tucked in tight. A bookshelf held books and CDs. *The Horse Whisperer, Hannibal*, Bryan Adams, Madonna.

"Angie changes the sheets every week," she said. "When he comes home, I want his room to be ready."

While I was searching for a comment, Morgan said, "I'm sure he'll appreciate what you're doing."

"Angie keeps the room nice, don't you think?"

"How long has Angie been with you?" I asked.

"Before Yankee sent her, it was all me. But it's a large house for one person to keep up."

I didn't bother to repeat my question. "Did the detectives search the room?"

She stepped over to the CD player and punched a button. Chris Isaak's "Wicked Game" came on. She strolled over to face Morgan, untying her hair. She fluffed her hair once with her hand, shook her head, and draped her arms around his neck.

"Dance with me," she said, melting her slim body against his. "Tomorrow is Sunday, and every woman should dance on Saturday."

"My pleasure," he said. The two of them fused as one, his eyes catching mine, but only for a flash. Morgan would not risk hurting anyone's feelings. The man would stub a toe before he killed an ant.

I'd seen and heard enough and went searching for Angie. She was in the living room, laboring over a jigsaw puzzle of a six-pack Zeus grasping a lightning rod in his outstretched hand. An empty chair rested beside her. Angie and Elaine did puzzles together.

"How long has she been like this?" I said.

She didn't look up. "Like what?"

"Two counties away from sanity."

"Who made you the judge of sanity?"

"I'm not judging. Just observing."

"Don't go twistin' words on me." She looked up from the puzzle. "She dancing? I hear the music."

"She is."

"She likes to dance. Especially to that song. Dance with about everybody who ever walked through that front door, so don't be thinkin' you special, although Mr. Morgan, he just might be. He looks at people like they're angels, and you look at people as if you want somethin' out of 'em."

"Does Ms. Callaghan have any reason to believe that foul play was instrumental in her son's death?"

"Not that I know. I never knew her son, but his disappearance destroyed her. I was hired about five years ago. Mr. Yankee pays me well. She might belittle her brother, but his money keeps her in this grand old house. I imagine it's her part of the family money, but he manages it for her.

"She thinks he's comin' home. They never found his body, or what was left of it. It would have been better if they had. Without a body, there's no closure. No funeral. Without the body, hope creeps into the soul. Let her live with that, you understand me? It's too late now for her to learn that he died, to have someone like you dig up his soggy old bones after all these years. You find out what happened to him, you don't be tellin' her. You come to me first. Understand?"

"I work for Yankee Conrad."

She glanced at the puzzle, tried a piece but withdrew it. "Don't gimme that. You come to Ms. Angie."

"She thinks that tomorrow is Sunday. Is she always that confused?"

"What's wrong with thinkin' that tomorrow be Sunday? Who don't like Saturdays? We just make up them days, anyways. She tol' me that she and Christopher used to dress up and go to church every Sunday, no matter he and his friends be out till the early mornin' hours the night before. They never missed church and always looked their best."

"Does she still go?"

She sat back in the chair, granting herself a break from the puzzle. "*We* do. That woman was made to walk into a church. And come Monday mornin'? She be sayin' tomorrow's Sunday. But she ain't as far gone as you think. In some places, she's not gone at all. You be careful around her. And my advice?"

"Yes?"

"Leave us alone. We just two women sittin' in this house doin' puzzles. Ain't no way anything good come from any of this. Just no way at all." She studied the puzzle as if seeing it for the first time. She leaned forward, plucked up a piece, and placed it into a cloud above the head of Zeus. "Imma namin' you Calm."

"Calm?"

"Hm-um. There always be a calm before a storm. That's what you is. That's all you ever gonna be. Now, you go, Calm. You get out of our lives and don't be ever comin' back."

6

The next morning I rolled out of bed in the dark, careful not to disturb Kathleen and Joy. I ran over the bridge connecting my island to another island. The illuminated pink hotel— what F. Scott Fitzgerald, after his visit, called the "hotel in the wilderness"—glowed in the black sky, reminding me of Elaine's reference about being stuck in the past. A fishing boat puttered beneath me, heading out silently from the silky channel, its anchor light a low-trailing star. It was a flats vessel heading to the shallow shores of the bay, where the captain would fight the morning heat as he stood in the sun casting for fish lying in the cool shade of the mangroves.

I ran south on the packed sand of the beach. The unseen sun radiated the soft underbellies of low clouds, leaving the bottom half ember pink while the top half remained a characterless shade of white. Off Paradise Grille, someone searched for seashells, their miner's cap lamp sweeping the smooth, uncolored sand.

Angie's parting comments reverberated in my head. I picked up my pace, betting that the physical ache of my muscles would focus my thoughts. Elaine Callaghan wouldn't

28

be of much use, and Angie was as much a spiritual advisor as a live-in companion. I couldn't see either aiding the cause.

As we drove away from Elaine's, Morgan and I discussed that Elaine believed Christopher to still be alive. I suggested that was a documented disadvantage of not conducting a funeral, of experiencing a formal sense of closure. He said it went deeper. That she seemed to possess a guarded secret that was rooted in more than the mere lack of formal closure. Morgan always heard notes higher on the scale than I was capable of hearing. He saw flocks of birds in the distant horizon that I swore were clouds. And so I listen to him because he hears what I cannot hear. He sees what I cannot see.

He had emerged from his bedroom dance with a picture of the *Ms. Buckeye*. She was a classic lady, her hull gleaming in the sun as she moored peacefully in Midnight Cove. But what had caught my eye was the boat in the background. Sundown's boat. The registration numbers were visible and matched the numbers that Hendren had given me.

Before finding Sundown, I needed to drop by and check on Harbor House, where Morgan and I were adding two more bedrooms. One was designated for women who sought sanctuary. Morgan had initially allowed a woman who feared physical abuse from her boyfriend to stay a few nights. She had no friends in the area as she had just moved to Saint Pete with her boyfriend. Word had gotten out. Prior to her, our guests had been immigrant families, usually transitioning from one housing option to another.

The smaller bedroom was for Domingo, who for room and board was our newly acquired live-in *chargé d'affaires*. Morgan knew Domingo, a name meaning "born on Sunday," from his sailing days. Domingo was a thin man who spoke in short sentences and carried a long knife. When Morgan heard that Domingo was looking for dry ground to experience his retirement years, he offered him the position. Morgan and I were thrilled with the arrangement as it made our commitment more manageable. If we had families and women sleeping there at night, we needed staff there as well.

An hour later, while Kathleen slept—my wife harbored a natural disinterest in the early morning hours and was dumbfounded by those who did not share her sensible view—I sat with Joy between my legs, both of us facing the bay. As birds smacked the water, I read *The Story of Crabby Bill and Lobster Lou* to her. She kept touching the pages, as if she could will things to be real, and for a moment, I understood Elaine Callaghan.

But I still thought she was nuts.

THROUGH A FRIEND OF Morgan's in the Florida Department of Highway Safety and Motor Vehicles, I learned that *Seaduction,* Sundown's 1985 Carver aft cabin, had been sold seventeen years ago.

I located the boat using a cross directory and finding the marina listed as an address. It was registered to Frank and Molly Shellstrip. As I walked down the floating dock, I spotted the boat with a woman reading on the aft deck. The Carver was still in good shape and she'd been rechristened *Off Key.* I introduced myself and explained that I was looking into a tragic accident years ago and understood that her boat was at the scene, and while she did not own it at the time, I'd like to ask her a few questions about the previous owner.

"Permission to come aboard," she said.

She introduced herself and said that she and her husband, "an up-and-coming seventy-year-old musician," lived on *Off Key* seven months a year. The other five were spent in the Finger Lakes appellation of New York, an arrangement that had worked well for a quarter of a century. "We keep thinking we should do something different, but it's a good rhythm."

We sat across from each other on the shaded aft deck as gulls bobbed in the water below us. Molly, whose T-shirt read "Shine All Day," lived as cheap and as good as you possibly could. Boat dwellers have a monk-like appreciation of life, and Molly was no exception. Her wide and kind eyes lingered on mine as if our meeting was the center of her day.

I gave her what information I possessed about Sundown and the night that the *Ms. Buckeye* met her demise.

"Do you recall Sundown's last name, or still have papers from the sale?" I asked.

"Can I get you a beer or something?"

"I'm fine."

"Negative on the last name. I do have the bill of sale—it should be on that. You sure you don't want something to drink?"

"I'm OK."

She rose and went into the cabin, emerging a few minutes later with a manila folder.

"Sundown was her real first name. I remember that because I just assumed it wasn't, being unusual and all. Here you go."

She handed me a piece of paper. The previous owner was listed as Sundown Ackerman.

"Did she ever mention witnessing a fire?"

"No."

"Did she give you any indication of what direction she might be heading after she sold the boat?"

"You sure I can't fix you an iced tea or something?"

"You know, an iced tea would be great."

She sprang up and returned a moment later with two glasses of iced tea, each with a fresh-cut lemon wedge clinging to the rim. She plunked a glass on the white plastic table next to me.

"Sundown said she was thinking of doing a B and B," she said. "Something small, maybe one of those cottages at the end of the island, south of Twenty-First. You could pick those up pretty cheap back then, but no more. Frank and I looked at doing that a few years back, but I wasn't sure I wanted to be making someone's bed every day."

The area she was talking about is at the southern tip of Pass-a-Grille Beach. It is crammed with charm and has water on three sides—the bay to the east, the narrow channel to the south, and the Gulf of Mexico guarding its western flank.

"Phone number?"

"Sorry."

"Any groups she was involved in? Crowds she ran with?"

"No—wait a sec. Now that I think of it, years later she did invite us to some museum thingamajiggy. Said she volunteered there."

"The Dali?"

She scrunched her face. "No. Nothing like that. We're talking small. She was into local history."

"The Gulf Beaches Historical Museum?" It was a small museum on the island with its own interesting history.

"Search me. Better yet, search them. Maybe they know."

I thanked her for her time and left with the usual reminder to call me if she could think of anything else.

I climbed in my truck and swung out of the parking lot. It was close to one, and I debated between going to the museum or lunch. But the museum had limited hours—I wasn't even sure it was open that day—so I opted to dash there first. When your luck is running, you want to ride it as far as you can.

It turned out that the museum and lunch came as a package.

7

The museum sat on a sandy toenail of ground behind a white picket fence that had blue dolphins with crooked smiles hung on it. It was 1:45, and the sign indicated it closed at two on that day.

I reached down, flipped the rusty latch, and stepped through the small gate. Even if I found Sundown, she might not advance my cause. My next stop would be Midnight Cove, where the *Ms. Buckeye* had been moored. That wouldn't provide anything of substance, but it needed to be done. Mysteries have a touch, a scent, and I'd yet to feel that familiar tinge. A shiver trembled me at Elaine's, but it was foreign and unrecognizable —gone before it could be identified.

I swung open the salt-eaten door and stepped into the museum. An older woman talked animatedly to a man with a Roman-bust bald head. His black shirt draped from crooked shoulders. They were discussing the history of the museum, for the building itself commanded as much attention as the artifacts and photos it housed. I wandered into the wing with the stained-glass window that had once been the bedroom of Dorothy Harrison. She had transformed the stone church into her home and then gifted it upon her death to be a museum. I stepped up to the glass case, and she looked up at me from a photo of her sitting in a large wicker chair, her hair tied tight behind her. I tapped the glass a few times with my finger. Maybe you can touch the past. She didn't poke me back. That was probably a good thing.

"Greetings. Have you been here before?"

I turned and faced a woman in khaki shorts and a fluffy pink shirt. I'd not seen her when I entered and presumed she'd been in the back room. Her eyes were empty of assumption. She did not look away, nor did she try to talk with them. She had sweetly disordered hair and unlipsticked lips. I'll describe her face in detail later.

"I have," I said. "Numerous times." I was going to add that I donated yearly to Friends of the Museum but didn't see the point.

"Then you know the area we're in was once the bedroom of the woman who converted the church to her house. If you have any questions, let me know. But I do need to tell you, we close in ten minutes."

"I'm looking for Sundown Ackerman."

"Sundown Ackerman." She planted her hands on her hips. "Wow, that's one from the past. Last I heard, she was running guns in Mexico."

"Guns in Mexico?"

"One step ahead of the banditos. That's where the money is, and that's all that fast chick ever cared about."

"You knew her?"

"As well as one can know another."

"When did you last see her?"

She cocked her head. "Why the Q and A, Sherlock?"

"I'm investigating a boat fire two decades ago that claimed a life. She was the only witness."

Her eyes widened. "Why now?"

"The family is looking for closure."

She stepped closer to me. She arrived with a faint whiff of—I couldn't place it, but it was familiar.

"Why now?" she repeated.

"The victim's mother is losing her grip. My search is the last-ditch effort by the family in what is likely a futile attempt to reconstruct what happened that night."

"Are you police? You don't look, you know, all po-li-cee like."

"I was hired by a member of the family."

"The victim's mother?"

Her questions seemed a little pointed, but I went with them.

"No. The victim's uncle."

She nodded. "That makes sense. Yankee. He was always one to tidy up loose ends. God knows Elaine was always making them."

"Pardon?"

"Just explaining the family dynamics."

It took me a moment. "You're Sundown?"

She gave me an infectious smiled and curtsied. "That'll be me."

"Running guns in Mexico?"

"You like that? What adventuresome little girl ever dreams of growing up one day to be a museum docent?"

"I see your point."

"Do they still even have banditos in Mexico?"

"I'm not sure. You might want to check that out."

"Naw. Those days have passed."

Roses on the beach. That's what she smelled like. Kathleen and I had taken a late afternoon stroll on the beach the previous week. Kathleen had picked up rose petals left from a wedding. Sundown's perfume—a tad heavy for my taste—smelled like rose petals on the beach.

"You knew, or know, Elaine?" I asked.

"Heard of her."

"Can we go someplace and talk?"

She cocked her head. "Sure. But I need to get some fuel. I've been here since ten with nothing but a banana a hungry monkey would pass on. Who's my date?"

I introduced myself and suggested we go to Dockside. It was less than a mile away and on interior water.

As I climbed into my truck, a van rolled by. The side of it read "Dan the Piano Man. You bang 'em, we tune 'em." A clean-shaven man sat behind the wheel, keeping his eyes straight ahead. A gold earring caught the sun. I couldn't imagine anyone trying to keep a piano in such a humid and salty environment. Maybe Dan the Piano Man lived in the area.

Sundown followed in a neon-green contraption that was more golf cart than car. A few minutes later we sat on the covered porch that extended over water and commented on the dolphins feeding along the seawall across the water. We ordered a pair of grouper sandwiches with salads. But she wasn't done.

"Your house dressing on the side and no pine nuts," she instructed the waiter, a young man who I noticed had been gaining about a pound—make that two—each month. "But add tomatoes and put the Gorgonzola on the side as well." It wasn't her first trip to the joint.

"I've seen you," she said after we surrendered our menus.

I dipped my head across the water. "I live over there."

"No. In the mornings, in the dark. You run on the beach. I've seen you when I'm looking for seashells. You keep your head down, like you're all serious or something."

"Where do we cross paths?"

"Just north of the jetty."

"Do you wear a miner's hat?"

"I know, dorky, right? But it frees up my hands."

"Dorky is efficient."

"Might be, but I don't think Madison Avenue's going to give me a ring. Whatja so serious about in the mornings?"

"Wasn't aware that I was."

"Hmm."

Between bites, Sundown explained how she'd lived on her boat *Seaduction* for three years, but then "transitioned" to land. And it had been her boat. Her money. Her adventuresome dream. The men came and went, but *Seaduction* was her baby.

"I mean a lot of guys thought living on a boat would be cool, but they just used it as an excuse to drink all day. They think they're living fast, but they're really dying slow."

"Miss her?" I asked.

She became contemplative, not a territory I sensed she was at home in.

"I do miss it," she said. Her eyes took on the glaze of someone lost in a waking dream. "The infinity of mornings. Waking up on the water—not just next to it, but *on* it, the waves lapping against the hull. The morning sun was so low on the horizon I felt as if I could stretch my arm out and touch it. And that it was doing the same for me—stretching its glowing rays over the water, warming my boat.

"Having to take my dinghy to shore during a January rain was pretty special, too. I'm glad I did it, though. It left a core of tranquility for life. A moveable morning. It's something the world can't take from me. I don't have much from those days. My father's navy knife—he was killed in a car accident when I was ten, and it's the only thing I've got of his—and a leather pouch with *Seashell* etched in it. It's great for keepsakes."

"Seashell?"

"That's the name of my tender—my dinghy. Goes well with *Seaduction,* don't you think? Plus, you know, I collect seashells. I changed the name a few months after the fire, which was when I relocated my boat. The previous name was *Little Sea,* which was OK, but it wasn't me."

"Do you remember that night?"

"Like yesterday."

"Care to relive it?"

"No."

"Will you?"

"Seeing as how you're buying me lunch."

"I don't recall that discussion."

She smiled, those unlipsticked lips driving me bonkers.

"Ask you something? How come you run so early?"

"Habit. How come you shell that early?"

She shrugged. "It's as good excuse as any to be on the beach before sunrise. You carry that magic moment all day."

"I agree."

"Then why'd you go with 'habit'?"

"I knew you could say it better."

"That makes as much sense as me running guns in Mexico." She dipped her head at my hand. "Just curious, you married?"

"Luckiest man on the planet."

"Hell's bells, you didn't need to be so confident about it."

"And you?"

"Oh, I got a man in my life. The only man I ever loved. Problem is, he loves his job more than me."

"He's making a mistake."

"Sure shootin' he is. But that's what we do, isn't it?"

"How well did you know Christopher Callaghan?"

She took a sip from her straw, her eyes resting on mine for an extra beat. "They say plastic is bad for the environment and all, but I hate these damn paper things. I'm thinking of packing my own straw." She flicked the straw with a finger. "Sometimes I'd go over to his boat for a drink; sometimes he'd come to mine.

"We were just friends. I know a lot of people think a woman and a man can't be just friends without the whole sex thing popping up—so to speak—but we were. I was dating another guy at the time. I wasn't one to cheat."

"How long had you known him?"

"Chris?"

I nodded.

"A year? He was in Midnight Cove before me. When I dropped anchor, he came over with a bottle of champagne to welcome me. We drained that puppy."

"Girlfriends? Boyfriends?"

"Me or him?"

"Him."

"No. He was pretty much a loner."

"And you?"

"Both. I mean we're only young once, right?"

"That's the curse. Did he ever make a pass at you?"

"Woo-zee, there's a phrase from a cave. No. That was odd because, well, I was a hot girl on a cool boat, right? We never got the time to really know each other. I mean, we'd go from one boat to another, but I doubt over the course of the year we did that more than seven, eight times. The movie of our lives is so much bigger in our minds."

A fighter squadron of pelicans rode the wind, their flapless wings shadowing the water.

"Tell me about the night of the fire," I said.

"Knew you'd come back to that. It was cold. I was inside cuddled in my bunk. The music was low, and I was reading *The Bridges of Madison County*—complete tearjerker if there ever was one. There was a light, like a glow, outside my window. I slept on the starboard side. I'm like that to this day—plane, concert hall, wherever I am I gravitate to the starboard side. I put on a jacket and scampered up the steps, and halfway out of the cabin I saw it.

"She was engulfed in fire off my port side where she was anchored. You know she was a woody, right? Know what my first thought was? How can something burn like that when it was surrounded, literally *floating* in water?" She swayed her head. "To think he was dying and I was thinking *that*."

"What happened next?"

"I called 911. I did it fast, but it took them a while. By the time the sheriff's boat arrived—it was the first boat—there was nothing left of the *Ms. Buckeye*."

I asked if she saw Chris that night.

She shook her head. "Not a glimpse. I don't think he made it out of his cabin." She shuddered. "What a terrible way to die and for me to witness. I relocated my boat a few weeks later to another harbor. I couldn't stay there. How can something be there and then not? Every time I'd look over to where the *Ms. Buckeye* used to be, there was nothing left but the buoy he anchored to. It was like he and his boat never existed. The water, the wind, all that we loved, didn't care. How do you accept that?"

We observed a moment's silence out of respect for a question with no answer. Pudgy waiter dropped by. He refilled our drinks without asking, which made me feel guilty about mentally ribbing him for his weight.

"I mean," she said, raking her fingers over the top of her ear, "on land, at least there's charred trees and dead weeds, something to mark the spot. But at sea?" She puffed out her breath. "Poof."

Hendren had made the same observation, that there wasn't even a crime scene to investigate.

"I thought you said you moved your boat a few months later, not a few weeks."

She looked momentarily lost as she searched her memory. "A few weeks, a month, something like that. I guess what I meant was that I didn't change *Seashell's* name until a little later."

"So you only met Chris," I spread my hands, "seven, eight times?"

"That's about right."

"Where does his mother, Elaine, come into it? Did you meet her?"

Her chest swelled and fell. "No, but he talked plenty about her. Said she was half-nuts."

"Why?"

"Why what?"

"Why was she half-nuts?"

She shrugged. "Christopher would say stuff. Personally? I think we're all half-nuts, so I might have tuned him out."

She excused herself. I settled the check and observed as a thirty-foot bowrider docked in front of me. A half a dozen people spilled out and invaded the restaurant. The captain and a younger girl, who I assumed was his daughter, stayed back and secured the boat, pushing it out with their feet to see how tight their lines were and if they needed to be adjusted. He said something, and she bent over and gathered in some line. Someday, that would be Joy and me. Or—my luck—Joy would love horses and scorn boats.

Sundown reclaimed her seat and scooted the chair forward, and then back again as if she was searching for a comfortable distance from the table.

"Elaine," I said.

"Elaine." She pronounced the name as if we'd started another chapter. "Christopher wasn't close to his father and had no siblings. It was just him and his mom growing up."

I recalled her earlier statement. "But you never met her."

"I never did. But he said she was odd, always collecting dumb stuff and wanting him to live in the house instead of getting his own place."

"That constitutes being nuts?"

"Half-nuts. Have you met her?"

I told her about Morgan's and my visit with Elaine but glossed over the parts where she touched Morgan and their dance in Christopher's bedroom.

"Soooo," she drew out. "You said your job was to what? Reconstruct what happened that night? How does that help anything?"

"The family seeks closure. Affirmation that he is gone. What did you know about Yankee Conrad, Chris's uncle?"

"Chris said he cornered the brains and money of the family. I never met the man."

"You remembered him pretty easily just a few moments ago."

She hesitated, but then jumped in. "His name, you know? Like mine. Its unusualness makes it easy to remember. You said Yankee was looking for closure—why now?"

I had told Sundown that the family was looking for closure, not Yankee. I decided not to tell her about the medallion. I had no reason to withhold information from her but felt it wiser to say less. Maybe those sepia lips were clouding my judgment of her, but something about her answers sounded off-kilter.

"He believes that his nephew is long dead and perhaps one final inquiry will settle the matter."

"Seems a little weak to me," she said.

"You ever lose a child?"

"Hey, no need for that."

"I didn't mean to be curt."

"No need for that, either."

I leaned back and flicked a piece of my bun I'd saved onto the floor. Harry, the resident pigeon, toddled over and pecked at it.

Sundown said, "And that was the only reason he gave you for looking into Christopher's death? Final closure?"

"That's it."

She seemed to consider that, but instead of challenging it

further, went with, "And what's the plan, report back to Yankee?"

"If and when I learn anything. So far, all I've done is talk to the lead detective at the time and you."

"And Elaine."

"And Elaine."

"I remember him—the detective. He still around?"

"Retired."

"We were on the shore looking at where the *Ms. Buckeye* had been, and he said, 'Out, out brief candle.' I'll never forget that—him standing there in his storm-tossed hair and saying that."

"*Macbeth.*"

"Pardon me?"

"He was quoting Shakespeare."

She bobbed her head. "He did have a certain air around him, like a man walking in a life that wasn't his. He kept asking me questions about whether I ever saw Christopher swimming to shore, like he thought maybe Christopher faked his death or something. Pretty bizarre. Burn your home, leave your car, and vanish, right? I could never see any reason for him to do that. He was a nice guy. Sweet. Gentle. There was nothing to spook him out of his life."

"But you only talked with him seven or eight times. Why so sure?"

She clasped her hands in front of her. "I mean, there could have been, what? Enemies? Debt issues? I don't know. I think everyone—and I totally get this—just doesn't want to accept that he went up in flames. That one second you're sleeping in your boat and a minute later, it's all over. No one wants to believe life is that fragile."

I asked her if there was anyone else I should be talking to. She reminded me that it was a long time ago, and there were no other boats in Midnight Cove. It was home only to the *Ms. Buckeye* and *Seaduction.*

"Those were happy days," she said. "Floating under sun by day and the moon by night. Every week a man in his boat would motor by and check his crab traps. Outside of him, there was no hint of the commercialization of life. The peace I took from that spot stays with me."

"Your moveable morning."

"My moveable morning."

I told her to give me a call if she thought of anything else. A question had popped in my mind while she was talking earlier, but I couldn't recall it. As I drove away, I couldn't shake her casual reference to Yankee Conrad. He was not a man who summoned casualness from others. I stuck it in the basement of my mind, where I collect things with no firm meaning yet do not want to throw away.

8

Kathleen and I were having dinner at Mangroves in downtown Saint Pete. The intoxicating sights, smells, and sounds blended together like a luscious Meritage wine.

I could taste the food with my mouth closed. Hear the thrum of the street with earplugs in. See the crowd with my eyes shut—the strolling groups of threes and fours, couples holding hands, conventioneers, and young women outdueling each other in high heels, short skirts, and bare midriffs. The Museum of Fine Arts across the street draped with royal banners proclaiming a special exhibition. Children climbing the giant banyan tree in Straub Park, its massive limbs covering the cut grass. Tinted-glass cars cruising the street, and waiters dressed in black dashing about. It was both glorious and boring. Where had the magic gone?

"Let's split," I said. "We haven't taken a week in a year."

"Sure. I'll just skip teaching, toss Joy in a papoose, and hit the road."

"Exactly."

"And why this sudden Kerouacian urge?"

I took a drink of whiskey and marveled at how the good side of booze never loses its magic.

"Hey, I'm talking to you."

"I hear you."

"But?"

"I think it'd be a wise thing to do before there's a reason to do it."

"OK. That's a little weak, but it's got a ring to it. Who's talking, you or the whiskey?"

"It's a duet. When I'm done finding that there's nothing more to discover about the death of Chris Callaghan, which should be another day or two considering he's been cold since Clinton, we do the papoose bit and hit the road."

"North or south?"

"Why not east or west?"

"You're a north and south man. You move vertically."

"I didn't know that."

"Now you do."

"North. We'll get a cabin and hike."

"You don't hike," she reminded me. "You run."

"Anything else you'd like to tell me about myself?"

She pondered the question. "That's probably all you can handle for now. You're at a dead end, aren't you?"

"Twenty-four years ago a boat goes up in flames and takes the owner with it," I said. "Case closed."

"Except now someone wants half a mil for the real story, which is likely nothing more than a scam to rip off desperate people, one who has a tenuous grip on reality and would pay such money just to sustain the heartbeat of hope. You've talked to a few people, came up empty, and now you want to drive off the set."

I bobbed my head. "That sounds about right."

"You're not motivated."

"Come again?"

She leaned in across the table and took a finger over my forehead, brushing back what I assumed was a random lock of hair. "You don't believe there is a crime. But there is. Not in what happened twenty years ago, but someone is torturing a grieving mother. Rally yourself. That is one bad person, and they deserve your wrath."

"You really don't think I can move east or west?"

"You're a sun tracker. Find the scum who's blackmailing a childless mother. Follow your nose like you follow the sun."

I struggled to see Elaine Callaghan as a childless mother. For some reason, that reminded me of when Yankee Conrad requested confidentiality from me. I hadn't been aware that I'd also put his comment in basement storage. What was he afraid that I might find?

I READ TO JOY THAT NIGHT UNTIL HER HEAVY EYES COULD NO longer hold the day. Until her breathing was more silent than the night. She slept between Kathleen and me, and when I saw that she had crossed over, her tiny hand clasping my finger, I turned the light off. I woke at 5:30 a.m. from a seamless night, which had been occurring more often. I think holding a child's hand while falling asleep had something to do with that.

The next morning the high tide made the beach unsuitable for running. I avoided the beach and took the bayside road both directions. At the house, I ground coffee, showered under the outdoor showerhead, and yanked a dead palm frond off a tree. Morgan was at the end of his dock, deep in his morning meditations. The sun struggled for altitude and a pod of dolphins surfaced in rhythm, their watered gray skin breaking the flat surface. I grabbed a hat, a cup of coal-black coffee, and went to the end of the dock. An osprey had used it as a latrine. I hosed off what I could and then settled on the bench, tilting my hat to shield the sun.

I had dropped by Midnight Cove after lunch with Sundown, but it was no good. It was just a stagnant bay, and in no manner gave up her secrets. No boats were moored there, although crab traps dotted her placid surface.

The crab boat that checks the traps in front of my house drifted to a stop. It was slack tide, and he easily pulled up the trap marked by the green buoy, emptied it, and throttled on to the next trap. I remembered the question I'd meant to ask Sundown. I stood, glanced over at Morgan, who occupied a different planet, and went inside to make sure Kathleen was stirring. She taught a class at ten and Bonita, our sitter, arrived at nine fifteen. Kathleen required a good thirty minutes of drowsy consciousness before feet on the ground became an attainable goal. Even then, it seemed to her a cruel and unjust world that would commence each day with the forlornness of having to leave one's bed. I wolfed down three eggs and then went outside and picked an orange hibiscus flower. I placed the flower in a vase and wrote a love line to Kathleen.

The city was due at Harbor House for final occupancy inspection. I wanted to be there in case any issues arose. But first I had a stop to make.

BRADFORD WILKINSON'S LEGS STUCK OUT FROM under the chassis of a 1965 red Mustang. He looked like the bad witch on *The Wizard of Oz*.

"Binger?" I said, invoking a nickname he claimed he earned by winning a homemade bong contest in high school.

"Hold on a sec."

A clanking sound of metal on metal came from under the car. His legs started backing out and finally his head. He squinted up at me.

"You owe me forty fuckin' bucks," he said.

"It was after midnight."

"According to your busted watch."

Binger and I knew each other from our drinking days in Fort Myers Beach. That was the gap year after I left the army. The rule was that you weren't liable for anything you said after midnight. We both left the booze and the beach in an attempt to start over. His passion was cars, and as long as he tackled them every day, he kept the bottle at bay. Last I'd seen him, he was toiling on his cars seven days a week, entering shows, and hanging around with car guys, a fraternal order of men who lived a life of gleaming chrome, flaring tail fins, and dual stainless exhaust manifolds.

For a brief time when he moved north, he had a commercial crabbing license. I told him I was looking for whoever had the trap rights to Midnight Cove twenty-four years ago.

He rubbed his hand across his stubbled chin, leaving a trail of black. "I know the water. It's a nice, protected bay. Seven or eight traps there when I was in the business, and it don't change much. Those rights go back forever, so chances are someone's been trapping that cove for longer than twenty-something years. You're gonna wanna talk to Vicky Esposito. His family has more traps than I got grease guns. He—assuming he's still alive—will know who had that area. I wouldn't be surprised if it was him."

"Vicky?"

"I suggest you stick with Vic."

"Know where I could find him?"

"Riptides."

"He owns it?"

"Hell no. He just rents a stool."

I got a description of Vic Esposito—"Sounds like he just walked out of a Jersey bar. What more do you need?"—and headed to Harbor House to meet the city inspector. He had already left by the time I arrived, although I had confirmed the time the previous afternoon. He hadn't liked the elevation of an outside drain, and a permit would not be granted until it was changed. I was ticked that I missed him. I checked in with the guys doing some punch-out items, but they had the wrong color of paint. Money spent with no progress.

THE INSIDE BAR AT RIPTIDES IS A PINE-WALLED ROOM with a stone fireplace and opened doors fronting the Gulf of Mexico. There is no air conditioning. No heat, either, except for the stone fireplace. It had been lugged down from New England, hadn't a clue what it was doing in Florida, glared with contempt at the patrons, and couldn't wait for someone to haul its stony ass back to Massachusetts.

It was two thirty in the afternoon. Binger had told me that most of the crabbers he knew hit the bars on the way home.I ordered an iced tea from the bartender. I have no desire to have a day on the calendar that would forever be my last drink day, so I keep to my rules. I often break them, but not often enough to go directly to jail and not pass Go. Winston Churchill said that he took more from alcohol than alcohol took from him. That is a worthy goal.

Around three, an older man who sounded like he sang baritone in a Jersey quartet strode in, his gifted instrument leading the way. A matchstick of a man wearing a red baseball cap accompanied him. They took up positions to my left, facing the nonexistent doors to the Gulf and the homesick fireplace. The bartender presented them a pair of beers.

"How's the classes coming, Cedar?" the older man said.

The bartender placed her hands on the bar.

"Two finals this Friday."

"Didja ever see that movie *Back to School*?"

"Can't say I have."

"That's my type of school."

"Vicky, I'm guessing that if it's your type of school, then it really isn't school."

"Wouldn't bet against you. I was never much good at that stuff."

"You study?"

"Hell no."

"What ju' expect."

"Cedar, why don't you just snatch you a rich man?" his companion in the red cap said. "You can have anyone you want."

"What's that got to do with her getting an education?" Vic— or Vicky—said, flashing a disapproving glance at his friend. He turned back to Cedar. "You get your degree. And as much as I love seeing you here, I won't shed a tear when you're gone. That don't mean I won't miss you, *capisce*?"

Cedar dipped her head. "Thank you."

I scooted down a few stools. "Vic Esposito?" I asked. He had a forward tilt to his body, his barge-wide forehead leading the way.

"Why you wanna know?" he said. "You with the IRS?"

"No."

"Child support services?"

"No."

"Looking for an aging porn actor?"

"Wish I could help you there."

"Makes two of us. What can I do for you, young man?"

I introduced myself and said Bradford Wilkinson had told me where to find him.

"Don't know the name."

"Binger."

"I'm with you now. Binger still got his ass under a car?"

"He does."

"Good place for him to be. He never liked crabbin' that much, and a man's no good at something he don't like."

"I'm looking into a boat fire that took a life over twenty years ago."

"The *Ms. Buckeye*?"

"You remember it?"

"Not many boat fires claim a life."

"Did you work that area?"

"I owned those rights for nearly thirty years. Had about five traps in there. They was good, but mostly I liked going to check them. It was a pretty little cove. Type of place you loved to go in and hated to leave."

Cedar came around. "Be careful," she said to me. "You hang around them you'll be old and cranky."

"What I ever do to deserve that?" Vic said.

"I'm teasing you, Vicky. I wish everyone was the gentleman you are."

"That's better."

"Refill?" she said to me.

"Thanks." I pushed my plastic cup toward her and turned my attention to Vic. "What can you tell me about the fire?"

Vic fished into his pocket and brought out a cigarette. You could smoke in the bar, as the open doors didn't constitute being inside. He reached for an ashtray—a hollowed-out porcelain alligator—and dragged it in front of him. He lit the cigarette and craned his head back, blowing smoke into the air. A couple of sweating guys came in from the beach volleyball court, calling out to Cedar before they took their stools.

"What can I tell you?" he said. He took another long drag, letting the smoke trail out of his mouth at a measured pace. "One week she was there, next she wasn't. Know something about fire on the water? It don't exist. Like it never happened."

Hendren and Sundown made similar observations.

"Did you ever talk to Chris Callaghan, the man who died on the boat?"

"Nah. I was there for business, you know. Hit the traps and move to the next. I wasn't making social calls."

"Did you—"

"That was a nice boat, though, the *Ms. Buckeye*. And she was a looker, a real player. Classic lines and a beam wider than an elephant's ass. I remember thinking a man living on a girl like that is one lucky fella. And Midnight Cove was paradise this side of heaven. You find a place like that, you don't tell nobody, know what I mean?"

He took another drag from his cigarette and eyed the two young men across the bar as they teased Cedar.

"What time did you usually check your traps?"

"Pardon?"

I repeated my question.

"I hit Midnight early. Nice place to start the route. I'd be there seven thirty a.m. most days."

"Did you notice another boat there?"

"I'm sorry, your name again?"

"Jake."

"Why the bullets, Jake?"

I explained that the family of the man who perished on the *Ms. Buckeye* had retained me, and I was trying to put things to rest once and for all.

"For once and for all," he said. "Good luck with that. I'm more of a beer-bottle philosopher—that's knowin' that the questions are more permanent than the answers."

He eyed the loud men, took another hit from his cigarette, and stubbed it out in the alligator's tail.

"Excuse me," he said.

Vic Esposito rose from his stool like a gnarly oak sprouting out of the ground. He strolled around to the other side of the bar at a leisurely pace. He planted himself between the two shirtless men and placed a large hand on the back of each of them. He bent over, wedging his head between them, and spoke words I couldn't hear. He righted himself, patted—more like a slap—the man on his right, and came back to his stool. The young men were quiet, their heads hung over their beers, one of them glancing nervously at me.

He reclaimed his seat and reached for another cigarette.

"Friends of yours?"

He grunted. "Damn young bucks. Ah, fuck, they're good guys. Just gotta grow up, know what I mean."

"Looks like you put the fear of God in them. What did you tell them?"

"That you're my lover and if they didn't behave around Cedar, you was gonna plant a wet one on their lips."

"Interesting. You use that line often?"

He smiled, revealing his smoker's teeth. "Nah, just pulled it out of my ass. I told them if they didn't treat a woman like a woman, there'd be blood on the floor."

"There are two of them," I pointed out.

"Like I can't count? I told them they'd win, but also told 'em you never want to be in a fight with someone who don't mind losing. My daddy used to say that, and I think those boys understood."

I nudged my iced tea.

"Did you notice another boat moored there as well?"

"*Seaduction.*"

I let out a low whistle. "You got a young memory for an old man."

"Beer drinkin' will do that. That was one fine boat name. She was plastic, though, not the same breed as *Ms. Buckeye.* They was about—I dunno—couple hundred feet apart."

"Did you ever see any unusual activity around the *Ms. Buckeye*?"

"At seven thirty a.m.?"

He likely spent little time in Midnight Cove. His job was to get in, check his traps, and hustle out. Why I thought he was worth the effort escaped me. I wondered what to cook for dinner that night, and decided to pick up shrimp and grits at Dewey's. Sometimes it's a treat not having to cook. Kathleen, who couldn't pick out the oven in a lineup with dishwashers, would be fine with my decision. No effort, no complaints. It was the cardinal rule of a great marriage. Right after having a ballistic crush on your significant other.

Cedar switched out Vic's empty mug with a fresh beer, giving him a wink in the process. He dipped his head at my iced tea. "What's your excuse?"

"I reserve my pleasures for the later hours."

"You know the story, right? Man goes to the doctor and says he wants to do all he can to live longer. Doc says, 'You drink?' Guy says, 'No.' Doc says, 'You smoke?' Guy says, 'No.' Doc says, 'You eat fatty foods?' Guys says, 'No.' Doc says, 'You chase skirt?' Guy says, 'No.' Doc looks at the guy and says, 'What the hell you want to live for?'"

"I appreciate the words of wisdom."

"Those later hours are under no obligation to make an appearance."

I stood, gave him my card, and asked that he give me a call if he thought of anything else.

"I do think they knew each other, though, now that I think about it."

"The two boats?"

He nodded. "I never saw whoever lived on the boats, but *Seaduction*? She had a tender. I don't remember the name."

"*Seashell?*"

His face crumbled. "Naw. That's close, but that's not it."

Then I remembered that Sundown had renamed her dinghy after she moved out of Midnight Cove.

"*Little Sea?*"

"Might be. Yeah, I do think that was it."

"What makes you think they knew each other based on *Little Sea*?"

"She wasn't always home."

I sat back down on my stool. "Come again?"

"She—*Little Sea*—was sometimes tied to the *Ms. Buckeye*. Remember, early morning, right? So I presumed that whoever lived on *Seaduction* was spending the night aboard the *Ms. Buckeye*. They had a nice thing going on there in Midnight Cove all those years ago. When she went up in flames, I felt bad for whoever lived on *Seaduction*. I mean when I found out that fella had died, I felt terrible for him, but ain't it funny how you feel more bad for the living than the dead? I guess we just figure the dead are done feeling."

Sundown had told me she went to see Chris maybe seven or eight times and denied any romantic involvement.

I asked Vic, "Was this fairly often?"

He sucked in his lower lip. "Enough times that I remember it like that. I can't swear on my mother's grave, but I bet *Little Sea* was tied to the Chris-Craft at least half the time. But remember, I was there one day a week. Could have been coincidental."

"Did you ever see the dinghy for the *Ms. Buckeye* tied to *Seaduction*?"

He gave that a second. "I don't think that was their arrangement."

I thanked him again, took two steps toward the door, and turned around.

"One more," I said. "After the fire, did *Seaduction* leave Midnight Cove? A few weeks or months later?"

He clawed his fingers over the side of his face. "No. She stayed. I remember that 'cause she looked so lonely. Like someone who'd lost her playmate."

Sundown had told me she pulled up anchor a few weeks

after the fire. Or months. She'd been purposely vague on the timeline.

"You sure?" I said. "Two, three months later, *Seaduction* was still anchored in the cove?"

"No doubt. She was the only boat there. I would have noticed if one day I pulled in and the cove was empty. She was there for at least a year after that. Hell of a lonely thing to see."

9

D id Vic have it wrong?

Memories are slippery little devils, creating fact from fiction and tricking us into believing things with such ardent conviction that even when we discover we are wrong, we cling to disproven beliefs. But he'd seemed confident that Sundown's boat was in Midnight Cove long after Sundown told me that she had pulled up anchor. Why would she lie? I thought about giving her a call, but it was late and I decided to confront her at the museum in the morning.

I read to Joy that night, but she was fussy and unsettled. I gave up on the books and hummed to her as she lay in the crook of my arm. I wanted her to have days lit by the sun and nights dimmed by the moon so that when she closed her eyes and was on her own, she would enter a world of white fluffy lambs and smiling dolphins, and I wouldn't have to worry because it's a terrible thing to lay a child in bed and worry what monster, what hideous nightmare might infect her virgin mind. She drifted to sleep, and I left her knowing I'd done all I could to craft her dreams, so that when she became untethered from the world, the barbarians would be turned away at the gate.

The following morning, I did five miles on the beach, although I didn't see Sundown and her dorky miner's hat. After the run I pummeled the punching bag with the pink smile. I took a couple of shots with my leg at the red *X* at the top of the bag. I couldn't do it as effortlessly as I did ten years ago, and that ticked me off. I came up a little low on each attempt. But the speed was good, and quickness is an underrated asset. I showered outside and had breakfast with Kathleen as Joy swatted at Hadley III's tail. Kathleen discussed her day—she had a class at ten as well as two, and planned to do research in the library after that. I told her I was going to visit Sundown again in an attempt to merge Vic's memory to what she had told me.

We kissed and departed the house. I half expected to see a woody wagon in the driveway, a golden retriever with a tennis ball in its mouth, a mailman strolling down the street, and a cartoon bluebird peeping on my shoulder.

I STOPPED BY THE MUSEUM AND WAS GREETED BY THE MAN IN the black shirt draped from crooked shoulders, except today's shirt was coral. I told him I was looking for Sundown.

"Join the group. She was supposed to take the first shift today but never showed up." His voice was kind and sonorous. "We only found out when Daniel—he does some yard work for us, pretty good plumber, too, but I'd advise you not to hire him for any electrical work—anyway, he called and said the place was locked up tighter than a drum. So I hustled over here. I called her—it's not like her to miss a shift—but no answer."

I asked if he had Sundown's address.

"It's a few blocks south of here, on Third. But I don't have the number. She told me once she had a two bedroom with a postage-stamp front porch she'd painted blue. Said she lived on that stamp—her words, not mine."

I thanked him and left. As I got in my car, a clown pedaled by on a bike. His Rudolph nose caught the sun, and his white, pasty face looked sickly and contagious. Someone must have been having a birthday party—although it seemed a little early in the day. I went the opposite direction of the clown and took a left on Third Street. I parked the truck against the curb, thinking that I didn't want some plague-bearing clown ever performing at one of Joy's birthday parties.

The Caribbean-blue porch was easy to spot, as was Sundown's car parked in front of it. I bounded up the steps, covered the porch in two strides, and rapped on the door.

Wait. Repeat.

She might be out walking the beach. I dialed her number, but it went straight to voice mail. I decided to grab breakfast at Seabreeze. As I stepped off the porch, the clown pedaled down Gulf Boulevard in the opposite direction he'd previously been going. He rode proudly, his head up, his knees pumping, his orange hair flowing behind him, the most natural unnatural thing in the world.

I hate clowns. They spook me for I do not understand them. Like tournament fish hung from grappling hooks, they are humanity gutted and turned inside out, exposing our idiocy. I'd rather be stuck in an elevator all day with a playlist of Johnny Mathis Christmas carols than face down a clown.

I jumped back onto the porch and peered in the window. An outstretched hand lay on the floor. I took two steps back and kicked in the door. I rushed through the front room and to the kitchen. Sundown lay on the floor.

Now I'll tell you about her face.

Even in death, it evoked her name. Quiet. Soft. The laying down of the day. Her thin, unlipsticked lips were the pale color of feathery summer clouds. Four fine lines stemmed from the corners of her eyes. A line for the sun, a line for the moon, a line for the water, and a line for the wind. Her parted lips revealed white teeth that seemed eager to smile upon the world. Thick red hair fanned out on the floor like the blazing sky fifteen minutes after the sun had gone down. Her eyes—that had not looked away, nor tried to speak—now held comprehension. For death is the resolution of all of Detective Hendren's philosophies.

If my senses had been muted when Kathleen and I had dinner at Mangroves, they were now a Geiger counter stuck on a nuclear warhead. The hum of the refrigerator under the dominant tone of the air conditioning. My thumping heart. A passing car. Summer's damp feel and death's foul smell.

It appeared as if she'd been choked to death as her neck was bruised and discolored. But her home was now a crime scene, and I didn't want to explain my prints or impede the investigation by contaminating the cottage. I reached for my phone to call Detective Rambler, a man I'd come to know due to unfortunate circumstances, but stopped. Once he arrived, I was out of the loop. I wouldn't get another shot at her house. I wanted to snoop around before being escorted out, instructed to sit, and enduring hours of questions and waiting. I could explain one pass through the house, but not my fingerprints. I snatched a dishcloth, opened the cabinet door under the sink, and found what I wanted: one-size-fits-all rubber yellow gloves. I stretched them over my hands—one size my ass.

The main room held a few chairs, a couch, and a TV. The drawers had been opened and ransacked. No computer. Either she didn't have one, which was unlikely, or whoever murdered her had taken it. There was no phone, either.

The guest bedroom had a bed and a dresser that was half-full. Maybe Sundown used it for extra storage for herself, leaving some drawers available to guests. I stepped into her bedroom. The bed was unmade. I tried to see it in my mind. Someone knocks? Did she open the door? Foolishly, I'd not tried to open the door before attacking it with my foot. I was out of my league, and the longer I stayed—they would somehow figure that out—the more questions they would pitch. I wanted to find what I was looking for and call the police.

I found it in the top dresser drawer in her bedroom under a mess of panties and socks. Sundown had told me at Dockside that she kept her "keepsakes" in a leather pouch with *Seashell*—the name of her dinghy—etched on it. The pouch was opened as if someone had gone through it, but I doubted anything was missing as it was stuffed with seemingly random mementos. Next to it was a large knife in a leather sheath. Her father's navy knife. I stuck the pouch and the knife under my shirt and made my way out of the cottage, taking the gloves off and stuffing them under my shirt before going outside. I didn't need some neighbor telling the police that I walked out of her home wearing yellow rubber gloves—good luck explaining that. I placed the gloves, leather pouch, and knife in the center console and called Detective Rambler.

I don't believe in an afterlife, but while waiting for Rambler, I prayed that Sundown woke up on the water, the glowing morning sun at the end of her outstretched arms, the waves lapping the hull of her boat, her moveable morning having followed her into the arms of God.

10

Rambler trudged out of Sundown's house and shook his head at me. When he arrived, he'd instructed me to lean against my truck and not to move—"And I mean not one goddamn step." Rambler, a man with heightened spatial awareness, took everything in but had little patience for any person or object once it had served its purpose.

Yellow police tape fenced off Sundown's home. Men and women in uniforms and white lab coats hastened around with serious faces. A van that read *Crime Lab* was parked directly in front of the house.

"I had nothing to do with this," I said when Rambler joined me in propping up my truck. It was a variation of the opening line I'd delivered upon his arrival.

"Yet here you stand," he said. "Let's hear it."

You have my word, I'd told Yankee Conrad when he stressed confidentiality.

"I dropped by because I'd gone to the museum and—"

"Yeah, yeah. You told me. What you muffed was why you wanted to see her in the first place."

"I didn't muff anything. I didn't tell you."

"See? That's what we've got to work on."

Rambler and I first met when he accused me of killing the man who I believed had abducted and killed my sister when we were children. He couldn't nail that on me, because I didn't do it. He recently helped me when I investigated the death of Andrew Keller, a friend of mine who sought my help in arranging a rendezvous with his former lover, Elizabeth Walker. While I'd been retained by a U.S. marshal to look into Keller's death, Rambler was rightly ticked that he was cut out of the loop. There was more, but that's enough.

"I had no hand in this," I said.

"That's not the point. You can help this investigation or hinder it. Your choice."

"There is—"

"If I find that you hinder this investigation, that you're holding back, those friends you stash in high places won't dare touch you. Understand?"

"I do."

"No, you don't. Talk."

"Not if you're going to have that attitude."

He wiped his forehead with the back of his hand. "Goddamn heat. I'd give anything these days to be a Canadian Mountie, a cool breeze and the whole town upset because of a dead elk. From the top, and take your time with it."

I'd had time to come up with my story, and I sold it with everything I had. But lying is an article of clothing that has never fit me well.

He eyed me warily. "You tracked her down because—help me out here—you were interested in doing work for the museum?"

"I've been a contributor for years."

"A contributor?"

I nodded.

"And so you came to her house this morning because no one could get hold of her and she wasn't at the museum."

"That's right."

"Kicked in an unlocked door."

"I assumed it was locked."

He blew out a long and low whistle. "You are one dedicated museum contributor. Tell you what, Jake-o. I don't believe a thing you're telling me."

Calling me Jake-o was new for him. We stared at each other for an uncomfortable moment.

"I can prove that I contribute to the museum."

"I need you at the station to make an official statement."

"Can't you just take it here?"

He didn't bother to answer.

RAMBLER KEPT ME FOR THREE HOURS. TWO AND A HALF OF those were sitting in a cracked plastic chair in a hall underneath a poster with mug shots of sex offenders. Funny guy. I wouldn't have minded sharing with him my investigation into the disappearance of Chris Callaghan—Rambler could be helpful—but first I wanted to run it by Yankee Conrad. That was not a call to be made inside a police station. I'd been unable to reach Yankee Conrad before entering the station.

When I finally walked out the front door, the heat sucker punched me. I connected with Yankee Conrad halfway home. When I told him that Sundown Ackerman had been murdered, there was a long silence on the phone. I thought I'd lost him, but then he said, "Proceed."

But it sounded as if he were steeling himself more than instructing me.

11

D inner that night was booze, bread, cheese, Miles Davis, and a woman beside me. It was all I could manage. It was all a man needs. Kathleen didn't mind. She'd sneak in a bowl of cereal before crawling into bed.

We sat on the screened porch as the tourist sailboat *Fantasea,* her sails harnessing the campfire sunset, drifted past the end of the dock. I'd just finished unloading the day on her. I didn't tell her that Sundown's eyes were wide open, her hair splayed on the floor, that the smell of death overshadowed the smell of rose on the beach, and that she had died reaching for the rising sun and I was afraid if I touched my daughter, all that would bleed into her. The basement of my mind was too full for that, so I stuck it in the attic—a far creepier place.

"And I thought I had a rough day because I had two classes and a department meeting," Kathleen said.

"You had a department meeting?" I said, slamming the door to the attic of my mind.

"Jonathon, again, insisting the curriculum stick to the Harold Bloom canon of literature."

Jonathan was the squirrel-brain department head. He had

the hots for Kathleen. It gave me great pleasure to skewer him at holiday parties.

"It will be a giant step forward for literature when Johnny boy steps down," I said.

"Only death will separate him from his guardian post. Are you OK?"

"Literature has survived far worse."

"Stop it. You know what I mean."

"Not if her association with me got her murdered."

"Even if her death was related to the boat fire—hard to imagine as that is—you haven't made enough ripples to pique anyone's interest."

I poured more Jameson into my glass. Rambler told me that the time of death was between 5:00 and 7:00 a.m. He dropped that because after getting clearance from Yankee Conrad, I'd marched straight back to his office and spilled everything on him, except Yankee Conrad's name. I did it without preamble. He never interrupted, nor did he ask who I was working for. He'd told me that Sundown had not been sexually molested, and he didn't believe the door had been locked. "She fought for her life, but she was no match for the skin under her finger-nails. He wore gloves. That shows premeditation." They dusted the place, but no hits. The neighbors said Sundown left the house early in the morning to walk the beach, but often took her trash out before leaving. As her trash was not out, it was assumed that her assailant entered the house at the earlier part of the timeline.

"She didn't live far from us," Kathleen said. Her voice brought me back, for I'd been staring vacantly at the red blinking channel marker. "It's terrible to know that such violence can be so close. That someone's life is ending in a nightmare while our days go on with startling indifference to the pain around us."

"Every man is—"

"Be careful," she said, not interested in dueling ideologies.

"That's the plan."

"Better yet?"

"Yes, ma'am?"

She leveled her eyes on mine. "Be yourself."

We both knew what she meant, but it's funny how you leave the details unsaid. How you grow to totally accept the stranger within, and if you're lucky, as I am, the other person in your life embraces that stranger, and that is part of her love for you, for she loves both of you as one, and that's something you've never been able to do.

SLEEP FOUGHT ME THAT NIGHT. I COULDN'T TAKE THE chance of my dreams bleeding into Joy. I gathered her in my arms, got out of bed, and walked around to K's side of the bed. I nestled her next to Kathleen and tucked the sheet in tight so she couldn't roll off. I went to my garage, unlocked the gray steel cabinet, and took my gun out.

I had vowed to never carry a gun again, but someone had to meet the barbarians at the gate.

WHILE RUNNING THE NEXT MORNING UNDER A brightening sky flecked with planets and stars, Kathleen's words pounded in my head with every step.

Be yourself.

I slowed down to a walk. I never do that. Then it happened: The stranger within kept going. He was out. Free. But I wasn't surprised; after all, I'd literally unlocked him the night before.

I sat on a bench that had a plaque dedicating it to some-one's memory, but it was too dark and I couldn't make out the name. My stranger sat next to me. I stared at the dark waters of the Gulf with his composed presence balancing my labored breathing.

There was one less person on the beach that morning. But to the waves, the scurrying sandpipers, the heavy moon, the thick tropic air that I inhaled like warm pudding, it was just another day. I believe the least of us to be more than all of those together. That is why the blood in my dreams haunts me so. But we're not going down that rabbit hole.

An hour later I sat at the counter at Seabreeze with the air conditioner blowing on the left side of my face. I would have preferred open windows, but no one asked me. Eggs, crispy bacon, hash browns drowning in onions, buttered toast with jelly, and two cups of coffee later and I was in look-out-world mode. Marci cleaned away my yolk-stained plate. I folded the paper—I'd been reading the obituaries, about the only thing I have interest in anymore—and placed it off to the side. Sundown's small leather sack, *Seashell*, sat on the counter to my left. I opened it. Her passport was in it. Sundown was an island hopper and had stamped most of the eastern Caribbean ports. I started sorting the other items, a hodgepodge of souvenirs and pictures.

A torn ticket from a high school football game—Sandy Springs Tocobaga High School. A picture of teenage Sundown sitting in front of a Christmas tree with, I assumed, her brother and sister. A couple of pages of class notes. One appeared to be a math class as it contained strings of numbers. The other page said *English Lit* at the top and contained names from spy novels. George Smiley. Jackal. Nancy Drew. The Hardy Boys. There was a photo of a cocker spaniel. Sundown, her brother, and the dog sitting in the front yard of a house, the sun beaming on their faces. A high school mug shot of another girl, with writing on it. "Sundown, good luck to a 'swell' girl and my best friend. RMA. Patti." An empty envelope with a return address: Patti Carmen, 518 Hall Rd., Sandy Springs, Florida.

"Refill?"

"Excuse me?"

"Can I warm it up for you?"

"Thanks." I nudged my cup toward Marci and away from the scattered debris.

"Looks like high school stuff," she said. "Like when you write on everyone's photo how much they mean to you and how you'll remember them forever. Thing is? You do remember them forever."

She twirled around and bustled back into the kitchen.

I read the writing on the back of another picture.

"Sunny, we know, don't we? Stay cool, girl, and thanks for being there for me. Love you madly. P.S. You, me, and Patti forever." I turned it over and looked into the face of a Hollywood-handsome man leaning with debonair confidence into the camera.

Chris Callaghan, like his mother, was one decent-looking person.

I put the picture down and rubbed my hands through my hair. Sundown and Chris went to high school together. They had known each other for years. When he died, it was not the death of a person she saw "seven or eight times," but that of a lifelong friend. She would have been devastated.

I pushed my coffee away, suddenly disgusted with—I didn't even know what to be disgusted with. I flipped the picture over and read it again. "You, me, and Patti forever." I noted the serial commas. CC was a proper writer.

"What did you and Sunny know?" I mumbled.

I called Yankee Conrad and asked him if Elaine had ever lived in Sandy Springs, Florida. He said that Elaine and her then-husband, Richard, had lived there while Richard worked at a nearby government facility. They'd kept their family house in Saint Petersburg. "The house you met her in was built by my great uncle after the crash of '29. He finished it October of '31."

"What age was Christopher when they lived in Sandy Springs?"

"Junior high through high school. He lived with his mother. She and Richard divorced soon after moving there. Why do you ask?"

I didn't feel like offering an explanation as I was still chasing shadows. "If it means anything, I'll let you know."

"What have you found?"

"Nothing of substance," I said, annoyed by his insistence.

An empty breath passed between us. "Remember discretion," he said.

I threw out an empty promise, and we clicked off. Yankee Conrad was not a man to succumb to urgency, yet I sensed it in his tone. I punched a few searches into my phone. There was still a Carmen listed on Hall Road in Sandy Springs. I considered calling first, but it was too easy to lie on the phone, especially when an unknown caller is asking prickly questions. It was a little over an hour drive, south and then east into the pancake-flat Florida scrubland. I checked in with Kathleen, cleared my schedule with Morgan, and told Bonita that I'd be out most of the day.

"You be careful, Mr. Jake," she said in her braid of Spanish and English. "Florida drivers are mad."

I assured her I'd be fine and headed out the door to see if Patti Carmen still resided in Sandy Springs and if she really did remember Sundown forever.

12

S andy Springs boasted a proud brick courthouse in the center of the town square with statues of long-deceased soldiers scattered on the lawn. Will there ever be a courthouse surrounded by statues of teachers, doctors, artists? Or must we sacrifice blood—inglorious as the cause may be—to be granted stone immortality? Baskets crowded with colored flowers and trailing vines hung from black gooseneck lampposts. Shops and restaurants lined the four sides of the square. I decided to kill time and have lunch before hitting Patti's address. If she worked, I had a greater chance of finding her at home later in the day.

I pulled into angled street parking in front of the Pirates' Deck restaurant. As I walked through the front door, I glanced down at my feet. *JCPenney* was laid in brick. The Pirates' Deck had started life as a downtown department store.

A blackboard by the front door listed the entertainment schedule. On weekends, the place rarely came up for air. A tin-stamped ceiling hung high over my head, a narrow balcony dotted with two-top tables rimmed the interior, and an elevated stage occupied the rear of the main floor. My salad was crisp, the fries hot, and the homemade tuna second only to mine. Best of all? No pirates.

I knocked on 518 Hall Road at four thirty, five thirty, and six thirty. A cross directory indicated that the woman I was searching for, Patti Carmen, owned the house. Whether she lived there was another matter. I decided to spend the night so I could hit her house early the next morning. I texted K and found a room at the Tocobaga Inn. It was a single-story motel that boasted air conditioning and internet. There was a lot of "Tocobaga" in the town. The Tocobaga tribe once lived on the land before being told by germ-bearing men with superior means of killing each other that they had no right to the land of their forefathers. Maybe the liberal sprinkling of their name was our statue to them. I settled in for the night, thankful that I kept an overnight bag in my truck, a habit left from years in the army. I kept a book in the leather duffel bag as well, but couldn't remember what it was or even when I'd placed it there.

That night I sipped whiskey and read *The Meditations of Marcus Aurelius,* wishing I'd paid more attention to what I kept in my duffel bag. But I got this: "For nowhere either with more quiet or more freedom from trouble does a man retire than into his own soul . . . constantly then give to yourself this retreat."

I drank that thought until I owned it.

AT EIGHT THE NEXT MORNING, AFTER A FIVE-MILE RUN ON country roads where pickup trucks kept chasing me into the high grass, I again knocked on 518 Hall Road. And again at nine thirty. Ticked at myself for not having more information, I headed back into town where I'd spotted a bookstore earlier. K's birthday was rounding the corner, and she collected first editions.

A Novel Experience was a large bookstore in a small town. As I opened the single-pane glass front door, chimes jingled above my head. The chimes were an odd assortment of hardware, including what appeared to be discarded jewelry—a gold anchor on a necklace, a starfish—that created a light tinkle sound due to their lack of weight. An antique desk sat off to the left. Several rooms broke off the main area, and narrow steps led to—according to a sign with an arrow—More Great Books! I didn't see anyone and wandered around the main floor. In a back room, I found a hardcover first edition of Pat Conroy's *The Prince of Tides* that Kathleen would love. I didn't have her whole heart; she reserved a chamber of it for tormented Southern writers—all the better if they were also Irish, Joyce's "an unfortunate priest-ridden race." For myself, I discovered a copy of James Crumley's *The Right Madness*. I decided to give it to Morgan as he'd mentioned once that he'd never read it. I'd lent my copy out years ago never to see it again.

The annoying beep of a dying smoke detector went off from upstairs.

A woman bounded down the stairs, cussed under her breath, and planted herself behind the antique desk. She popped open a laptop even though double screens sat on the credenza behind her. A collie curled on the rug next to her. One of its hind legs was wrapped in a white bandage. A water bowl next to the dog read TIPPY. You'd think I would have noticed Tippy when I first entered.

A man pushed through the front door hugging a box overflowing with books. "Where do you want these, Patti?"

The woman flicked her eyes up from the laptop and seemed surprised to see the man. "What do you got there, Brandon?"

"Books."

"You don't say."

"Garfield estate."

"I thought we had them all."

Brandon, about the same age as the woman behind the desk, said, "Some man just dropped these off. He said we missed them the first time through. He saw me get out of my car and said he knew I worked for you. He told me to tell you not to sell them until he works out the pricing with you. Got it? He doesn't want them listed yet."

"Who gave them to you?"

"My arms aren't what they used to be, Patti."

"Stick them upstairs on the sorting table. Anything promising?"

He glanced down at the box. "*The Robe. The Day of the Jackal. The Big Fisherman. How Green Was My Valley. The Quiet American.*"

"Wonderful. That stuff will never—"

"*Mrs. Miniver. From Here to*—"

"That's enough. Upstairs table, and thanks."

I'd been in the middle of the store, and the woman unfazed by the narrow steps had yet to notice me. I strolled to the front of the store and faced her. She wore a white blouse with the sleeves rolled up to her midforearm. A cup of black coffee rested to her right. The inscription on the mug read "Drink like you give a damn." A stack of leather bookmarks with the store's name on them was next to an adding machine that came out of the same decade as some of the books that Brandon was lugging up the creaking steps.

She glanced at the books I held.

"Sorry I wasn't here to greet you when you arrived," she said in a pleasant but robotic tone. "Can I help you find anything else?"

One of the twin screens was on screen-saver mode. It displayed a picture of three people by a boat on a sandbar. One of the people looked like Chris Callaghan, but the picture flashed to Tippy wearing a Christmas bow before I could be certain of what I'd seen.

"I'm not sure," I said. I gave her cash, and she placed it in a black steel box. She handed back my change. "Are you, by chance, Patti Carmen?"

She arched her eyebrows. "What can I do for you?"

Brandon bounced downstairs. The smoke detector beeped. He glanced at me and then said, "What's next, boss lady? You got a nine-volt battery? I can take care of that right now. You also mentioned something about the light in the women's room."

"Ronny put a new bulb in, and it still doesn't work."

"Ronny screw the right end in?"

"Take a look if you would. I also got Rodriguez working on the freezer at ten thirty. I'd appreciate if you met with him. That stuff is out of my circle of competence, and I don't want to be talked into something I don't need."

"Roger that. How's Tippy?"

"Taking her to Kim's later. Should get the bandage off."

"Need me to watch the store when you're out?"

"Appreciate it, but Suzanne's got me covered."

"How about that battery?"

"Damn thing started going off yesterday just as I was closing up. I meant to pick up one on the way in this morning—but you know how that works. I'll run out and pick up a pack."

"I'll give you a call on the freezer after Rodriquez takes its temperature. Get it?" He smiled and marched out the door.

"A freezer?" I said. "Is that some new method of preserving books?"

She laughed. "Not that I know of, but it wouldn't surprise me. The freezer's at the Pirates' Deck."

"The restaurant?"

"God help us if there's a real one in this forsaken crossroad."

"You own that as well?"

"That and half the town, which I'm sure you observed, is a far thing from bragging. I believe you asked my name?"

"Patti Carmen?"

"In the flesh."

Her daffodil-blonde hair was hacked short on the sides, her bangs trimmed well above her eyes. An uneven part with darker roots ran down the middle of her head. She leaned in on the desk, ready to bat away whatever issue I presented to her— just another item in a day stuffed with busted light fixtures, broken freezers, books that needed to be categorized, a pesky smoke detector, and a trip to the vet—so who's got time to color their hair?

"I'd like to ask you about Sundown."

She leaned back in her chair.

"And you are?"

I gave her my name.

"What about her?"

"Have you heard?"

"Heard what?"

"I'm sorry to have to tell you this, but she passed away."

Nothing.

"Patti?"

"Sundown?"

"I'm sorry to bring you the news."

I repeated my condolences, with the creeping realization that Sundown was not a distant name from the past.Patti's face pinched in pain, and she bit her lower lip, struggling to maintain her composure. She shoved the adding machine a few inches away from her—stupid thing that it was—and clawed her hands across the top of the desk.

Her eyes narrowed. "How did she die?"

As I spoke, she clenched her hands and her face went cold, battening down the hatches.

"I need a minute," she interrupted me. She stood and teetered out the back door. I pretended to look at books. A few minutes later she returned through the same door she had exited.

"Who are you?" she demanded. "And I don't mean your damn name. How did you find me?"

"I'm looking into the death of Chris Callaghan. Does his name ring a bell?"

That brought another round of silence. I was hitting her with body blows, although I did not know why and it certainly was not my intention.

"That was a long time ago," she snapped. "Why are you looking into it now?"

"The family wants closure. One last investigation to help Elaine—that's Chris's mother—come to terms."

"How did you find me?" she repeated. Her words corresponded with another beep from the neglected smoke detector.

I told her about Sundown's keepsakes and added that I'd tried her home late yesterday and that morning.

"Yeah? Well, my days start early and run long. Sorry I can't help you."

"I didn't ask for your help."

"Not yet, but you didn't drive here to"—she nodded at my books—"buy another tale of Mr. Conroy's dysfunctional family. Are you with the law?"

"No. Yankee Conrad hired me. He was Chris's—"

"I know who the hell Yankee Conrad is. Only decent person in Chris's life." I fished for my wallet and extracted the picture of Christopher with the writing on the back. *P.S. You, me, and Patti forever.*

"Does this mean anything to you?"

She snatched it from my hand, her eyes locked on the photograph. She started to raise her head, but then kept it down.

"Patti?"

She raised her head, her eyes burning mine. "You went through her stuff?"

"I'm trying to find who killed her."

"Isn't that a job for the police?"

"And they may talk to you, but now it's you and me."

"You think her death is related to Chris's?"

"I have no assumptions."

She turned the photo over a few times, as if she were perplexed that it only had two sides. She shrugged and handed it back to me. "Long time ago. I don't remember much from those days."

"I think you do."

"I don't care much what you think."

I leveled my eyes at her. "We're on the same team here. Can we talk?"

The door opened, ringing the dangling chimes that hung over the frame. A tall woman with striking features and a curvaceous figure walked in. Patti looked up at her. As she did, tears welled up in her eyes.

"Suzanne," Patti said. "Mr. Travis and I are going to run over to Woodstock. You OK for a few?"

"What's wrong, Patti?"

"It's . . . nothing. I'll tell you later."

"You sure?"

Patti took a deep breath. "I'm fine."

Suzanne tilted her head and ran her fingers up her neck, fluffing up her chestnut hair. A sense of déjà vu possessed me— but ran right out of my head and clear into next week before I could catch it.

"And who might you be?" she asked in a chesty voice.

As I introduced myself, Patti rose, grabbed her purse, and headed for the door. She opened it and then turned to me.

"I don't have all day."

I picked up a leather bookmark. "May I?"

"Comes with the book."

"Remember, Patti," Suzanne said from behind us, "to stop by the pharmacy and get a nine-volt battery."

13

A triple-spindle milkshake machine stood next to a flat grill behind the counter in the rear of the Woodstock Café. Bottom dollar it had been there since Ike was president. A radio sat next to it, its thin silver antenna searching the airwaves for a Telstar signal. The establishment had started life as a Deep South pharmacy when pharmacies had lunch counters. If walls could talk, these girls would howl.

Patti and I each claimed a backless, cracked blue vinyl stool on a silver base. She ordered coffee from Calloway, an older man with a wrinkled face and a smooth white apron. He and Patti had exchanged greetings when we approached the counter. They chatted while I eyed a cinnamon pastry under a domed plastic lid.

"You own this, too?" I asked Patti after Calloway shuffled away.

"No, and I don't want to. I need a place to relax that is someone else's problem."

"It's a great spot." And it was, for those silent howling walls spoke forgiveness, forging into good what had once been bad. "You, me, and Patti forever," I said.

"We were best friends," she said, keeping her eyes on the mug or, more importantly, not on me. "That's all. It was a long time ago, and it seems even longer than it was."

"The writing on the picture—what was it that Chris and Sunny knew?"

She flashed her eyes at me. "Oh, we knew lots. Who was breaking up, who had a hard crush on who. Stuff like that. Those were high school years, when love was ten times love and sad was ten times sad. Life doesn't stay that intense. At first I thought that was tragic, but now I think it's for the best."

"We can't burn that hot forever."

"Or stay that cold."

"Calloway?" I said. He stopped wiping down the grill that couldn't possibly become any cleaner.

"Yes, sir?"

"I think that cinnamon Danish has my name on it."

"I believe it does."

"Two forks and a knife, if you don't mind."

Calloway plucked my prize with metal tongs and placed it on a scratched white plate. I repositioned it between Patti and me.

"Help yourself."

"Shame on you," she said. She cut off a piece and I followed. The radio with the searching antenna emitted tinny advertisements.

"Tell me about when you met Sundown," she said, catching me in midchew.

I swallowed and then explained how I traced her boat, stumbled upon her at the museum, and our lunch together. Patti listened patiently while occasionally biting her lip. I was clueless as to whether she gnawed in response to my words or was worried about the light in the women's room at the Pirates' Deck.

"She lied to me," I concluded.

"Excuse me?"

"She told me that she didn't know Chris that well. That he was just a guy on the next boat over. But he wasn't. They were good friends before they moored their boats next to each other. She told me she rarely took her dinghy to his boat, but I've got a witness that remembers her dinghy being at his boat more often than she let on. She told me she moved her boat after the fire, but I confirmed that, too, was a falsehood. Why?"

"I don't know."

"That's a pile of untruths."

She flipped open her hands.

"Can't imagine a reason, right?" I said.

She squirmed in her stool. "I don't understand what any of . . . those days have to do with Sundown's death."

"Maybe nothing. But if in some manner Sundown's death is tied to the past, then you're the only surviving member. What was the secret?"

She puffed her breath out, and I took the opportunity to stuff more Danish into my mouth.

"Chris was gay," she said. "Big deal, right? But this is a small town, and it was different then. The three of us ran together. Chris knew he had to get out of Sandy Springs. He and Sundown were close."

That didn't answer my question of why Sundown lied, but I gave her some rope. "Tell me about them."

"They packed up and headed out after graduation."

"College?"

"UF, but they both dropped out after a year. Chris's parents divorced soon after he moved here. His dad worked at the government facility out on Route 29. He and his mom stayed here so he could finish high school, but after that the two of them moved back to Saint Pete. I think Chris decided he'd rather live with his mom and travel than the whole overblown college thing. I was the bittersweet recipient of sunset postcards from the far edge of every continent."

"Did you keep in touch with him?"

"Not really. The postcards got fewer in between. Fine with me. I didn't really need reminders of what I was missing. They both ended up in Saint Pete. And"—she tilted her head—"here I sit."

"There's no need to leave."

"Small towns are for leaving, right? But people split because they're trying to leave their old selves behind. I'm not sure it works like that."

"What did Chris's father do for the government?"

"I don't know."

"Where is the government facility?"

"Told you, Route 29, a road out of town that leads to nowhere. I haven't been by it in years."

"Sundown and Chris certainly stayed in touch if they were both in Saint Petersburg."

"Guess so," she said with an air of indifference.

"Why would Sundown lie to me?"

"You already asked that."

"And you never answered."

"I did. I said, 'I. Don't. Know.'"

"How about a guess?"

She hesitated. "I can't think of anything."

I registered my disbelief in her statement by observing a moment of silence before asking, "Did you and Sundown stay in touch?"

"For a few years. Maybe a decade. But nothing recently. I doubt I spoke to her in the past five years. Sad, really, when you think of it."

Maybe she was being truthful with me, and I'd driven a long distance for nothing. I switched tracks. "How well did you know Elaine, Chris's mother?"

"Well enough. We—Sundown and I—would go to Chris's house. It was a big old antebellum off of Holly Road. Elaine was . . . I guess colorful is the word. Bohemian."

"I met her," I said. "I don't believe she has both oars in the water."

She bobbed her head a few times. "Left the cookies in the oven too long—however you want to spin it. But who among us can throw stones, right?"

"They were close, mother and son?"

"They were."

"Too close?"

She eyed me. "What do you mean?"

"Did their relationship seem unusual?"

"I was a teenage girl. What did I know about a son's relationship with his mother?"

"But looking back?"

She took a piece of Danish and then pushed the plate toward me. "The rest is yours. Looking back? Who's got time for that? We had fun. I remember one day we all drove over to Saint Pete Beach—Elaine, Chris, Sundown, and Harlan, he was my boyfriend at the time. Yankee took us out on the *Ms. Buckeye*. It was a beautiful day. We anchored off a sandbar. I'd never been in water so large and so warm. Elaine had packed a lunch for us. We spent the day on that boat. Life was good, and it was all for us. But then life moved on, and took some of the good with it." She flicked her eyes to me. "It sucks when you hit the age when you start sentences with 'I remember.'"

"Beats 'I forget.'"

"Yeah? Well, that's next. Do you think her death was in any manner related to her history with Chris? You insinuated that, didn't you?"

"Is there anything else you can tell me that may shed some light?"

"Sorry." She straightened, as if suddenly aware that her

posture had given in to the challenge of sitting on a backless stool. "You know, I really need to get back to the salt mines."

We stood, and I told her I appreciated her time and gave her my card. We walked back to A Novel Experience, commenting on what a terrific job the town did in maintaining the flowers hanging from the lampposts. She stopped and faced me before entering her bookstore. She thanked me with emotion and a note of finality the situation hardly warranted.

"You OK here?" I asked, for I sensed the news of Sundown's murder hit her harder than she let on.

She mustered a weak smile. "Never better."

She scurried into her store, closing the door behind her as if to make sure I didn't follow. Along with the bad freezer, a dog that needed a vet, and a busted light fixture, she now had an old friend to mourn. I couldn't blame her for wanting to distance herself from me.

Plus, she still needed to get a nine-volt battery.

14

I did a loop around the town square before heading out in the opposite direction I needed in order to get home. I felt I would be leaving with more questions than when I'd arrived, turning my back on the very thing I should be facing. I cruised a few side streets and found Holly Road and what was likely the antebellum home that Elaine and Chris had lived in during their tenure in Sandy Springs. It was restored to its Southern glory, white Doric columns projecting grandeur that was both misplaced and indigenous.

The homes thinned out, and I took a different road back into town. A high chain-link fence with barbed wire in the shape of a *V* at the top bordered the right side of the road. It continued for half a mile until it broke for a concrete drive mapped with cracks and weeds. It appeared to be surplus government property—the well-maintained fence gave it away. I wondered if it was where Chris's father worked and the reason the three of them moved to Sandy Springs. I checked my GPS. Route 29.

I did a U-turn and pulled into the drive. A gate blocked me from going any farther, but it was partially open. I got out of the truck, swung the gate wide enough to allow my truck to pass, and continued down a single-lane road. The road bent once for no apparent reason and ended at a two-story yellow brick building. It had a flat roof with security cameras at the end, but I doubted they were still operational. An old green pickup truck with more miles behind it than in front of it sat by the building. Its driver-side door was open and a Black man sat inside munching a sandwich, one leg dangling out the door. He spotted me and put his sandwich down. I swung my truck to the side and got out. We met between vehicles.

"I'm sorry, suh," he said. "But this is government property and is closed to the public." He stood motionless, a slender man unswayed by my presence. His voice was thin, as if he shared it with the wind, and his milky eyes kind and soft.

"But here you are."

"Yes, suh. They pay me to walk the grounds twice a week, but I'm here nearly every day. Don't want to give them any reason to be replacing me. I was just having my lunch before setting out."

I introduced myself. He said his name was Joe, and we shook hands.

"I apologize for intruding. I was in town meeting with Patti Carmen and was taking a tour before I left."

"Patti tell you where this was?" he asked.

"She told me about it. One of her friends' fathers used to work here."

"Used to ain't even close. This place been locked over a decade now. Goin' on two."

"You know Patti?" I asked.

"Everyone knows Ms. Patti. She owns 'bout everything except the churches. She'd be too smart to go inda business with God, but don't you be tellin' my wife I said that."

"How long have you been walking the grounds?"

"I jus' finished my lunch. I'm about to start out."

"I meant how many of those shuttered years?"

"Oh. Past five or so. Started when McClatchen got the bug and his children moved him up north to be closer to them. Not a bad job, really. A few bucks a week for walking a couple of miles, and the steps are good for me. I need the work. My truck's on its final days. It dies and my wife has no way to visit our grandchildren till I get me another one, and I don't know how I'm gonna do that. My daughter up and moved to Montgomery on account of a job. The virus chased both her and her husband out of their old jobs. It was like the world pulling away."

I nodded toward the brick building. "What did they do here?"

"Top secret stuff," he said with a twinkle in those soft eyes. "I like sayin' that 'cause folks always be axin me. Officially it was a warehouse, but the scuttlebutt is it was some sort of think tank where they worked on missile guidance systems and trained secret agents. You know, that Cold War stuff."

"Cold War was a long time ago."

"Yes, suh. That's what they be sayin', but I'm not so sure about that. Seems the Russians be hacking something every day."

"You're a wise caretaker," I said.

"If you don't mind me axin, what was it you were seeing Ms. Patti for?"

"I'm afraid that I was the bearer of bad news. An old friend of hers died. Someone she hadn't seen in years."

"You an officer? You got out of your truck like a man not afraid of his next step."

"I served, but I'm not with any law enforcement."

He took a moment with that and then said, "How did Ms. Patti take the news—that her friend had died?"

"She was hard to read. I guess they'd fallen away from each other."

"That seems to be part of life. She was out here 'bout two weeks ago."

"Patti?"

"Yes, suh. She placed some flowers up on the ridge that runs across the north of the property. Finegan's Ridge, on account of the General Joseph Finegan once camping his troops there after he headed north to the battle of Lake City. It's a pretty spot. Years ago they used to do Civil War reenactment up there even though there was never a battle here." He swung his head. "I ain't the smartest man, but I never understood why men would reenact anything about war except its ending."

"You're smarter than you give yourself credit for. Why did Ms. Patti put flowers up on the ridge?"

"I axed her that when I saw her at the Pirates' Deck—that the restaurant she owns. I play banjo in a band there on Friday nights. She said she just like picnicking at that spot. Been doing it for years with friends. She and two other women was up there."

I'd asked Patti about the government property. *I haven't been by it in years.* I couldn't see a reason for her to lie on such a simple matter. Maybe she deemed it not worth the effort.

"You mind taking me there?"

"Not a-tall. I need to be makin' my rounds anyways. Be nice to have a little company."

We hiked a narrow path through trees suffocated with kudzu vine. Joe said he'd never seen anything suspicious when doing his rounds, yet he was required to file a report every week saying he'd walked the circumference of the property. We climbed up a rocky path where he unlocked a small gate.

"I oil this lock every so often," he said. "Not required to, but I'm in charge of this property, and my daddy used to say that any job worth doin' is worth doin' right."

We'd arrived on a plateaued surface that held a sweeping view of a green valley with heavy-leaved trees. It was high ground—for Florida. Two drooping bouquets of flowers rested by a small stone.

"This is the spot," Joe said.

"How long did they stay?"

"Not long. They waved at me and I waved back."

"Did you recognize the other women, besides Patti?"

"One of 'em was Patti's old friend. The other one—she was tall."

"By tall, do you mean Suzanne who works in the bookstore with her?"

"I'm afraid I don't know her."

"And the other woman, the old friend?"

He nodded. "She's the one I recognized. Used to hang around with Ms. Patti when they was teenagers. I saw her at a house when I was layin' bricks."

"What house was that?"

"Old antebellum on Holly Road. I laid the brick patio they have out back. I put down bricks for nearly fifty-five years."

"Was that the Callaghan house?"

"That's the name," he said excitedly. "Someone axed me the other day, and I couldn't remember it for the life of me. Nice place now. The new owners fixed her up good. I know they wouldn't had to do anything to that brick patio, though. That patio be here when Jesus come back—I don't mean that in vain."

I took a moment to string together what he'd told me.

"The woman who laid these flowers—you remember her from when she was young and visiting the Callaghans?"

"Yes, suh. She was a nice girl. Had one of the prettiest faces you'd ever see and a name to match, although I wasn't starin' or anything. I was raised never to look a White woman in the face."

"The times are a-changing."

"Yes, suh. I believe I read that someplace."

"And this girl—woman—was up here with Patti two weeks ago laying these flowers?"

"Um-hum. She, Patti, and another woman—the tall one. She changed a little over the years, but God was kind when he gave me my eyes. I see now jus' as well as I did when I laid my first brick at fourteen."

"You got a name to match the face?"

"Sundown. A man don't forget a woman with a name like that." He'd been maintaining eye contact with me, but now he gazed over the distant fields, his head a little higher, his breezy voice firm. "They could tell me not to look a woman in the face, but my mind belongs to me.

15

Well, bust my britches. Patti had flat-out lied to me. Just as Sundown had. Does anyone tell the truth anymore?

I sped back into town, my anger at Patti outweighing my curiosity about why she lied. I'd thought we'd gotten along well. Even shared a cinnamon roll. Patti not only kept in contact with Sundown, but apparently she, Sundown, and Suzanne—I was guessing there—had a picnic at Finegan's Ridge two weeks ago. I thought of Sundown lying to me regarding her friendship with Chris and couldn't imagine why the three old friends—at least the surviving two—had been so secretive. Whether any of that had anything to do with the death of Chris Callaghan was another matter.

Suzanne peered up from behind the desk after I burst through the front door of A Novel Experience.

"Can I help you?" She spoke in a flat tone, as if her mind was a universe removed from her body. Smudged makeup marred her face.

"Patti here?"

"No."

"Know where she is?"

"You might try the Pirates' Deck."

"Appreciate your time."

I started for the front door.

"Hey."

I spun around. "Yes?"

She dropped her eyes. "Nothing."

I hit the door and jaywalked across the street to the Pirates' Deck. It was empty except for a few late lunch stragglers. I marched back to the kitchen. A man slumped on the floor next to a freezer with its back off. An assortment of tools was scattered around him.

"Have you seen the boss lady?" I asked.

He glanced up at me, his eyeglasses halfway down his nose. "Nope. Brandon said she'd meet me here, but she's been a no-show."

"She do that much?"

"Do what much?"

"No-show."

He snorted. "I'm surprised she's not on the floor with me now, stickin' her head in this thing. Glad she ain't, though."

"Is Brandon here?"

"Not unless he turned into a mouse and crawled into the wall."

"You Rodriguez?"

"The one and only."

"Have a good day. By the way, Brandon says you're the best."

"I tried to talk Patti out of this SABA. It's seventy-two cubic feet. She'd be better off with two smaller ones in case one breaks, but what do I know, right?"

I decided to stay in one place, take a deep breath, and let Patti surface. It was a small town—she couldn't have gone far. I grabbed a barstool. A petite young woman with purple hair tied in a ponytail planted herself across the bar from me. She'd not been there when I'd first entered. A sign above her head read "When the virus is over, I'm still drinking alone."

"What'll it be?"

I ordered a beer—I deserved it—and said, "I don't suppose you know where Patti is, either, do you?"

"Patti, Patti, Patti," she said. "Everybody's always looking for Patti. You think this town would just slip away without her."

"Just a question."

She plopped a foaming auburn ale in front of me. "No."

"Expect her back soon?"

"I don't keep tabs on my mom."

"You're her daughter?" Patti hadn't looked old enough to have a daughter legally standing on the work side of a bar.

"You're a quick one."

"I was talking with your mom earlier and wanted to ask her a few more questions before heading out of town."

She rested her hands on her hips.

"She's gone."

"Gone?"

"You're familiar with the word, right?"

"Gone as in not here or as in—"

"Gone, baby, gone. She had business to attend to out of town."

I took a sip of beer and considered the woman—presumably Patti's daughter, but I wouldn't put money on it.

"I just shared coffee and a cinnamon Danish with her. She didn't mention leaving."

"How sweet. You her probation officer or something?"

"Do you know when she'll be back?"

"Nope."

"Know where I can find her?"

"See previous comment. Might as well stop looking for her."

"What makes you think I'm looking for her?"

"Do you hear yourself?"

I pushed my unfinished beer across the counter and reached for my wallet. "What do I owe you?"

"Why the attitude?"

"Beers and lies. You pay for one and the other is complimentary. Your mother left town and you don't know where or when she'll return?"

She planted her elbows on the counter, folded her hands in front of her, and rested her chin in the cradle of her fingers.

"Tell you what," she said. "Beer's on me. That way both are complimentary."

I slid my card across the shiny counter. "I gave her one already—but in case she tossed it."

She reached for the card, but as she did, I pulled it back. I grabbed a pen, wrote a note on the card, and handed it back to her. She picked it up and examined it.

"I saw the flowers on Finegan's Ridge," she read. She crinkled her nose, and I saw her mother in her. "Is it part of a poem or something?"

I'd been studying her for any sign of recognition, but I'm notoriously bad at reading people, an unfortunate trait that has never kept me from quick and inaccurate judgments.

"It *is* a poem," I said. "But I don't understand it. Tell her I need her help. And—"

"And what? You come in peace?"

"Tell her I think Sundown would want me to know the rest of it."

Her eyes narrowed and she shifted her weight. "Sundown, her friend?"

"The same."

"What about her?"

Her friend. Not her old friend.

"Have her call me."

"And if she doesn't?"

I laid a ten on the counter. "She will."

As I walked out the door, I glanced at another sign above the threshold.

"Think of it: Someone is quarantined with your ex."

96

16

Patti texted me the next day, just as I'd gotten done hanging a screen door at Harbor House. She asked if we could meet at Sundown's house at six that evening. I took it as an admission of guilt that she'd lied to me about not keeping in touch with Sundown.

I found her sitting on Sundown's sun-slanted front porch when I pulled up against the curb at 5:55. I ambled—I didn't want to appear confrontational—up the steps and took a seat on a weathered wood rocker. A bottle of scotch sat between us. She appeared to be a lap ahead of me.

"Rocks or neat?" she said.

"Rocks."

She fished ice out of a bucket and poured scotch over a wreck of cubes.

"To Sundown."

"To Sundown." We clanked glasses.

The air was thick, and beads of sweat trickled down my chest. A trembling palm frond registered a breeze, but I didn't feel it. Faint music carried out of the house from an open window, and thunder rumbled from behind us. It was a good spot and a fine night for scotch.

"When was the last time you were here?" I asked.

"Couple weeks ago."

I let out a low whistle. "Sweat Pea, you are one fine liar."

She tilted her head at me. "Why, thank you, *Sweat Pea*." She crossed a leg over another and leaned back in the chair, her eyes holding mine.

"I'm sure there's a good reason for misleading me," I said.

"You mean lying?"

"I was being considerate."

"You first," she said. "How did you find Finegan's Ridge?"

I told her the story of driving through town and running into Joe, the caretaker.

"Really?" she said, curling up the left corner of her lip. "That's it? You just turned into the facility, trip over the banjo player for Uncle Al, and that led to us being here?"

"Uncle Al?"

"That's the name of the band Joe plays in. Packs 'em in every Friday night."

"No. You not being truthful led to us enjoying this evening together."

She puffed out her breath. "She died a few feet behind me. I don't know how I can sit here and drink her scotch. But we always said that if one of us went first—and that's generally the way it works—that we needed to carry on. To live life even fuller, for now we live for the deceased as well as the living. I believe that, and I don't believe much."

"And so we carry on."

"Can I just get it out?" she said.

"The stage is yours."

She cast her eyes down to the floor. "Chris used to say that. He liked theater. *Loved* theater. But he added a twist to it. He'd say, 'The stage is yours, and the theater is empty.'"

"A bit nihilistic."

"That was Chris."

"You have an audience of one."

She gripped her sweating tumbler with both hands. "I had a baby in high school." Her voice was flat and void of emotion. "I was sixteen. I wanted to keep her and I did. But she died at eight weeks old. SIDS. Sudden infant death syndrome. I'll never get over that. How I put her to bed and the next morning she was still there, just as I had laid her down the night before. I waited an hour past when she usually wakes up—I thought she was just sleeping. But when I stirred her, she was limp in my arms." Her body shuddered. "She felt the same. Weighed the same. But she was gone."

She took a sip of her drink, her head buried in the empty promise of the golden liquid. "Life is weightless." She shot her eyes up to mine. "That's what I learned in high school. Terrible thing for a sixteen-year-old girl to discover. I feel more sorry now for my sixteen-year-old self than I did then. We buried her on Finegan's Ridge. Me, Chris, Elaine, and Sundown. No one else knew."

"Did you—"

"Now I lay me down to sleep," she said. "I pray the Lord my soul to keep. And should I die before I wake, I pray the Lord my soul to take." She let out a blast of breath. "What a holy pile of shit. I didn't want the goddamn Lord to have my baby. She was mine. To this day, I can't watch a baby sleep. I always poke it."

Thunder rolled in the distance like a sustained chord from a pipe organ. After a silent measure I said, "I'm sorry for your loss."

"I see her sometimes, when I see a woman about the age she would be. I can't help but wonder if her life went some-where else. If I've passed her on the street. In a store."

"We don't know."

"Yes, we do. We just don't accept it."

"Your parents?"

She gave a heavy sigh. "When I realized I was pregnant, I moved in with Chris. Elaine took me in just as my mom was kicking my 'whore-ass' out. Elaine was the only one outside the three of us who knew. I don't know how I would have survived without that woman's support. I dropped out of school. Told everyone I had mono."

"Your father?"

"My parents divorced when I was six."

My gaze wandered over the street. Elaine had been an integral part of the lives of Chris and his friends. I was getting someplace, but like driving in a foreign country, I didn't know where.

"You were trying to ask a question?" she said.

"You answered it, but here's another. Harlan, the boy you were dating when you all went out on the *Ms. Buckeye,* was he the father?"

She nodded. "A worthless piece of charming white trash."

"But charming trash knew."

"Yeah. I told him I lost Amanda. That was her name. But he didn't give a flying fuck one way or the other. I apologize for my salty language. There are parts of my life that bring out the sailor in me."

"I take it this was after your glorious day on the *Ms. Buckeye?*"

"That would be right."

"And your sojourn to Finegan's Ridge?"

"Amanda's birthday."

Patti's eyes tracked two bicyclists as they pedaled down the street, weaving back and forth in a pattern of lazy indifference. A chain on one of the bikes clanged with every rotation. A boy on a skateboard skimmed by going the opposite direction, his body lean and without motion.

"Why not tell me the first time around?" I said.

"Just didn't."

"I ran into your daughter at the Pirates' Deck."

"She knows. I had Melinda when I was eighteen. I thought having another would help me get over Amanda."

"How did that work?"

She smiled at me. "Pretty damn well. Melinda's the joy of my life. I got a daughter and a best friend to boot. I couldn't ask for more."

"Melinda's father?"

She shook her head at me. "You're going to have to throw the towel in on the men of my life; God knows I have. I'm no good at 'em. Find me a good-looking one that can't hold a dollar bill and I'll flip over him. Or I used to. I learned my lesson. Between A Novel Experience, the Deck, and the UPS store—I own that, too—I keep myself busy. Own a four-family, too. Turns out I'm unlucky in love and lucky—and damn good —in business. The bookstore doesn't make much money, but it's a quiet place to work. I run expenses through it, which keeps my taxes on the other two hovering around zero." She cut me a look. "Zero, that's about as much chance as I have of finding a guy with half a shot of common sense."

"You're still young."

She cocked her head and creased her forehead. "You feeling bad for me? Telling me I'm a failure just because I don't share my bed at night? Piss off."

"I didn't mean it like that."

"Typical male."

We each took refuge in our diluted drinks.

"Can I help you with anything here?" I offered, trying to crawl back into her good graces.

"I appreciate that, but I'm not sure what I'm into. I'm the executor of her estate."

"Joe told me there was a third woman at Finegan's Ridge."

"Melinda would go up with us. Melinda once said if Amanda hadn't died that she'd never been born."

"There's some truth to that."

"No," she said, taking a swallow. "There's all truth to that."

A thought slipped in my mind, but it vanished without a whisper. I didn't chase it. Instead, I went with, "Sundown."

"What about her?"

"Do you know of any reason someone would want to kill her?"

"Haven't a clue."

"Haven't a clue or you'll tell me more later, after I accidentally trip over the truth?"

"That was one and done. I haven't anything more."

"There's always more."

She searched my face to see if I was bluffing, which I was. I had no reason to believe that Patti was holding anything back —other than her previous lies.

"She was murdered," I said. "Maybe random. Maybe not."

She glanced down at the floor. "She told me that Richard had contacted her."

It took me a second. "Elaine's ex-husband?"

"The same."

"Why would—"

"They had an affair."

"Sundown and Richard? Chris's father?"

"That's right."

"Imagine. And just a minute ago there was nothing more."

She humped her shoulder. "It seems a pretty private thing, and easy to misconstrue. It's not like we had nothing to do in a small town except screw each other's parents and bury babies."

"I didn't say that."

"Be a fool not to think it. It was after she'd been to college for a few years. They had a fling one summer. There was only about twenty years between them, and Sundown was always into older men. And Richard Callaghan—he was serious swoon material. Between him and Elaine, you could see where Chris got his killer looks. But there was more. He was kind. Thoughtful. The perfect damn man."

"How did Chris feel about that?"

"He'd come out of the closet around then, and I think his father's sexual escapades were the furthest thing on his mind."

"How close were Sundown and Richard?"

"It was a fling. They had no illusions."

"Elaine?"

"Can't help you there. I'm not sure if she ever knew. They were long divorced by then." She cut me a look. "There you have it. Our own little *Peyton Place*. Unfortunately for you, none of this has anything to do with who murdered Sundown."

I wasn't so sure about that. I added a few cubes to my drink, poured God's gift over them, stood, and walked over to the end of the porch, pushing my body through the air heavy with water and salt. I sat on the railing, picking a spot that had a supporting spindle directly under my weight. The late afternoon sun shafted a yellow ribbon down the street, and another roll of thunder indicated that the storm would blow south of us.

"Did Richard ever circle back into Sundown's life?"

"Not that I know."

"Harlan double back into yours?"

Nothing.

"Patti?"

She hesitated. "He dropped by the bookstore about a month ago. Said he was passing through—total shit, no one passes through Sandy Springs—and just wanted to see how I was doing.

"Said, 'Do you remember Amanda?'" She bit her lower lip and swayed her head. "Unfuckingbelieveable. He said he was sorry for deserting me and all that, and he just wanted to make peace with his past. He said he wanted to see Sundown, too. I think that was his reason for dropping by—he wanted to know where she lived."

"Was there anything between them?"

"We all dated, but not really. She always warned me that I saw more in him than there really was, and she was right. I had no earthly clue why he wanted to see her."

"But you asked."

"She said he knew he was a jerk and wanted to make amends."

"And did you? Give him her address?"

"Sure, and then gave her a heads-up call. She didn't mind. She called a few days later and said he had dropped by. Said he wanted to apologize for being such an ass back in the day."

"Seems a little lame."

She shrugged. "There you have it." She stood and took a step toward the street. She ran her finger down a wood post flaked with paint. As if the act of touching it in some manner connected her to Sundown.

"All the small-town gossip," she said. "The lies. The cheating. The buried baby. The replacement daughter. The Bobbie Gentry flowers on a ridge." She cut me a look over her shoulder. "You satisfied, poking around my sorry-ass life?" But her voice fell flat of her blustery intent.

"I met a successful businesswoman who is respected in her town and is blessed with a beautiful daughter with whom she works every day. Looks like the top of the world to me."

That earned a weak smile. "Thank you. We do get better at spinning things as we age." She leaned against the post, the sun glowing on half her face and the other half shadowed. "I thought drinking whiskey—scotch, whatever—on Sundown's front porch might be a good idea. Now, I'm not so certain."

I was having trouble accepting what Patti claimed was Harlan's reason for wanting to meet with Sundown.

"How can I reach Harlan?"

"Why? So you can check out my story?"

"No. I want—"

"He owns a nightclub—or whatever you might call it—downtown. The Encore. Tell him I sent you."

I stood and walked toward her. "How long are you here for?"

"Probably a couple of days. I booked a room around the corner. I didn't want to stay in the house."

"If you'd like dinner sometime, give me a call. Beats eating alone."

"Meet the fam and all that?"

"That's how it works." The thought that had vanished without a whisper came back around. "You said Melinda accompanied you and Sundown to Finnegan's Ridge?"

"What about it?"

"Joe told me he didn't know the third woman. That she was large. Your daughter—"

"That would have been the last time. Suzanne came up with us. Melinda couldn't make it. Suzanne and I went to the University of Florida together and lost touch. We reconnected a few years ago, and she's a good friend. Nice to have new-old friends seeing as how I apparently won the last-one-standing award."

RAMBLER CALLED ON THE way home.

"We got the autopsy," he said. "She was struck in the carotid artery and an arm wrapped around her neck from behind. Mean anything to you?"

"Guy knew what he was doing."

"He likely used strangulation to elicit information. Still no sign of her phone or computer. You know of any reason why such a gentleman would be visiting our hamlet?"

"No."

He hung up.

Why am I surprised that people lie when I do the same?

17

K athleen was reading to Joy before putting her to bed. I
worried about her going to sleep some night and not
crossing through to the new day just as Patti's baby, Amanda,
had done years ago. And I'd been worried about bad dreams.

Hadley III rubbed up against my leg, which she rarely did.
Kathleen's attention had shifted to Joy, so the cat was moving
down the list in its search for affection. I went to the fridge and
took out a piece of cold fish. Breaking it into pieces, I placed it
in her bowl on the screened porch. She sniffed it, considered
me, and then nibbled a few bites before slinking out the cat
door and into the moonless night. I put a Billie Holiday album
on the Magnavox and turned it low.

Kathleen staggered out of our bedroom and collapsed on
the chair next to me.

"I don't know who was more tired, Joy or me."

"Call it a night?"

"I'll rally."

She would. Kathleen possessed a tremendous capacity to
brighten as the day moved on. I, on the other hand, am a

windup tin soldier, charging out of the gate every morning only to grow weaker with each step.

She pushed her empty wineglass toward me. "Hit me with a smidge." As I poured French grapes into her glass, she said, "Have the police found anything else on Sundown's death?"

I'd explained to her, over a fresh shrimp scampi dinner—it was a little heavy on minced garlic, but I couldn't control myself—my latest encounter with Patti.

"Rambler called," I said in conclusion. "The man who choked Sundown knew what he was doing."

"Clarify that."

"He entered with the intention of killing her."

"So you have three friends—four if you include Harlan—one dies in a tragic boat fire and the other is murdered. And the murdered one, years ago slept with the father of the one who died in the fire. Oh, and a baby who never saw her first birthday. A mess, but I'm sure there are bigger ones out there. Can you imagine Joy having a baby in sixteen years and then losing it?"

We were quiet a few minutes, Billie's tortured voice struggling to find us.

"Can you just imagine?" Kathleen repeated, and I knew the thought had taken her like a riptide.

She stood up and motioned for me to scoot over. She nestled next to me, her warm body pressed against mine. She laid her head on my shoulder and snuggled her face into my neck. Her breathing slowed, and I thought she might nod off. But then she lifted her head and kissed me. Our breaths were stale with the wine and the too-much garlic and the tiredness of the day. I've said it before, but it warrants repeating—a dirty kiss is a damn good kiss. She positioned herself so that her legs straddled mine and wrapped her arms around my neck. I stood, and she hiked her legs around my waist.

I walked us into the spare bedroom as our tongues, silent to each other for most of the day, engaged in a frantic duel driven by the unquenchable thirst of the heart. She matched my insatiable appetite for her with her own dark passions as we tangled with no one in charge. A crucifying bolt of fervor decomposed us to dust, and in that flash I understood how Patti saw her deceased daughter in the eyes of strangers, but it is a mystery why it came to me then.

I DID FOUR FAST MILES THE NEXT MORNING ON A DARK BEACH and was in front of my computer before the sun cracked the cotton-candied horizon. I had no reason to suspect that Sundown's death or the ransom letter was related to Richard Callaghan's work decades ago for the government, but the more I knew, the more I could rule out.

Sandy Springs Logistics and Research Base, closed for seventeen years, had provided logistics and support for MacDill Air Force Base in Tampa. "Logistics and support" was military jargon for planning and fulfilling military movement and missions. It covered a lot of territory. Joe had said the "scuttlebutt" was that the facility worked on missile guidance systems and agent training. MacDill itself was founded under army command in 1939, before the creation of the air force as an independent service in 1947. Garrett and I flew out of it numerous times, as it was headquarters for both the United States Central Command (USCENTCOM) and the United States Special Operations Command (USSOCOM), which we served under.

I'd called Garrett and asked him to see if he could gather more information on Richard Callaghan. Garrett would go through Colonel Janssen, our former colonel who we did contract work for after we checked out of the army. I'd ask him myself, but he'd hang up on me. I'd been the one who made the decision, for both Garrett and myself, to disengage from him.

And here I was crawling back.

YANKEE CONRAD PULLED INTO THE GRAVEL PARKING LOT at Harbor House at 9:45. I'd called him earlier, and he suggested he drop by. He claimed he wanted to see "the good work we were doing."

The city inspector had just left, giving me a green light on a handicapped ramp I'd installed leading up to the back porch. It was nip and tuck with the elevated porch—another few inches higher and we would have been required to put a rail around it. The inspector also approved the drain. Now that his nagging interest lay in someone else's property, I could punch out the water lines I'd rerouted under a bathroom sink that abutted an outside wall. I wanted an outdoor shower, which are apparently destructive to the planet. Dirty kisses and outdoor showers are damn good living.

Yankee Conrad stretched his lean body out of a spotless white four-door sedan, gave the property a visual once-over, and strolled to the back porch where I stood in the shade. A few feet away, heat radiated off the earth, angry that it couldn't burn me.

He joined me in refuge from the sun. "Welcome to the house of the tired and poor," I said. "'Your huddled masses yearning to breathe free.'"

"'The wretched refuse of your teeming shore,'" he added, quoting Emma Lazarus's poem. "'Send these, the homeless tempest-tost to me. I lift my lamp beside the golden door.'" His eyes rested on mine. "Mac always liked that. It's good to see what you've done with his place."

"You knew him?"

He skipped a beat. "We had the pleasure. I see you removed the antiaircraft gun."

Mac—Walter MacDonald—had been the man who owned

the property before his death at age ninety-four. I'd met him while tracking down the man who had kidnapped my sister and only sibling from a Florida hotel when we were children. We'd bonded the first time we met—one of those rare occurrences when you meet someone and instantly form a deep and trusting friendship. Upon Mac's death, he gifted his property to the county for the purpose of serving immigrant families and "all those who seek help." That's a wide net. He appointed Morgan and me as trustees of the ample endowment he funded to support the mission.

The antiaircraft gun.

Mac hated seagulls. During World War II, he'd witnessed the eyes of his fellow sailors pecked out of their heads as they slowly died while floating off Iwo Jima and Okinawa, their kapok life vests conveniently keeping their bobbing heads facing God. Mac had a 1950s antiaircraft gun that he'd nicknamed Sallie-Mae mounted at the edge of the pond. When he'd let a few rounds go at unsuspecting gulls, I suspect he was shooting at more than the birds. Ironically, Mac's eyes blazed with life. I recalled hardly being able to take my eyes off his, for they glowed with a goodness not of this world.

He'd also worked for the Office of Strategic Services, the predecessor to the CIA. Yankee Conrad's casual mention of Mac reminded me that there was more I didn't know about Yankee Conrad than I did know.

"It was a bear," I said. "I left it at the curb. They claim to pick up whatever a homeowner leaves out."

Yankee Conrad chuckled and smiled, twin moves I'd never witnessed in him before. "One can only imagine," he said, no doubt envisioning the crew of a county's trash truck staring at a Cold War relic nearly the size of their truck.

He asked what I'd learned, and I repeated what I'd told Kathleen the previous night. He was a good listener and never interrupted.

"Do you know what Richard Callaghan, your ex-brother-in-law, did at the government facility?" I asked.

"He was a bit of a shroud. A man whose soaring intellect was undermined by his Cary Grant persona. I lost track of him after he and Elaine divorced."

"Did you know that your nephew, Christopher, was gay?"

"Likely before he did. How did you unearth that information?"

I told him about my conversation with Patti.

"I can't imagine it factoring into anything," he said. "Do you?"

I ignored his question. "When you first asked me to look into his death, you indicated that you and Chris were close."

"Correct."

"Did that change in any manner after he came out?"

"Absolutely not. If anything, it made us closer. He was more comfortable with himself. His internal struggle was over, his personality free to soar. He was, likely for the first time in his adult life, permitted to be himself. And as I said, he was a delightful young person."

He paused and then said, his eyes holding mine, "In many respects, I was a second father to him, and he to me—a son I never had."

A great blue heron glided to the edge of the pond, its prehistoric wings giving two majestic flaps to initiate a ballerina landing. It took a tentative step, and then froze in its hunting position. The bird survived by utilizing a motionless attack. I believed that Yankee Conrad, for a reason unrevealed to me, wanted me to be like that bird. It was not a natural state for me.

"Sundown apparently had a brief fling with your ex-brother-in-law," I said.

That arched his eyebrows. "I remember her. She was an attractive young woman who looked and acted older than her years."

"How did Richard Callaghan take the death of his son?" I said, mixing topics in an attempt to catch him off guard.

Yankee Conrad squinted at me, although his face was shaded. "Who takes such things well? How about a tour of your property?"

I dropped the subject and gave him the ten-cent tour. As he was preparing to leave, I said, "You knew Mac?" He had deflected the question earlier.

His gaze wandered over the pond. He stood transfixed and mired in his thoughts. I sensed he was more familiar with the property than he let on.

"We had the opportunity to engage in business together," he finally said. "Why do you ask?"

"What type of business?"

"Business."

"I believe he was in the OSS."

"He was. Sundown's death is most disturbing," he said. "Have you been in contact with the police?"

"I have. No leads at this point."

"You have a man there?" he said.

"I do."

"Keep me apprised on what they know."

He drove away a few minutes later. I planted myself in the middle of the driveway as the swirling dust of his car misted the hot air. I wanted to make sure that Yankee Conrad saw me watching him.

18

Patti rang as the final swirl of glistening dust from Yankee Conrad's car settled back onto the gravel drive.

"I think I found—or didn't find—some things that might help you," she said. "Sundown kept a diary. I—"

"Where? I didn't find one."

"Under a floorboard in her bedroom. She'd told me before that she kept it there. I wasn't sure I wanted to read it—who knows what she said about me—but we both know that debate didn't have legs. I'll skip the incidentals. She said that Harlan came by and they reminisced about the old days and she showed him that medallion you mentioned."

"Reminisced?"

"I know, right?" Patti said in a perky voice. "I would never tackle that in my diary, but Sundown was always a good speller. But that's hardly the point. She said—hold on a sec, I'll read it to you." The line went quiet, and then she came back on. "You there?"

"All ears."

"She wrote, and this was over a month ago, 'Harlan dropped by. Hadn't seen him in years. He has a club downtown. He's still an egotistical bully. What did we ever see in him? Can't believe that I used to be jealous of him and Patti. Neither of us would give him a second look today. It's like we grew up and he didn't. He asked if I had anything of Chris's, and I showed him Chris's medallion. We reminisced about the boat fire. He asked if I ever saw Chris's rich uncle anymore, and I said no. He wanted to know if his uncle was still alive, and I said I'd lost track of him.'"

"That's it?" I asked.

"A week later she wrote, 'I can't find Chris's medallion, and I wonder if I misplaced it or if Harlan took it.'"

I mulled over what Patti had said. Could it be that simple? I'd not mentioned the medallion to Sundown when we met and now wished I had. A sickness formed deep within me as, like a chessboard, I saw the alternative moves that might have opened.

What might have been prevented.

"Her last entry—she noted the time as 11:25 p.m.—she wrote, 'He fears his great secret is coming undone, that they'll find her. I feel so bad for him. He still owns my heart, and it pains me to see him so worried. So not in control, so unlike him. He asked if I had the papers he gave me, and I told him I did. He reminded me what to do with them if anything happened to him.'"

"He?" I said.

Pause.

"Richard," she said. "Richard Callaghan was the only man she ever gave her heart to." She punched her breath out, and I was surprised it didn't blow right through the phone. "He was the love of her life."

I recalled when Sundown and I had lunch. *Oh, I got a man in my life. The only man I ever loved. Problem is, he loves his job more than me.*

"That's hardly what you originally led me to believe," I said, while wondering what else Patti was withholding.

"I thought I was protecting her, isn't that stupid? But now maybe it helps find who killed her."

"Had they seen each other recently?" I asked.

"Or just talked. I don't know. I do know that Richard traveled extensively."

"What are the papers she mentioned?"

"I haven't a clue."

"What was she supposed to do with them?"

"I don't know."

"Patti?"

"I'm straight as an arrow with you."

"That'll be the first time," I said, unable to resist. "Who is 'her'?"

"Who?"

"You said Sundown wrote that Richard was afraid that they would find her. Who is he referring to?"

The line went dead.

"I'D LIKE TO MAKE A PARKING LOT BESIDE THE HOUSE," Domingo said after Patti hung up, leaving me staring at my worn shoes. I hadn't been aware that he had approached me—or that my shoes were in such a dire state. "We can surface it with a load of crushed seashells."

Domingo's wide-brimmed straw hat darkened his face. A knife in a leather sheath hung from his shorts. I'd asked Morgan about it after our first introduction. Morgan had explained that while he lived on a sailboat, he always kept a knife on his shorts. I'd been afraid that Domingo's knife might scare some of the clientele, but it had not. He was far too personable, and I'd witnessed him using his knife for everything from slicing fruit to pruning trees. Its practicality and handiness could not be denied.

"You're good to go," I said.

"And a circular drive in the front for drop-offs."

"How big?"

He withdrew his knife and tossed it about twelve feet. It stuck in the ground like a guided missile. "To that point."

"Hold on a sec." I jogged to my truck and came back with the knife Sundown said had belonged to her father. I had never removed it from the center console. I showed it to Domingo.

"What can you tell me about this?"

He took it from me and gripped it in his hand, flipping it over a few times.

"It's a Cattaraugus 225Q. Standard military issue from the second war. Still a lot of them out there. Younger guys in the services like them. Heavy knife. Made for bush work. It is a good survival tool. It has a deep belly for skinning. It's got three layers of steel and a one-fifth-inch-thick blade." He bounced it a few times in his hand. "The center of gravity is behind the guard, not in front of it. It's more of a sporting knife than a killing knife. But it won't fail you in battle." He ran his finger over the blade and handed it back to me. "It has a good edge. Where did you get it from?"

I told him about Sundown. He did not flinch at her death.

"And this was her father's?"

"It was." I'm not much with knives, so I added, "Would you like it?"

He flipped it in his hands a few more times. A similar move by me would have resulted in a permanent loss of fingers.

"I think I will like this knife. Thank you."

I started to leave and he said, "Are you aware of the false wall in the loft?"

"You're telling me something I don't know."

We went inside and up the stairs to the narrow loft that overlooked the living room and open kitchen.

"Here," he said, running his hand over a panel of wood. "I noticed yesterday that this panel was not aligned with the others." He took his new knife and gently probed the crack between panels. His hands did the rest, and the panel swung open. Its hinges were ingeniously mounted on the inside.

The open panel revealed a room no deeper than three feet. It was lined with empty shelves, except for a *Look* magazine from 1965. Candice Bergen's face framed the cover. She laid on her hands with a few blades of grass poking up. Strands of hair rested on her black turtleneck sweater. There's something about a '60s cover girl—that first generation to capture its youth in color and broadcast them to the world, and subsequently the first generation to learn that having a colorized youth did not grant immunity from aging. "It is a good room," Domingo said. "I will clean it. I will also adjust the hinge so it does not draw attention to itself. Do you wish to discard the magazine?"

I was about to say yes but instead went with, "No. Keep it for now."

19

As I pulled open the front door to the Encore, a black SUV swung into the no-parking zone in front of the bar. I tripped a wire somewhere. They would have to wait until I talked to Patti's former boyfriend.

"Is Harlan around?" I inquired of the young woman behind the hostess stand. Her mile-long hair draped in front of her. She flipped it over her shoulders with both hands. The move was too choreographed to have any effect beyond comical.

"Maybe. Maybe not," she said. "It's ten dollars for the entry pleasure."

"Entry pleasure, as in cover charge?"

"You know, like at Disney. Instead of Do Not Enter they have Cast Members Only. It's all in the branding."

"Doesn't feel the same."

"Last week it was an enjoyment fee."

"Does anything stay the same?"

"Sure."

"What?"

"Ten bucks."

I reached into my wallet and handed her a bill. "Would you

tell Harlan a friend of Sundown's is at the bar? I'd like a few words with him."

"Friend got a name?"

"Just deliver the message."

She pouted her pink lips. "Chill, Sonny. I'll see if I can rustle him."

"Sonny?"

"I like naming my patrons."

"Are you Cher?"

"Who?"

"Tell Harlan he's wanted."

I took a seat at the bar and ordered a Jameson on the rocks from the bartender. A man dressed in black approached me from a door next to a glassed-in cigar lounge. His open shirt revealed a pharaoh's collection of necklaces. The sleeves of his shirt were turned up once above his wrist, revealing a different pattern than the shirt itself. A tattoo snaked up his neck, and his disheveled hair looked as if every wild strand had been meticulously positioned. Introducing Harlan: a man who checked himself twice in the mirror before gifting himself to the world.

"You looking for me?"

I introduced myself, and he took the stool next to me.

"I'll take one, Bev," he said to the woman who had served my whiskey. She reached high for a bottle of bourbon, poured two thumbs, added a single cube, and placed it in front of him.

He faced me. "What can I do for you, bud?"

I told him I was looking into the death of Christopher Callaghan.

"Double C," he said, shifting his weight on the stool. "That's what we called him. Man, you are digging up some old shit. Why me?"

"Are you aware Sundown was murdered?"

"Word got around. Just terrible. She was a beautiful woman

—in and out, know what I mean? I can't imagine why anyone would do that to her."

I asked him when he last saw her.

"Oh geez." He swung his head. "That's a tough one. Year or so back? I ran into her in Sandy Springs."

I took a sip of whiskey and situated myself on the stool so that I directly faced him.

"I did a little homework," I said. "You're overextended here. You were late on your last three real estate taxes. You bought this right before the pandemic. Terrible luck."

"What's it to you? Besides, things are picking up, not that it's your business."

"Do you remember Elaine Callaghan?"

"You're pulling names out of your ass."

"Is that a yes?"

"Get to your point or get out."

"Someone is trying to extort her."

He blinked and spread his hands. "Sorry I—"

"How about Yankee Conrad?"

His eyes churned with hesitation and wariness. He'd already lied to me regarding when he last saw Sundown, and now he needed to decide whether to double down or fold.

"Name sounds familiar. Sorry I can't give you more time."

He started to stand.

"Sit down, Harlan."

"What did you say?"

"You met with Sundown a few days before she was murdered. I got a friend who's a detective. Phone call away. You want to talk to him? It won't be here. It will be at the station."

He reclaimed his seat, tented his hands in front of him, and fanned his fingers while he stared at the counter.

"Sundown showed you Chris's medallion," I continued. "You stuck it in your pocket, and now you're trying to tell a grieving mother that you have information on her long-dead son."

"I don't know what the fuck you are—"

"Patti found Sundown's diary. She wrote that you dropped by a week or so ago and that she showed you Chris's medallion."

"Yeah, so I dropped by. But I didn't take any damn medallion."

"You have already established your lack of credibility."

"I don't have to listen to this shit." He sat up straighter on his stool. "I went to see Sundown just to get reacquainted. I don't care what she wrote in her diary. Yeah, we talked about Chris, Patti, and the old times; that's what people do. She showed me the medallion that Chris had left her, but why the hell would I want it? I had nothing to do with trying to get money from anybody."

"Why did you lie when I first asked you when you'd last seen her?"

"I don't want anything to do with a murder investigation."

"You're a real friend."

"And you're a real pain. You can find your way out."

The purpose of my visit was not to administer justice or provide retribution. I was there to see if there was a viable reason to believe that the medallion held any real clues as to what happened to Chris Callaghan. Two distinct thoughts surfaced: Harlan had stolen the medallion and, as evidenced by the SUV waiting for me outside, that was the least of anyone's concerns.

Regarding the SUV, I had a good guess who was in it, although I tried not to think of her. It wasn't hard; I'd been practicing for years.

"Tell you what, Harlan. I'm going to tell Yankee Conrad that he can forget about the medallion. That there is no evidence it is tied to the death of his nephew."

"I don't give a squirrel's tit what you tell him."

"You should. Apparently you pelted Sundown with a few questions about Yankee Conrad—the guy you just said whose name sounded familiar. Why would you be interested in him after all those years?"

"You are way out of line."

"Extortion is a felony."

"You got the wrong man," he said, but his voice wavered and lacked conviction.

I wanted to give him a way out with a thread of dignity. "Can I assume there'll be no more ransom notes?"

He kept his head down, his hand wrapped tight around his drink.

"Yeah. Assume what you want."

"Then we're done," I said. "As long as we have an understanding that if any item, threat, or insinuation of someone having information regarding the death of Chris Callaghan ever rises again, and such information is available for a sum of money, I'll be back."

But I'd gone too far threatening him on his home turf. He tilted his head back. "You wanna play games? Try this on: if I ever see your face again, Beverly will claim you tried to solicit her. Isn't that right, Bev?"

Beverly had been keeping her head down in front of us, washing glasses. She lifted her head. "Told you, boss, he offered me a hundred bucks. I told him I'm not that type of girl—and to get his greasy hands off me. I've seen him in here before, harassing and fondling the girls. They'll vouch for me." She spoke in a light and breezy voice, fully aware of her power, her unjustified believability over mine. Guilt by accusation.

I looked at Harlan. "You run a classy joint."

"If only we could keep scum like you out."

He started to walk back to his office.

"One more thing," I said.

He turned. "What?"

"You ever bother to go to Finegan's Ridge?"

"Up your ass." He continued toward his office at a leisurely pace.

I turned to Beverly. "Would you have really done that?"

She shrugged. "You'd be wise not to find out."

"You'll have to forgive me if I'm not a repeat customer."

"Be a fool if you were."

"So to get this straight, I'd be wise to leave and a fool to return."

"Sayonara."

As I walked out the door, the hostess called from behind me, "Thanks for coming in, Sonny."

THE BLACK SUV SAT IDLING IN THE NO-PARKING ZONE, exhaust fumes puffing out of its rear end. The front passenger door swung open. A man popped out and opened the back door. "Take a seat."

"Why? You don't want them anymore?"

"Inside, smart mouth."

I did as instructed. This was not the first time the man or, more importantly, the person inside, had orchestrated such an arrival. I had no clue why or how I'd drawn her attention, but her presence indicated I was in far deeper water than I'd thought and—as I had surmised, perhaps a bit late—the medallion was the least of anyone's problems.

20

Natalie Binelli, dressed in her trademark navy skirt and white blouse, nestled in the far corner of the black leather seat. A pile of papers rested next to her. She snapped shut a laptop on her knees and placed it on the floor.

We'd met nearly ten years ago when she, working undercover for the FBI, helped to imprison Raydel Escobar. Escobar had tried to blackmail the U.S. government with an incriminating Bay of Pigs letter that he'd come to possess. She'd been reaching for her gun during our first—and only—kiss. She'd kept the gun high on the inside of her thigh. My groping left hand got there first. Since then, we'd worked on several cases together, but none as steamy as our inaugural partnership.

At one point, I thought she might be the one.

"Jake."

"Natalie."

"Care to tell me what you've been up to?"

"If you recall, I don't do car conversations."

The suit who opened the door was still outside, granting us privacy. But it was a government vehicle and likely wired. We exited the car and strolled across the street to South Straub

Park, our strides at first synchronized. On the far side of the grassy park, Tampa Bay lay dead in the summer doldrums, a jointless piece of gray concrete. A nonsense exchange from our past dropped into my head. I'd accused Binelli of being from Yale.

Fuck Yale. I'm from Vassar.

"To what do I owe the pleasure?" I said.

"Face recognition software," she said.

"Come again?"

"It's when we pick up a face and—"

"I know that part."

"You visited a facility in Sandy Springs, Florida."

"You're joking." I had assumed those cameras were no longer in use.

She shook her head. "The FBI does not acknowledge humor. We scan facial recognition of all trespassers and visitors on government property. It gets crunched and then forwarded to anyone who is on record as knowing or interacting with the suspect. A caretaker at Government Facility 4A281 reported a visitor—identified by our software as one Jake Travis. I got an email."

Good to know that Joe took his job so seriously. Who would have guessed?

"Suspect?" I said.

Her eyes rested on mine. She'd aged a little, and I wondered what she thought of me. A thin gold chain rested on her chest and vanished into her shirt, hiding behind the third button that was the first button doing its job. She always wore that gold chain, and I couldn't remember what was at the end of it. I didn't know if I'd forgotten or I'd never known. That's a lie, partner, and as big as they come. I'd never known, and I'd always ached with primitive desire to find out.

She nodded to a bench. "Take a seat. And tell me why you dropped by Sandy Springs Logistics and Research Base."

"Why care?"

"It's been closed for over a decade, which makes your unexplained presence even more curious."

"Why you?"

"Are we going to sit here and ask two-word questions all evening?"

"Are we?"

She rolled her eyes and crossed her legs, dangling her foot. She wore an ankle bracelet that I doubted was within FBI guidelines, but she'd always cut her own path. She'd told me once that she'd entered college as a theater major but went into law enforcement after the random murder of both her parents. I wasn't sure I had that right and had never bothered to revisit it. We rarely discussed our personal lives.

"I'm in counterintelligence now," she said. "We had some leaks that stemmed from Sandy Springs years ago, before my time. It's a cold case that neither the army nor the FBI commits resources to. But when I saw you bound out of your truck and stare stupidly into the camera, I thought, golly gee, look who we have here. You didn't think the cameras were operational, did you?"

"Stupidly?"

"Best I can do."

"I'm afraid your trip is for nothing."

"I'll be the judge of that."

I told her that I'd been asked to investigate an extortion case and recapped what led me to the closed research facility—Patti and A Novel Experience—as well as my conversation with Joe and our trip to Finegan's Ridge.

As she listened, her eyes wandered over the park and to the water and then did what all eyes do when confronted with water—they rested. A breeze brought a whiff of her perfume, and it snapped me back to when we had lunch at a restaurant in Washington, DC, along with another FBI agent. The man had mentored her career, but unbeknownst to us, he was in collaboration with a nefarious art dealer, Agatha Christie, who lived aboard his yacht *The Gail Force*. Christie specialized in murder for hire. Like two hormone-charged kids in a boring science class, Binelli and I couldn't keep our eyes off each other. In the circles of our lives, we were never closer than that day.

Or I'd foolishly assumed she shared the same emotional tug. And if she did not, I don't want to know.

"That's it?" she said after I finished. I couldn't help but think my rudderless thoughts had bled into her. How could they not? "You dropped by out of what—boredom? Random chance?"

"Wish I could give you more."

"You always had a dog's nose for a case. Give me the name of the players again, and don't leave anyone out."

I recited, again, Yankee Conrad, Elaine—I added Angie this time—Sundown, Patti, Harold Hendren, Patti's daughter Melinda, and Harlan. I even threw in Molly Shellstrip and Vic.

"Any names trip an alarm?" I asked.

"How about the man who worked at the facility? I don't think you gave me his name."

"He was Elaine's husband at the time. They divorced soon after they moved there."

"That's right," she said, calculating the names in her head. "Someone's trying to extort her—dangling a medallion to extract money from her for information on his death because she refuses to believe he's long gone. But you think you solved that."

"That's right."

"And it's become the least of your issues, seeing as how Sundown was murdered."

"Double right."

"And the man's name who worked at 4A281?"

"Richard Callaghan."

Her eyes widened. She uncrossed her legs, planting her feet firmly on the ground.

"Richard Callaghan?"

"You know of him?"

"Son of a bitch," she said.

"Not that I know of."

"But you've not met him, right?"

"That's correct. I take it he rings a bell?"

"He bangs the drum." She swung her head. "You really don't know?"

"I do not."

"Richard Callaghan keeps tabs on an operation of foreign operatives living in this country. It's called the Network. Men and women who work covertly for foreign governments—read the former Soviet Union—within the United States. They are largely inactive until called upon by their government.

"We—he—knew these individuals were working for foreign interests. Richard befriended some and turned them. He allowed the others to carry out their jobs, feeding them false information."

"He runs sleeper agents in the field," I said.

"Some of which he has not revealed to us. Double agents. Triple. Quadruple. People with shifting and unpredictable loyalties. He was—likely still is—their handler. From what I hear, he's gifted in getting people to trust him.

"He's become too powerful. Which is exactly why we want to shut him, and his operation, down. He was instructed to tell his agents that their services were no longer needed and to reveal those in the Network he had turned, and those he had not."

"But the best-laid plans."

She sighed and puffed out her breath, lifting her bangs. I did remember that trademark move.

"Handlers get close to their agents. These are not relationships one can easily dismiss. About a month ago we did a litmus test. See if some of the agents were still active. First one, then another bit. Apparently Richard didn't follow through. They responded to updated codes. Nor did he turn over any names."

She swatted away an invisible bug from her face. "Furthermore, it appears that his foreign counterpart has learned that some in the Network—his agents—have crossed over. We've got bodies starting to float."

"Foreign as in Russian?"

"Correct. But as you know, we do not consider the former Soviet Union to be a country in the political sense. It is an organized crime state, loosely controlled by Putin, who is following a classic autocrat playbook."

"Certainly someone questioned Richard," I said.

"He insisted his agents had vested too much of their lives to simply walk away—that they were irreplaceable. It was a contention hard to find fault with. He wants to keep them active."

"Sounds like solid judgment to me."

"People lined up on both sides. Those who thought he was wise and those who saw nothing more than a relic who had disobeyed direct orders and therefore could not be trusted."

"And you?"

"I only know him through his files. Money was not a factor in his career, and he never displayed wealth beyond his paycheck. I think he, like many handlers, developed deep relationships with his agents. They were his life's work. He also knew that it took years, even decades, to cultivate such relationships. While the current powers might vote to deep-six it, the next Washington cast might wish to resurrect it. Success is often just outlasting the current regime."

"Richard was doing what he thought was best."

"But that doesn't fly within the beltway," Binelli said. "The good operatives—and Callaghan is among the best—never play by the rules. That creates constant tension. Now Richard's gone under. We can't raise him. Some think his life is in danger."

I thought of Sundown's diary saying Richard had paid her a visit. That wasn't something I was prepared to share with Binelli. Not yet, at least.

"Why the cavalry?" I said.

"One of the sleepers, who had been a double agent for us, was murdered a couple of weeks ago. Strangled. His residence had been searched. We believe he might have been in contact with Richard prior to his death, but Richard never uses phones, so it's difficult, at best, to recreate past events."

"They're onto him," I said, my mind racing in a thousand directions.

"Four days ago, another asset was neutralized."

"Do you hear yourself?"

"A person was murdered."

"Slow strangulation?" I asked.

She nodded, her eyes drilling mine. "Richard Callaghan warned us months ago that the mastermind behind the Network, who initially placed the agents in the U.S., had discovered that some of them are no longer loyal to Mother Russia."

"So grab the list and let them know. Protect those who have helped you the most."

"We don't have a list."

"Come again?"

"Richard is the only person who has the Network, and he's gone deep."

"You're telling—"

"Skip it," she said. "He's old school. He doesn't trust his own people, and he might be right."

"He would have placed information with someone."

The words hadn't even left my lips before they opened a portal into a new world.

"Absolutely. We believe he has core allegiances within the agency, but they have not stepped forward. Anonymity—I have learned—is true power."

"You didn't get that from Vassar."

She cocked her head and smiled. "You remember."

"I do."

She paused a beat. I thought the corner of her lip turned up, but maybe not. "No, that wasn't in the syllabus. Any suggestions who he might be close to?"

"No."

"Why did you say slow strangulation a moment ago?" she asked.

"Lucky guess."

"Bullshit."

"No one's heard from Richard?" I asked to fend off her accusation.

"Agents in the field have cat senses, and Richard is no exception. It's likely his counterpart in Russia has put a target on his back. Would love to sever his head."

"Do you have a name?" I asked.

"Just a code name. Remember this is a man in the employment of an organized crime state with a closet full of nuclear warheads."

"All this from Sandy Springs Logistics," I said.

This time there was no denying the thin smile that cracked her lips. "Sandy Springs was a Cold War artifact. The name was purposely misleading. Apparently that was the thing to do in the day. The army ran counterintelligence training and data crunching. Richard Callaghan, who likened himself to a certain Ian Fleming creation, trained men and women in social integration."

"Pretend I don't know."

"Social integration: how to stroll the Champs-Élysées on Monday, munch on a Wiener schnitzel in Berlin on Tuesday, worship in Istanbul on Wednesday, down a stout in Belfast on Thursday, and smack an eight-iron at the Old Course at Saint Andrews on Saturday without ever drawing attention to yourself."

"Busy week."

"That's why he was—is—so good at what he does."

I thought of the pictures I'd seen of Elaine and Chris, all the places they'd traveled.

And I wondered.

"Social integration," I mused, more to myself than to Binelli. "And if one of those assets wanted to disappear, did Richard teach that as well?"

"Most definitely. That is why it's been so hard—impossible if you judge us by our results—to locate him. He was the teacher. The master of blending in and disappearing."

We were quiet for a moment, the nightlife staging around us like a background film.

"I understand there was a murder not far from your house," she said, snapping me out of pinball thoughts that were struggling to form a pattern.

I told her about Sundown. I omitted the diary and any mention of Richard Callaghan. I had my reasons.

She opened a small handbag she'd been clutching. She reached in and pulled out her phone, tapped it a few times, and turned it to face me. It was a picture of a bearded man unaware that his picture was being taken. I gave it a casual glance.

Dan the Piano Man.

"Who am I looking at?" I asked.

"An international button man, favored by Russian oligarchs. Jean-Baptiste. Goes by Baptiste."

"John the Baptist."

"He baptizes, all right. We believe he's being paid by

Richard's counterpart to rinse the Network. Your woman, Sundown? It was likely that she, in some manner in which you are not sharing with me, was a threat to the Network. She—"

"I never—"

"Please, don't." She let her statement hang as her eyes rested on mine. "Richard Callaghan and Sundown Ackerman were lovers, but you know that, don't you?"

"I—"

"What else are you holding?"

"Nothing."

We held each other's eyes, and I sensed that she'd grown more powerful since I'd last seen her.

"He did Sundown," I said. "Strangulation."

She bounced her head a few times. "That's where you got it from. Have you seen him before or since?"

"No."

"Might want to watch yourself."

"You indicated earlier that he doesn't trust his own people and he might be right."

She took a deep breath. "We have issues. We're working on them."

"What can you add to that?"

"Nothing your imagination can't handle."

"Any portraits of Richard's counterpart? The man who created the Network, is behind the killings, and who might be going after Callaghan?"

She pecked at her phone and turned it toward me. It held the picture of an older man in a white suit. He was at an outdoor party where men wore $1,000 suits and women wore $2,000 dresses and fountains gurgled around them.

"Got a name?"

"Goes by Condor."

"Doesn't look like Robert Redford."

"All we got. No location. Prefers living on boats. Not the type of man to ever get caught. He's old school, like Richard. A man who has survived in Russia despite the torrents of political change."

"Did he pick the name?"

"We don't know. Ask him if you see him. Better yet?"

"Yes?"

"Kill him."

21

Condor

C ondor stepped out of his private stateroom aboard *Sea Mistress* and greeted the morning with an appreciative breath. He found this part of the earth to be comparable to the Mediterranean ports of southern Europe. A little warmer, the air a little thicker, but there was no disguising, no matter what spot on earth one occupied, the voluptuous days created by the incestuous relationship of sun and water.

Murdoch approached him from behind.

"Did he find anything yet?" Condor asked without turning around.

"No. He said her computer had no files or trace of the Network."

Condor faced his assistant. "She kept it somewhere else," he said. "He foolishly thought, like most people of his generation, that she would have her life on a hard drive. Such instruments are burdensome. Dangerous. He would have told her that. Trained her in that regard."

"Or she didn't have the information. They were lovers. Why would he endanger her?"

"He loves only his work. Get Baptiste on the phone."

Murdoch reached for his phone while Condor stared at the glass towers designed to reflect the sky they invaded, as if man was afraid to make a statement.

Condor had been in the game ever since his aunt, Raisa Gorbacheva, introduced her physically flawed—albeit unnoticeably—but exceptionally bright nephew to her husband two years before he ascended to power. Fluent in German and English, Condor had mastered French during a bohemian year slumming in Montmartre, where he indulged in enough sexual and artistic exploration to appease him for a lifetime. That was over forty years ago, before the wall fell. Before the dreams crashed. There were so few of his generation left.

Sitting in the back row of a theater in Bonn in the 1970s, he'd been mesmerized by *Three Days of the Condor*. The movie, based on a novel titled *Six Days of the Condor*—Hollywood being king of "shorter is better"—was about a bookish young man who outfoxed the brightest and the best. A man dedicated to survival and the pursuit of truth. He saw himself as that man. Possessive of that instinct. Those rare gifts. When his associates gave him the nickname, he didn't contend.

He had survived by intuitive intelligence and fearless adaptation—twin qualities he took from the movie and thought were sorely missing in the world. But the decades had taken their toll, and he'd tossed in the towel on the truth part. He chose in his later years to embrace Voltaire's dictum, "Cherish those who seek the truth but beware those who find it."

That left survival.

Now, at age seventy-three, he stood on the deck of his 116-foot Azimut yacht—courtesy of a Russian oligarch who ran human traffic through Saint Petersburg, Russia—in a marina in Saint Petersburg, Florida. Life is irony. He was dressed in dark linen pants, an off-white silk shirt, and soft leather Italian shoes with no socks. The pants and shirt would be worn for one day before being laundered. That was supremely important to him. Condor felt a man had an unquestionable obligation to control what little he could.

He considered his younger associate.

"I'll take the papers now."

Condor abhorred reading things on an electronic device. A sexist to the core, he preferred to save his eyes for the bodies of women and the art of men. If others wanted to take the world's temperature through tiny handheld devices, he had no problem with them. But he was a man immensely comfortable with himself and unnerved by the opinions of others.

His peers, most of them long departed from the field, had had no interest in a project that had taken decades to spawn. If it was a Monday, they wanted something that could be accomplished by Friday. And then, courtesy of Northern California, the silicon chip arrived and the world warped to *now*. There was no Friday. No tomorrow. Such shortsightedness made an ideal opening for someone who excelled at the long game. And the Network was a long game, indeed. Only now, decades after its birth, was it bearing fruit. Only now had his agents reached positions of power. Their jobs serendipitously made that much easier after the president of the country found himself up to his eyeballs in debt. A few discreet loans and they had him by the balls. Pity that the institutions of democracy had prevented the man from stealing a second term.

The Network.

Condor had learned of his counterpart in the U.S. A man who had identified his creation, and—much to Condor's admiration—instead of shutting it down, had attempted to turn many of the assets. Condor had to assume that the man had succeeded in a fair number of cases. He'd even secured a picture of his capitalistic counterpart—a good-looking man who Condor nicknamed Romeo. Condor had tracked the man, calculating that if he neutralized him, the Network could be left intact, or at least reconstructed.

Still, unwilling to bank on his success, Condor had acted to eliminate those agents he thought were most susceptible to American charm. If he threw out a few babies with the bath-water—so be it.

Now, with Romeo's lover dead, he faced the very real threat that on any given day, arrests would be made across the country, and his beloved Network, the magnum opus of his life, would collapse. He had to sever the head. Fast. That would buy him time to assess the damage.

He took a sip of Costa Rican coffee. Murdoch placed two newspapers in front of him. He handed Condor the phone in his other hand.

"Talk to me," Condor said.

"She knew nothing," the voice on the phone said.

"Did you look for the obvious? If he left something there for safekeeping, he might not have hidden it."

"I saw no list of names."

Condor rubbed his eyes. *No list of names. Did the man really say that?*

Baptiste said, "We have another problem."

"What?"

"The man who visited her? Who led me to her?"

"What about him?"

"He was picked up by a government vehicle last night. Downtown."

"How do you know this?"

"Standard black SUV. And he's ex-military. I can tell."

"Did he spot you?"

"Not a chance."

"Don't be cocky. Follow him. Maybe he will lead us to Romeo."

"We have him."

"Romeo?"

"My assistant followed him when I stayed with the woman."

Condor knew that the man often hired local help. He didn't care. He paid him an exorbitant fee, and if the man needed to recruit the whole damn Red Army, that was fine with Condor.

"What are my instructions?" Baptiste said.

"As soon as it is feasible."

"The other man?"

"What of him?"

"What shall I do if he gets close?"

Condor took his time with that. Was the man hunting Romeo, thinking that Romeo was running the Network, or did the man believe that Romeo was looking to expose the Network?

Did it matter?

"Deliver the package first. If the second one still shows interest, eliminate him as well."

He disconnected.

He opened a dossier that Murdoch had left waiting for him next to his breakfast. He extracted a picture of Richard Callaghan—Condor preferred to stick with Romeo—and the woman known as Sundown. At first, he thought she, too, might be in the business, but had decided they were lovers.

Romeo and Juliet.

But the other one—the tall woman with striking features. Baptiste had sent him pictures of her and Romeo on Juliet's front porch. Who was she? They appeared comfortable together. Another lover? But wouldn't the woman—Juliet—be jealous? A ménage à trois?

Ah well. A man has to have his pleasures.

22

"Clowns! Magicians! Come one! Come all! New disguises!
New hand tricks! Yes, even new noses! Magicians and Clowns
12th Annual Southeast Convention. One Day Only!"

I stared at the bulletin that someone had placed in my front
door, like the lawn-care people do. But clowns? What
misguided marketer would blindly pass out flyers to a clown
and magic convention? I wadded up the flyer, but then thought
of the clown pedaling through the neighborhood the day that
Sundown was murdered. I glanced at the other homes on the
street. None had the fluorescent yellow flyer stuck in their door.
I unfolded the crumpled paper. It was today at the Palladium,
in downtown Saint Pete. Then I saw what I'd missed in my
haste to toss it. Across the bottom someone had scrawled
"Looking forward to meeting you."

In case you missed it the first time around: I loathe clowns.

"I'VE BEEN TO IT," MORGAN SAID WHEN I SHOWED HIM THE
invitation. I'd called over to have him join us for breakfast.

"For what earthly reason?"

"It's a great place to learn new magic tricks."

"You don't do magic."

"No one does," he said. "But I do illusions. My father taught me. Looking for company? I can be free by late afternoon."

"Clowns and magicians." Kathleen took a sip of coffee that I knew was too strong for her, but I don't compromise on coffee. "Mind if I tag along as well? It certainly sounds more interesting than grading papers that examine decaying morality as a central Southern gothic theme in Flannery O'Connor's later works. I'll see if Bonita can stay a few hours longer."

And that is how Kathleen, Morgan, and I ended up at the Magicians and Clowns 12th Annual Southeast Convention, or, to put it in less formal terms—we went to Clowntown.

The Palladium, a ballroom erected in the 1930s—during the middle of America's long winter of 1929 to 1945—housed small to medium venues. It was little more than an oversized barn with a stage at one end. Kathleen and I attend the Florida Antiquarian Book Fair there every year, but that sacred event marked the only times we'd been there. The three of us entered through the front door and paid the twenty-dollar admission fee—a little steep, I thought. A young girl with flowers in her hair, who looked as if she'd wandered out of *The Canterbury Tales*, collected our money. Instead of handing us a ticket, she interlocked her hands and two plastic flowers popped out—I hadn't a clue where she had them. She gifted one each to Morgan and me. Morgan's had a smiley face on it. Mine was a skull and crossbones.

"Nothing for me?" Kathleen said in jest to the young girl.

The girl stood and ran her hand down the side of Kathleen's head. "Such pretty hair, my lady." She brought her hand in front of Kathleen's face, and a yellow rose was in her hand. "You deserve a rose."

She was a talented little urchin.

Kathleen gave a small curtsy. "Thank you, my child." She stuck the rose behind her left ear. We stepped into a crowded auditorium stuffed with rows of magic booths, costume booths, prop booths, and colorful balloons that floated above spaghetti strings. A concession area hugged the right wall. We each took a map of the auditorium that listed the individual booths as well as a schedule of events. Apparently there was to be a clown parade in about an hour. Somewhere men were golfing. Fishing. Hunting wild boar in Africa.

"Where do we start?" Kathleen said.

"I'm grabbing a wiener and a beer," I said.

"Party pooper." Kathleen wrapped her arm around Morgan and gazed into his eyes. "Let's be magic."

The two of them skipped off toward the first aisle, and I split in the opposite direction, the appeal of a mustarded hot dog and a beer propelling me through the crowd.

Refreshed and fueled, I left the sanctuary of the roped-off eating area and ventured into the maze of booths. Two aisles were magic tricks and the gear necessary for those tricks. A third aisle was costumes and makeup artists. It was there that I bumped into Kathleen. She'd been transformed into an elf princess—I'm flying blind here, having never really seen an elf princess. Her hair was pulled tight from her forehead and braided in a long, single rope. Her fake pointy ears and long eyebrows were blushed the color of her skin.

"Charming," I said. "And what magical powers do you possess?"

"I am Alida, Princess of the Green Valley." She touched the tip of my nose with her finger. "I am sovereign over all first kisses. I have two hearts. One, I lend to young lovers."

"And the other?"

"Alas, although it is for me, if I ever kiss any other than my true love, both my hearts will cease to beat, and there will be no new love in the world. Because of this, I am afraid to kiss. I am the first kiss for lovers, but I, myself, have never shared the poetry of another's lips."

"I've never done it with an elf princess."

"But what if we are not to be? Would you risk all future love?"

I studied my wife, who was all the magic I could handle. "Unless you are willing to lose two hearts, you will never learn to love with just one."

She bowed her head. "Yes, my lord."

"Just to be clear here, your heart has never been plucked?"

"Methinks your mind wanders."

"Me knows so. Where is your spirited companion?"

She dropped her mythical voice. "He got sidelined at a booth of card tricks. There seems to be no aspect of wizardry and painted faces that does not fascinate him."

Morgan popped up beside us. "The clown procession starts in a few minutes," he said excitedly. "Has anyone made contact with you?"

"No."

"So nothing to indicate there's a reason to be here?"

"I met this hot elf."

"Alida," Kathleen said to Morgan as she curtsied.

The canned music stopped, and a woman took center stage. She announced that the twelfth annual parade of clowns was about to commence. Oh boy. The lights dimmed, the music changed over to what can only be described as a classic cartoon soundtrack, and they came. And they kept coming. A single file of clowns from the door left of the stage. The lead clown rode a tricycle, his knees bumping far above the handlebars draped with rainbow streamers. Short clowns. Fat clowns. Skinny clowns on stilts. Red noses. Blue hair. Happy smiles and Jack the Ripper faces. Bald heads, and heads flowing with rainbow-colored hair and ears that only Dumbo's mother could love. A madding procession of painted faces and deranged humanity.

The clowns marched down the far aisle. The leader, never giving his horn a rest, turned the corner and started down another aisle before the last clown emerged from the door. The raucous crowd stood off to the side and cheered them on. I'm surprised Road Runner didn't dash past me with Wile E. Coyote hot on its trail. Beep, beep. I longed for another beer. It might have aided my appreciation of the moment—or mercifully dulled it.

The goose-honking tricycle clown finished the loop, dismounted his bike, and took the stairs to the stage. He rang a clown bell, a ridiculously large bell that made a high-pitched ringing sound. A net released hundreds of balloons, the lights dimmed, and Sinatra boomed "My Way." We were rocking now. The clowns dispersed into the crowd, doing sleight-of-hand tricks in front of children, who, I now realized, comprised a large part of the attendees. I turned to say something to my elf princess, but Alida and Morgan had taken a seat where a man was sketching a charcoal caricature of them. I headed off for another beer. Halfway to the promised land, a hand tapped my shoulder.

I turned to a white plastered face punctuated with a tangerine nose.

"Mr. Travis?"

"Mr. Clown?" I replied.

"Keep walking," he instructed. "Do not look at me."

We navigated down one of the crowded magician aisles.

"Let me guess," I said. "Bozo? Ronald?"

"Richard Callaghan."

I gave him a quick look.

"Please do not do that. Act as if we are discussing things of interest." He pointed at a booth of hat tricks. "You see?"

"Yes," I said. "Fascinating."

"You talked with Sundown before she was murdered."

"I had nothing—"

"I know that."

"The FBI is interested in you," I said.

"Tell them Condor is pruning the Network. Taking out those he cannot trust."

"They know. Why me?"

"I cannot trust my own people." He picked up a makeup case as if he were examining it.

"No. What I meant was—"

"I have my means."

"You're going to have to do better."

He hesitated. "You're Yankee Conrad's man."

What surprised me about his comment was that I wasn't surprised.

"Your country is confused as to what side you're on," I said.

"My country is confused as to a lot of things."

"But for our matter."

"That only attests to how deeply their assets have penetrated. We—don't look at me—need to protect those in the Network who are loyal to us. We owe them that. I owe them. I turn it over to the wrong people and they'll bungle it, likely getting even more killed. I have reason to believe my Russian counterpart, who created the Network, is pruning the list. He must be stopped."

"Condor?"

"You're doing better than we thought," he said.

"We?"

"Who is your source?"

"I have a friend in the FBI."

"Ms. Binelli?" he asked.

"You know her?"

"No organization can be trusted. Their infiltration is greater than we thought. I will facilitate communications until further notice."

"Rather presumptive of you."

"We need to make sure the house is clean before divulging names."

"What if I tire of playing cloak and dagger?"

"You can walk if you wish." He held up a deck of playing cards as if we were discussing them. "But that is all I can give you now. My reasons for choosing you will become clear to you at the appropriate time."

"Sundown?"

He broke his own instructions and leveled his eyes on me. "I will never forgive myself. It was foolish of me to see her, and she paid the price for my blunder."

"My deepest sympathies," I said. "I understand you were close."

"They have the list. Code names and buildings they work in. I left such a partial list at Sundown's."

His cold dismissal of my condolences told me more about the man than I wished to know. Patti had told me that Sundown wrote in her diary that "he" had visited her and left documents. *He reminded me what to do with them if anything happened to him.*

"How do you know they took it?" I asked.

Callaghan was quiet for a moment. We passed a booth that proclaimed, "Clown in a box!" It sold backpacks that held the contents necessary to duck into a phone booth and, forgoing the common and trite urge to emerge as Superman, burst forth as Touchstone from *As You Like It*.

"It's not where I left it. But there is a master list. The Gate-keeper has it. You have to understand the Network. It was designed to place Soviet agents in the echelons of American culture. Government. Education. Military. By *agent* I mean those who have a monetary gain to advance the interest of the Soviet Union and undermine the interest of the United States. It was conceived and operated by Condor. By its very nature, part of it was doomed to fail. Agents died. Lost interest. More than one decided they liked America better—well-stocked grocery stores and large bedroom closets should not be taken for granted in this world.

"We fed false information to those we were able to identify. Others, we turned. They are the most valuable assets."

We were midway down a crowded aisle. I kept my head low and close to his.

"But in the process, I compromised—sacrificed—my identity, and I'm afraid Condor knows me and I don't know him. A most awkward and threatening position. And now that he knows, we need to protect those who risked their lives for us."

"And you."

"And me."

"Or kill Condor," I pointed out.

"That would be most pleasant, but the man has eluded me my whole life. I see the painting, but not the artist."

We stopped at a booth that sold tarot cards. He picked up a pack as if to examine it while the woman who operated the booth talked with another woman.

"You said the list you left at Sundown's house was gone," I said. "Did you return to her house?"

"No."

"Then—"

"My son told me."

"Your son is dead."

"Please." He touched my arm. "We need to keep moving. Perhaps it is best if I tell you now why you have been chosen. Enough of the game. I told Yankee it carried too many variables."

We maneuvered through the thickening crowd as the cluster of clowns on the stage had disseminated onto the floor, pushing and shoving around us.

"My ex-wife, Elaine, was never well. She and Chris had a delicate relationship. That is one reason why I left. None of this can expose my son. He has the right to his privacy and his life.

He cannot be connected in any way. You must promise me this."

I wasn't prepared to make a promise to a clown I'd just met. Not without further information. My questions were lining up, and I took them in no particular order.

"You mentioned a Gatekeeper," I said.

"There is one—"

Richard Callaghan collapsed in my arms, his painted white face gripped in pain. I wrapped my arms around him. A knife, wet with his warm blood, protruded out of his back. A woman screamed and then another. I shut that part of the world off.

I laid him on his side on the floor and shouted for someone to call 911. A crowd of clowns and panicked people stood over me, their faces contorted, their mouths agape.

"Stay with me," I said to Richard Callaghan. But I'd seen the eyes of dying men before. "We've got an ambulance coming, Richard. Stay with me. Richard. Richard. Look at me."

I cradled him in my arms. I didn't want to pull the knife out, as it would likely cause more harm. There were two hospitals within a few blocks, but the seconds were ticking by like hours. A pool of blood gathered on the floor and soaked through my pants.

He spit blood out of his mouth.

"My son," he muttered.

"Where is he?"

"My son."

"Help me, Richard. Where is your son? Who's the Gatekeeper?"

"Naw . . ."

"Keep breathing, Richard. You'll see your son again. Do you hear me? Richard?"

He grabbed my arm, surprising me with his strength.

"A naw . . ."

His eyes rolled back. I let him go and shot to my feet. One

clown with orange hair walked calmly in the opposite direction even as those around him rushed toward the commotion.

More screams as I pushed and shoved my way through the crowd. I ran to where I'd last seen the orange-haired clown. I jumped on a table and caught a glimpse of him, still navigating calmly toward a group of side doors. Leaping off the table, and flattening a pair of clowns, I muscled my way after him, shoving and pushing everyone in my path.

"Hey, buddy, how about taking it easy?"

I glanced into the face of a clown with orange hair. *How many were there?* But he wasn't my clown. Had my clown turned back into the crowd? Was he that good?

I dashed out one of the fire exit doors and into the early evening. It was quiet. No cars shrieking out of the parking lot. Sirens were getting closer. A bald-headed clown leaned against the wall smoking a cigarette. He took a leisurely drag, craned his neck, and let out a long trail of smoke.

"Did you see anyone fly out of this door?" I asked him.

"Fly?"

"Did anybody just come out of this door?"

"Yeah, some clown walked out. I opened the door for him, you know, a nice gesture from a jester."

"Which way did he go?"

"Didn't do it for you, huh?" He glanced at a sheet of paper he was holding in his noncigarette hand. "He went that way. He had a large spoon. He heard the Super Bowl was in town."

"Did you get a color of his car?"

"Naw." Another glance at the paper. "Hey, did you hear about the two cannibals that ate a clown? One turns to the other and says, 'Does this taste funny to you?'"

"Want can you tell me about him? Height? Features?"

"Sorry, man. I'm on in ten minutes, and I don't know this stuff. I've had my head buried trying to memorize it. I gotta tell you, your reaction ain't real encouraging. I told them I hadn't done stand-up in years—shows you how desperate they are."

"Can you tell me anything about him?" I pleaded.

He took another drag of his cigarette, letting the smoke curl out of the right side of his mouth. "He looked like a fuckin' clown. What do you want me to say here?"

I headed toward the door to go back inside. From behind me: "My uncle just died. Yeah, I'll miss him a lot. He was a circus clown, and all his friends came to the funeral in one car."

23

Condor

"It is done?" Condor said over the phone.

"Finished," Baptiste said.

Condor registered a tinge of sympathy. First Juliet and now Romeo. Both by his hand. He had admired Richard Callaghan from afar. Cut from the same cloth but raised under competing ideologies, he often mused if they were really that different. He thought of the Thomas Hardy poem he'd learned as a young man—"Had he and I but met / By some old ancient inn." Condor knew what came next. He knew the first time he'd read the poem without having to read beyond its first two lines. He was twelve years old at the time and wondered why he understood such things. What that said about him.

"We have an issue," the voice on the phone said.

Condor rubbed his eyes and remained silent. His manner of registering his disgust for the needless posturing.

"The other man was there."

"Other man?"

"The one—ex-military—who entered the government vehicle."

Condor surveyed the harbor. Limp flags draped on the mast of sailboats like debutante dresses hanging in the closet the morning after the ball. He often operated in the theater where the job was, preferring to be close to the action in a world where most people assumed he would not be in the same hemisphere. But there was no victory in the phone call. The voice on the phone explained that Callaghan had died talking to the same man who had shadowed his lover. A man who Condor knew nothing of. Condor was not one to underestimate his adversary. Certainly Romeo had initiated his own defenses. Analyzed his odds. Planned accordingly.

"How long were they talking?"

"Not long. I—"

"The question, please?"

"Five minutes. Ten?"

"Enough time."

"We don't know what they discussed."

"Are you suggesting they discussed clowns?" Condor asked, his voice edged with a rare tone of frustration. "This other man?"

"He followed me out."

"You know this?"

"I do."

"Did you get a good look at him?"

"I talked to him."

"You talked to him?" Condor asked incredulously, realizing he was proliferating the type of conversation he despised.

"I was having a cigarette outside when he crashed out the door, looking for me. I told him clown jokes."

"Clown jokes?"

"You know. My uncle was a clown. When he died, all his friends came to the funeral in one car."

A smile formed on Condor's lips. Yes, Baptiste was good.

"Should I eliminate him?"

"Not yet," Condor said. "Follow him. Let us gather them in. We only want to do this once."

24

N atalie Binelli scraped a chair back and took a seat.

"Bagel?" I said.

She flicked her eyes up at me. Thick bangs formed an even ridge above her eyebrows.

"Half."

I scooted over a paper plate with half of an everything toasted bagel smeared with cream cheese. There are two types of people in the world: those who artfully spread the cheese evenly across the face of the bagel, and those like me. My bagels resemble little snow-covered Swiss valleys with patches of barren land and jagged mountains.

We were at an outdoor table on Beach Drive in downtown Saint Pete. She had called earlier to tell me that Richard Callaghan, dressed as a clown, had died at a clown festival, and could we meet. I did not divulge that he expired in my arms.

Earlier that morning I'd thrown away the bloodied pants I'd worn the previous night. A night I thought I was going to make love to an albino elf princess named Alida, who, although she had two hearts, had never loved. When do you think that opportunity will roll around again?

Garrett had called a little before midnight and informed me that Richard Callaghan wasn't on the colonel's radar screen, but I knew that by then. I'd brought Garrett up to speed and then dialed Yankee Conrad. A long silence followed after I informed him that Richard Callaghan was dead. He'd listened with gloomy patience when I reiterated the part where Richard referred to his son in the present tense. He hadn't seemed surprised by my revelation, but it was difficult to imagine anything surprising him. I'd also explained my visit with Harlan and pressed my belief that he had taken Chris's medallion, now the least of anyone's concern.

I told him that Richard referred to me as "Yankee Conrad's man."

"You misled me," I said. "Richard Callaghan was far more than an ex-brother-in-law who you 'lost track of years ago.'"

"I did," he admitted with surprising candor. "But not without reason, which I am not at liberty to reveal at this time."

"And Chris Callaghan is apparently alive—but you know that."

"You should proceed into the investigation of Sundown's death with utmost caution."

"Now would be an opportune time to tell me more."

"You handled Elizabeth Walker's affairs with aplomb. I must ask you to do the same here and reserve your judgment until the conclusion."

"Do you know where Chris Callaghan is?"

"I am not prepared to discuss him."

"Elaine?"

"Use your discretion."

Have you ever been in one of those horror houses at an amusement park and halfway through there is a door whereby you can ditch if it's too much for you? A wiser man might have ditched. Taken that door. But I have no claim to wisdom and am not one to cut and run. Yankee Conrad knew that. I questioned why I trusted him so explicitly, but he was a hard man not to trust.

But there was more. Once you are stained with the blood of another, you have an unquestionable obligation. A duty.

I'd decided not to parry any further with Yankee Conrad. We'd disconnected on an amicable note, both of us knowing we left more unsaid than said.

Binelli took a bite of the bagel and then dabbed her mouth with the napkin as some of the cream cheese failed to enter her mouth—more a testament to the sloppy preparation than to her eating etiquette. Although she went lightly around her red lipstick, it was an impossible task.

"How'd I do?" she asked.

"A minor smear."

She let out a sigh. "That's why I hate these damn things." She put the bagel down, snatched her purse, pulled out a small mirror, and touched up her lips with a corner of the napkin. Lips that, unlike Sundown's, blushed with color. She placed the mirror back in her purse and snapped it shut.

"Gimme that knife," she said, her eyes lingering on mine, for she'd caught me staring.

I handed her the white plastic knife, and she smoothed the cream cheese on her remaining bagel.

"You ever color outside the lines?" I said.

She stood, took off her blue blazer, and draped it over the back of her chair. "Boys are always jealous of how well girls color," she said. "Remember I told you we didn't have a copy of the Network and that Richard was old school? Richard Callaghan detested email, worshipped paper, and believed that once you place something in cyberspace, you're soliciting someone to steal it. Hack it. Heist it. Whatever.

"The interesting thing is that the agencies have come around to see his point. Clandestine meetings and secret codes right out of the cereal box are in vogue. My rambling leads to this: What was Richard Callaghan doing at the clown thinga-majiggy? Was he there to meet someone?"

"Maybe clowning was his true passion."

"There's always that." She paused a beat. "Richard Callaghan likely hid, or gave Sundown a document, perhaps as simple as a single piece of paper, that contained the Network. He'd be a fool not to have copies elsewhere."

"Any guesses where?"

"You said his ex-wife is still alive. What if she's in on it?"

"I don't think so." I pictured Elaine and Morgan dancing in Chris's bedroom.

We were silent for a moment as a delivery truck rumbled down the street, fuming the morning. The heat steamed off the pavement, still wet from last night's rain. Had Harlan taken other things—perhaps a seemingly meaningless list? What if—

"Hey, you still here?" Binelli said, snapping me out of my reverie.

"Why the meeting?"

"We have reason to believe that Condor is in the vicinity. I thought you ought to know, seeing as how you usually end up in the thick of it."

"What do you know?"

"A source—we're not totally hapless—informed us that he's on the prowl. But that could be anywhere from Miami to New Orleans. He's positioning to protect the Network. He took a giant step in that direction with the hit on Callaghan."

"Condor certainly assumes Callaghan would not permit his life's work to perish with him."

She pointed her finger at me like a gun and popped her lips. "Great minds," she said. "What's next on your plate?"

"Another trip to see Elaine, Chris's mother."

"You just rubbed her off. Why the change in heart?"

Good question, Natalie. Something about how Richard had

mentioned his former wife. His son. Richard Callaghan was a family man—in a distorted translation.

"Just to make sure I didn't miss anything the first time," I said, aware of the gap between her question and my reply.

"Keep me posted?"

"Always."

We parted, and I felt bad for not telling her. She'd find out on her own and it would, again, damage our relationship. But I had no choice. She would understand. She always understood, which is why I had such trouble not thinking of her.

25

Angie opened the door for Morgan and me.

"Ms. Angie," Morgan said.

"Mr. Morgan." She glanced at me. "I see you brought the eye of the hurricane with you as well. Ms. Elaine is expecting you. She's on the back patio."

We trailed her through the house of magisterial books and unintended pillows to the back patio. Elaine Callaghan sat erect on a padded wrought iron white chair under a green canvas awning. Beads of condensation wiggled down the side of a tall glass next to her on a table battling rust. A trimmed hibiscus bush by the fence sprouted bright red flowers, their opulent petals opened to the sun.

"Have you found my Christopher yet?" she asked before we had the opportunity to exchange pleasantries. A book and a single-stemmed rose in a thin cylinder vase sat next to her drink.

"No ma'am."

"Perhaps my brother should seek another man."

"That is his prerogative."

"I'll have a word with him. Angie, would you offer our guests a cocktail?"

Angie glanced at Morgan. "Mr. Morgan?"

Morgan dipped his head at Elaine's glass. "What is your pleasure, Ms. Elaine?"

"Raspberry iced tea, although it is only proper with a dash of light rum."

He turned to Angie. "That would be fine."

Angie looked at me.

"Iced tea," I said.

"Are you too good for us?" Elaine challenged me.

"I like iced tea."

"We both know there's a story behind that," she said. I smiled. It beat words.

Angie disappeared through the French doors.

Today's presentation was a low-cut harvest-yellow dress with thin straps. No shoes. Her hair was brushed over her right shoulder. She favored jutting her chin to the opposite direction, her left, exposing a smooth river of skin. At this point, it's best to walk away from explaining Elaine Callaghan. You had to see her. Smell her. Hear her. All your senses banging and clamoring at once. And then you would understand: more than just a sybaritic presence, Elaine Callaghan threatened to erupt into an orgasm with every puff of air she inhaled. The *Tampa Bay Times* had done an extensive article on a woman with persistent genital arousal disorder—a condition likely tied to a nerve disorder. It sounded like heaven. It was hell. It eventually drove her to take her own life. I could only wonder if Elaine Callaghan, in some manner, shared the same genetic code.

"How is my brother treating you?" she asked me, brushing the side of her face with her hand.

"I understand he told you about Richard, your ex-husband. I'm sorry for your loss."

161

"I know who Richard is, and he was no loss. Someone broke into his house and murdered him? Terrible."

Yankee Conrad had told me he would not be telling his sister that a clown had knifed her former husband while he himself was dressed as a circus creature.

"When was the last time you spoke with him?" I asked.

"Why? Am I a suspect?"

"No. I'm—"

"We hadn't spoken in years. Decades."

"Had he made contact with you in any manner over the past year?"

"I believe I answered that."

"A note? Anything?"

"A note? I like the sound of that. Slipped under the door, perhaps? That would be so like him, but no, no note. Tell me about my son."

"You first."

"Pardon me?"

"Why do you think he is still alive?"

"A mother knows."

"Something a little more concrete would—"

"Don't cross me."

"Did your ex-husband tell you?"

"Heavens, have you not been listening?"

I didn't want to push her too hard, for I sensed that underneath her Gypsy Rose Lee exterior, Elaine Callaghan was fine crystal and could shatter at any moment. I thought of revealing her ex-husband's reference to their son, but considered that it might do more harm than good. She did not need an ember of hope. She needed a bonfire of truth.

Angie returned and served the drinks.

"Have you been contacted in any manner?" I asked Elaine, after thanking Angie for my iced tea.

"Such as?"

"An unknown phone call? A letter? A package?"

"Hardly." She directed her attention to Morgan. "Did you feel the summer heat last night? It didn't leave with the sun but stayed and stirred the darkness like a sauce. Chris loves the warm summer nights. And this morning? The way the sun brightened the wax begonias, still wet with rain? The red hibiscus? All of it is him, and he is in all of it."

"I understand," Morgan said. "Did anything recently trigger his aura in your life?"

"Aura." She stood and walked over to Morgan. "Would you like to see my garden? I've been working on it all week. Tomorrow's Sunday and it always looks its best on Sunday."

"I'd love to."

She interlocked his arm in hers, and they strolled into the shaded and green pasture of her backyard, her bare feet scuffing the grass.

I recalled Angie telling me when we'd first met that Elaine always thought tomorrow was Sunday.

"Does Sunday ever come?" I asked her.

"Mmm hmm. I take her to church every week and lord, when that woman gets all dolled up, you should see her shine. She own every inch of that day. Now tell Ms. Angie why you came back when I tole you to stay away. Man like you don't be wastin' no time on two women sittin' around doin' puzzles."

"My question was sincere. Is there anything that recently made her believe that Chris is not dead?"

"Why you be axin that question?"

I didn't know how much to trust Angie. What if Richard had not intended that information regarding his son be shared with his ex-wife? What if I put Chris in danger by spreading the word?

But I refused to allow my trip to be in vain.

"Do I have your confidence?" I said.

"Why would I enter into a pact with you?"

"Because if a storm is coming, you want to be prepared," I said.

"I knew you before you was born. What storm you be bringin'?"

"Do I have your confidence?"

"I can keep my mouth shut, if that is what you are axin."

"Richard Callaghan did not die the way Yankee Conrad said he died."

"Oh?"

"He died in my arms."

"Oh, sweet Jesus." She rocked back and forth in her chair. "Sweet lord. I knew you was trouble. I knew it the day you crossed over the threshold. Don't be tellin' me you killed him."

"I tried to save him."

"You be God's crusader then. But you still trouble. What's this got to do with Ms. Elaine's son?"

"Before he died, he mentioned that his son might be in danger."

She hugged herself. "Oh lord, oh lord. Oh lord. You can't be tellin' her that. It would just destroy her. You can't be sayin' that until she see him."

"I have no plans to tell her. But I do need to make sure that she isn't holding anything back, even if it seems inconsequential. Was there any contact in the past few days that seemed unusual?"

She swayed her head. "No, sir. I can't think of anything. And I'm afraid she's slippin' further away. She had a terrible dream the other night. Said clowns were chasing her, makin' fun of her and all. Not like her to care what other people think."

"Clowns?"

"Yes, sir. Likely on account of the one that came to the door a few days ago. Maybe a week."

I leaned forward in my chair. "Tell me about the clown."

"Why would you—"

"Tell me about the clown."

Angie's lower lip trembled. She looked at me, her eyes wide. "He knocked on the door. When I opened it, he handed me a book and the rose." She dipped her head at the table next to where Elaine had been sitting.

"What color was his nose?"

"Excuse me?"

I repeated my question.

She squirmed in her seat. "Why you be axin me that? Orange—pumpkin-like, now that I think about it. He gave me a flyer about some clown show and said the book was a free gift."

"Did he ask for Elaine?"

"No, sir. He just said the book was a gift, gave me the rose, and left. I assumed he was going to other homes."

"And did he?"

"I didn't watch him. It's a nuisance when someone comes to the door. And I didn't know why he be givin' me a book. They usually trying to peddle something."

"Was there a personal note on the invitation?" I asked.

"Not that I know of. But I didn't really look at it."

"Do you still have it?"

"I threw it away and the trash done come."

"Did Elaine see the clown?"

"No, sir."

"Did the clown ask to see Elaine?"

"Why would he do that?"

"Did he?"

"No, sir."

"You can drop the 'sir.'"

"Yes . . . OK."

"The book?"

She nodded at the table where Elaine had been sitting, just as Elaine and Morgan returned from their garden stroll.

"Why, Angie," Elaine said, "you look like you've just seen a ghost. What has our friend been telling you?"

"Just that he believes your son is not coming back, and I tole him we don't tolerate that type of talk around here, Ms. Elaine. No ma'am, we do not."

Elaine cut me a stern look. "We certainly do not. Yankee is still paying you to find my son?"

"He is."

"Then find him."

"What book are you reading?"

"Pardon?"

I jutted my chin at the book.

"Oh, some old tome that Angie said a clown brought by. A real clown, Mr. Travis, because that's the world we live in."

She reclaimed her seat, reached into her glass, and fished out an ice cube. She brought it up to her neck and slid it down her throat and between her breasts and then back up the side of her neck and behind her ear.

"I like the heat," she said, looking at me with her dreamy eyes. "It fits me well."

"May I see the book?" I said.

"Be my guest. Apparently our clown was canvassing the neighborhood promoting some sort of clown and magician expo, or whatever you call a feast of fools."

I picked up the book. It was a first edition of Allen Drury's *Advise and Consent*.

Advise and Consent: Pulitzer Prize for Fiction, 1960. The central character of the book was accused of being a communist sympathizer while enduring confirmation hearings to become secretary of state. Despite the evidence against the man, the president presses forward, blackmailing the chairman of the hearings with a photo of the chairman that betrayed his brief gay experience during the war. The chairman—blissfully married with children—kills himself. There's more, but it doesn't matter for our purposes. Mixed political loyalties. Breached sexual boundaries. Did Richard choose the book randomly?

I didn't want to raise her suspicion, but I needed to make sure. I said to Elaine, "Did you happen to catch a glimpse of the clown from a window?"

Angie's eyes burned on the side of my face.

"No."

"Why would he leave a book?"

She shot me a look of disgust. "How on earth would I know? Keep the damn thing. I don't want it. All this talk of a clown. It was just some stupid way to promote their conference, or whatever you call a gathering of clowns. A herd? A school? A pride?"

It was then that I noticed a slim leather bookmark sticking out of the book. I knew what it was before I read it. Angie said something to Morgan, but my mind had left the room, and all I heard was the dying voice of Richard Callaghan.

"A naw."

A Novel Experience.

26

The lingering sun illuminated the mangrove shore across the rippled water as the light held the day like a summer with two Julys. Kathleen had just put Joy to bed. She'd been fussy all evening, dulling the sweet monotony of dinner, wine, air-spouting dolphins, and majestic white sails taut with the warm wind.

I put a record on the Magnavox, flipped the ceiling fan down a notch, and settled in the chair beside her.

"I'm hot."

I popped up and switched the fan back to its previous speed.

"Do you think it's something she ate?" Kathleen wondered.

"Maybe she was hot."

"I dunno."

Kathleen wasn't a "dunno" type of person. I told her that.

Her reply?

"I dunno."

"That's your best shot?"

She reached for her glass of wine but only shoved it a notch. "It's a good phrase. It requires little effort. It's nonconfrontational. It sums up all our reasoning, all our battles, in a simple and inarguable conclusion."

"But you have so much more language in you."

"Language, slanguage." She sat up and took a sip of wine. "Bonita said she didn't nap well today. Maybe she was just a country mile past tired."

"She wouldn't be the only one."

She yawned. "It has been a long day. I'm not sure I'll teach summer semester next year. What was I thinking?"

"That you were born to be in a classroom?"

"I dunno about that."

She picked up the leather bookmark from A Novel Experience. I'd recounted Morgan's and my visit with Elaine and Angie over dinner while Joy made a messy sport of eating. Kathleen had fought the good fight the first half of dinner and I the second half, but the seventeen-pound bundle of babbling, incoherent, and whining sounds had defeated us. Seventeen pounds. Never thought I'd see the day when one so small could master ones so large.

She turned over the bookmark in her hand. "You think Richard dressed up like a clown and delivered a copy of *Advise and Consent* to his ex-wife? Why would he do that?"

"I dunno."

"Hey, stealer-peeler. That's mine."

"Search me?"

"That's better."

"The bookmark doesn't really mean that Richard was at A Novel Experience," I said. "He and Sundown were lovers. Sundown and Patti were best friends, and she was bound to have some bookmarks in her house. It could have come from any of them."

"But why *Advise and Consent*? You flipped through it, right?"

"I did. No secret pirate's map with an *X* marking the spot.

That's not to say it's not a masterful reproduction of a first edition encoded in ways that elude me."

"You can turn it down now."

I turned the fan down a notch. Hadley III slinked in through the cat door, gave us a disinterested look, and sauntered into the house to do whatever cats do.

"Why would Richard want Elaine to have the book?" K asked. "She's a crackpot."

"I wouldn't go that far."

"How far would you go?"

"A cracked pot. But even a cracked pot can be useful. It just needs to be handled with care."

"Show-off," she said.

"I think he was spreading his information around in case something happened to him."

"Endangering those who mean the most to him? What a swell guy."

"Those are the only people he trusted."

"You're better off being a friend he didn't trust. Are you going to A Novel Experience tomorrow?"

"I am."

"What do you expect?"

"I can't imagine."

"Listen," Kathleen said. "What don't we hear?"

A dolphin blew and then another. Eric Clapton's eloquent rendition of "Autumn Leaves" swirled out of the open doors behind us.

"I don't hear the cries of a tiny person trying to make sense out of a wacky world," I said.

"Wacky world," she said. "Speaking of depth of language."

I stood and held out my hand. "Dance with me."

She peered over the rim of her wineglass. "You don't dance."

"Said the woman who claimed I only move vertically."

"It's true. You never—"

"Dance with—"

There was no need to finish my statement as she was in my arms, her head snuggled against my neck, her autumn hair in my face, and I breathed through my mouth because I could take more of her in that way. In an evening that lingered like a summer with two Julys, I held a woman I loved more than a thousand Septembers.

27

Condor

C ondor had been elated to learn that Saint Petersburg not only had the Chihuly Collection, but that he could purchase glass creations from the artist he had so long admired. His recent acquisition, two glass flowers and an aqua glass basket, refracted the morning sun. Condor wondered if the artist himself was ever so blessed as to see his creation in such radiance.

He switched his attention to the picture on his phone. "Is this the man he was talking to when he was eliminated?"

Murdoch stood to the side of the table. "Yes."

"Baptiste is certain?"

"He is," Murdoch answered. "The man has been step in step with us. It is time to be more aggressive."

Condor studied his employee, for it was rare of him to be so suggestive. He'd used Murdoch for everything from polishing his 8.78-meter Riva Aquarama that he docked in the Old Port of Marseille to killing three men in Saint Kitts. The men, working under the cover of medical students and funded by the CIA, had traced ransomware attacks to a warehouse in Moscow. Condor hadn't wanted to use Murdoch for that purpose; it was more in Baptiste's job description. But Baptiste had been in York, England, silencing a gullible Soviet defector who had been foolishly promised by MI6 that no one would come looking for her holed up in her modest flat off Green Dykes Lane. Murdoch had stepped forward.

"Where was this taken?" Condor said.

"Baptiste followed him to a house, a few blocks north of here. This other man accompanied him."

"The home?"

"We see no purpose in it."

"Yet, they went there."

"Yes."

Condor dismissed the line of thought. "You think he has a partner?"

Murdoch hesitated. "No. Not in that sense. This other man was—"

"Was what?"

"What do you call them? Hippie. Yes, he was more like a hippie."

"A hippie? Did he have flowers in his hair?"

"He wore a ponytail."

"Ah. I've seen you do the same. Are you, too, a hippie, Murdoch?"

"My ponytail is style."

"Style?"

"Vanity."

"His?"

"Authentic."

Condor was going to press on with the hippie reference but had strayed as far as his operating system would permit.

"Bring Baptiste on board. It is time to finish our business and be gone."

28

Three-quarters of the way around the square in Sandy Springs, I finally found an open space. The white car two vehicles behind me, which I'd first noticed a few blocks from the courthouse with dead soldiers, continued on and took a left on a side street. The driver had a baseball cap low over his face, and a gold earring caught the sun. All I could make of the license were the first three letters—JLV. Jesus loves vodka. Maybe an eight after that.

"Patti here?" I said as I stepped through the door of A Novel Experience, the annoying chimes dangling above my head.

Suzanne glanced up from the desk. I'd gotten the impression that Suzanne was visiting from out of town, but behold, here she was.

"She is not," Suzanne-from-out-of-town said in her alto voice. "May I help you?"

"When do you expect her back?"

"When she walks through the door."

"What time might that be, Suzie?"

"Don't call me Suzie."

"Ten? Fifteen minutes?"

"When she and Melinda are done doing the work schedule at the Pirates' Deck."

"I'll wait for her in the catacombs. If I get lost, Suzanne, please tell her that I'm here."

"And you are?"

I gave my name and reminded her that we'd spoken the previous week, a comment she chose to ignore. I took the squeaky steps to the second floor, where a farmhouse table in the middle of the room held stacks of teetering books. The door chimes jingled. I selected a book and made my way back down the narrow steps. Patti and Suzanne were conversing.

I approached them holding a first edition of *The Day of the Jackal*.

"That's not for sale," Patti said. "I just got it in." She held out her hand, and I surrendered the book. She placed it on the desk.

"Is there somewhere we can talk?"

"Why? Someone else die?"

I studied her face to see if she meant it rhetorically or if she knew of Richard Callaghan's death. "I was looking for a copy of *Advise and Consent*. Do you happen to have one?"

"You going to tell me you drove here to buy *Advise and Consent*?"

"No."

Patti folded her hands in front of her, waiting for me to speak and seeing no need to prod me.

"A visitor paid Elaine a visit and gave her a copy of *Advise and Consent*," I said. "Your leather bookmark was in the book."

"Can you jump ahead?"

"I have reason to believe that Richard Callaghan—disguised as a clown—rang his ex-wife's doorbell and presented her a copy of a book that has your bookmark in it."

"Really? What an active imagination you have."

"Do you know why he would visit her?"

"Got me."

"Had he been in your store?"

"Richard?"

I nodded.

"You think Richard Callaghan came by here?" she said.

"Did he?"

"No."

"I noticed last time I was here that you keep a detailed record of books you sell. Is that correct?"

"It's called inventory control."

"Can you tell me if you sold a copy of *Advise and Consent* in the past month or so?"

"Can you tell me why any of this matters?" Patti asked.

"Richard Callaghan was murdered two days ago."

Suzanne let out a gasp and jutted her hand out on the desk to steady herself. Patti cut a nervous look at her but then quickly came back to me. "Oh my god. How? Where?"

But my eyes were on Suzanne. "Are you OK?" I said.

"I'm fine," she stuttered. "It's just, well, first Sundown and now Richard."

"How did he die?" Patti asked.

"I'm not at liberty to—"

"Does Elaine know?" Suzanne cut in.

"She does," I replied, keeping my eyes on Suzanne, for I was afraid she'd come undone.

"My god," Patti said, hugging herself. "She must be devastated."

"She seemed less affected by the news than you," I said.

Patti smoothed her jeans with her hands. "Well, that probably attests to her state of mind more than anything else."

"I'm going to grab a cup at Woodstock," Suzanne said. The chimes above the door jingled before the last of her words left her mouth.

Patti raked her hand through her short hair.

"Fuck."

"Suzanne's taking it pretty hard," I said.

"Fuck."

"I sense a theme here."

Her eyes shot up to mine. "A theme? A *theme*? Suzanne comes for a visit and my old friends drop left and right and you call it a *theme*?"

I didn't bother to explain that I was referring to her language. It had been a poor attempt to lighten the moment.

"Did she know Richard Callaghan?" I asked.

"No. Never met him. But I told her he stole Sundown's heart and that despite Sundown's front, she never abandoned her dream that he would settle down with her."

"Why would anyone want to kill him?"

She shot me an angry look. "How the hell would I know?"

I let that go as well. "I'm curious as to why he would show up at his ex-wife's door with a copy of a book with your bookmark in it."

"Dressed like a clown?" Patti said. "You don't even know if it was him."

"I do not."

"We go to book fairs every year. Hand out our bookmarks. I can tell you that Richard—Mr. Callaghan—was not in this store. And even if he was, what does this have to do with your medallion assignment? I thought you were done. Harlan took it."

"Richard Callaghan mentioned his supposedly deceased son in the present tense. He indicated that he might be in danger."

Patti took a deep breath and raked her hand through her hair.

"Patti?"

"Fuck."

"We're back to that?"

She worked her lower lip. "Chris is dead," she said in a catatonic tone.

"Help me here, Patti. You could be a target."

"There's nothing to say."

"I think there is."

She reared her head back. "Oh, you do? I'm afraid it doesn't work like that."

"When was the last time you saw Richard Callaghan?"

"I told you. Years. Decades ago. You really need—"

"And Chris?"

"Chris?" She laughed as if I'd just said the most ludicrous thing. "I don't even remember. Maybe the picnic on the boat?"

"I think you're lying."

"I don't much care what you think. And as much as I'd desperately love to chat with you, I've got a zoo to run."

"How long has Brandon worked for you?" I asked. He was about the same age as Patti and Sundown, and it had occurred to me that with a little cosmetic surgery, Chris could have become a new person.

"Who?"

"Brandon. The man—"

"A few years? I don't know. Why?"

"How long have you known him?"

She swung her head at me and rolled her tongue in her cheeks. "You're just screwed up."

We were silent for a beat and then I said, "A killer is loose, and Chris might be in danger. You—"

"He's dead," she shouted at me. "Burned in flames decades ago. The hell is your problem?"

Every bone in my body told me she knew more than she was letting on, but she'd have to reveal it on her own.

"I'm sorry to bring you this news," I said.

She stared at the floor. "Please leave. Just go."

I headed for the door and turned before exiting. "Call me any time. I don't require answers in order to help you."

I walked out the door, the annoying chimes ushering me out. But I didn't leave. I sat in my car and watched as Suzanne flew out of Woodstock and raced back into A Novel Experience. I didn't know what the two women were discussing, but it wasn't books.

29

"We should add another bathroom," Domingo said. "We can build it out here." He motioned with his hand. "We will tie it into the plumbing through this wall."

We stood in the late morning heat that punished you for the temerity of being outside. While we had added one bathroom, Morgan and I already saw the error of our judgment. With the new bedrooms sleeping as many as four people, we needed additional facilities. It was a good time to do it, as we had no families staying with us. That could change without notice.

I calculated the hassle of going back to the permit office and expanding my request. While outwardly supportive of my cause, a few of the well-heeled neighbors had filed a grievance. They were not fond of the increased traffic on their secluded street of waterfront mansions. I'd offered to put in a secondary road to bypass their homes, but that sensible request had been rejected.

"Where would the wall be?" I asked.

He unsheathed the Cattaraugus 225Q and tossed it into the

hard ground. The knife pierced it like soft chocolate. The man could toss a knife. "There. Ten feet out."

"You're using Sundown's knife," I observed.

"When I get a new knife, I carry it until it is part of me. It is the only way to get comfortable with it. To know the feel. The balance. The weight."

"I'll go to the building board," I said, although seeking regulatory approval for another bathroom was the last thing I wanted to tangle with.

He said the dimensions were inside, and we headed around the side of the property. A four-door sedan pulled into the gravel drive, spitting up stones as it dragged its tires. Natalie Binelli bounded out of the car and marched toward me, her arms pumping. Her white shirt glared in the sun. Her eyes glared even hotter at me.

I patted Domingo on the shoulder. "You might not want to hang around for this."

"I will take your suggestion," he said and scampered into the house.

Binelli stopped two feet short of me, which was about a foot closer than she intended. She instinctively took a step back. She planted her hands on her hips.

"Morning, sport," I said.

"Richard Callaghan died in your arms?"

"Did I not mention that?"

"The *hell*, Jake?"

"We were enjoying bagels and—"

"Bullfuckingshit." She puffed out her breath, sending her bangs flying as if she were as disgusted with them as she was with me. "This isn't funny. Show a little respect. Think you can manage that? What is it with you? You have some image of yourself riding a stallion on the range?" She paced in front of me, hands still gripping her hips. "It wouldn't hurt you to play team ball. No one's going to pass to you if you never pass back."

"I know how it works."

She stopped in front of me. "Really? Do you? 'Cause I don't see that. You know how many times I've gone out on a limb for you?"

"I know."

"Then why did—"

"Edward Kent Franklin."

Edward Kent Franklin. He was the influential man at lunch with Binelli and me when we couldn't keep our eyes off each other. When Franklin's deeds were exposed, Franklin, a blue-blood Washington insider, had used a family revolver to pull a Richard Cory. The lesson? Trust no one.

She dropped her hands. "That is *so* unfair."

"It's not."

"That was a one and done," she said, but the anger had drained from her voice. "He was an exception."

"Not the first or the last. You mentioned that your people lined up internally—those who thought Richard Callaghan was wise to keep his secrets and those who thought he was being disobedient. What if there's another reason Callaghan didn't want to turn the list in? What if he discovered that the Network had placed someone in the agency? He hands over the list, and the double agents are exposed."

"Where'd you get that from?"

"You?"

"Me?"

"You said, over poorly presented bagels, and I quote, 'He doesn't trust his own people, and he might be right.' You encouraged me to use my imagination."

"Yeah? Well, I was running my mouth."

"No, you weren't."

"Fine. It's a theory we have. But I think it's pretty far-fetched."

"Don't confuse far-fetched with impossible."

She swayed her head and starting pacing again, but at half speed compared to her opening act. "We were expecting a message from him. He was always fond of clowns and magic—some quirk of his. When we heard of the murder at the clown convention—or whatever you call it—we pulled a video. Turns out they keep security cameras rolling in that building."

"Did you get a visual on the killer?"

"A clown, just like every other plaster-faced freak on the floor. But this one knew to keep his head down. So, to answer your question, no. But you're missing the point."

A whiff of her morning shower rode the breeze.

"Finding who killed Richard Callaghan is not the point?" I asked.

"We're watching Richard's death and—"

"When did—"

She shoved her palm in my face. "Do not speak unless directed to. Me and the boys are sitting around the table watching the video and someone says, 'Do we have any ID on who he's talking to before he dies? The guy who catches him in his arms? Looks like Binelli's buddy.'"

"I don't—"

"Binelli's buddy. First at the deserted facility and then cradling Richard Callaghan. Who, I might add, had a knife protruding out of his back."

She shook her head and looked away from me. We were silent for a moment as she defused.

"It's not you," I said. "You know that, right?"

"Wow. I feel so much better. You don't think I can keep a secret?"

"You drove out here to see me in person because you don't trust your own phones."

"No. Because I wanted to bash your face in."

"That, too."

She gave me an evanescent look that was equal parts hurt,

contempt, disappointment, resignation, longing, vulnerability, and a tinge of what could have been between us. That's a lot for a fleeting speck of time, but a woman can do that.

"You should have told me," she said.

"I wanted to get a jump and see if I could find anything first," I admitted.

"And did you?"

"No."

"No, no?" she said. "Or no, because you think some satellite is listening?"

"No, as in I'm clueless."

"Might be the only honest thing you said today."

"I told my daughter I loved her after she spit up on me."

She turned her head away, but not before I caught a glimpse of a smile.

I recapped what Richard Callaghan said to me. That his son was alive. That there was a Gatekeeper. About how I suspected Richard appeared at Elaine's door with a book and my trip to A Novel Experience.

She'd said her "people" weren't too thrilled that Richard died in my arms, and it took all her persuasiveness to convince them to allow her to question me versus hauling me in.

"You think his son is still alive and may have access to the Network?" she said after we completed our calm-down speeches.

"I do."

"Son of a gun." She slapped her hand on her hip. "What a perfect guise. A dead man holds the secrets. A dead man *always* holds secrets."

"His mother," I pointed out. "I don't see a father and son doing that to her."

"What if there was something greater at stake?"

"Like what?"

"God and country."

"That song still plays?"

"You'd be surprised." She let her breath out. "Let's stick to what we know. Someone followed Richard and killed Sundown. They also killed Richard, likely cutting off the contact of those in the Network who he turned."

"But he would not let his work die with him," I said. "He mentioned the Gatekeeper. But he certainly made provisions beyond a single person."

"And you think this bookstore is somehow connected? Patti —what's her last name?"

"Carmen."

"Like the opera?"

"Like the opera."

"She has a history with the family, right?"

"High school chums."

"Is it her?"

"I don't think so."

"Why so sure?"

"She's hasn't seen any of them in years," I said. "Let's get out of the sun."

I felt bad lying to her but, again, had a good reason. As we made our way to the back porch, I said, "You told me Richard distrusted email and loved paper. How did he communicate and store information?"

"A few years back, Richard—twice the age of the new wave of security experts—walked into a meeting with a few self-published titles in which the first and last sentences of the chapters gave the address and bank account of everyone around the table."

"Impressive."

"You have no clue. It was a grade school math book wrapped in a mystery, designed to help kids like math. The Hardy Boys meet Winnie Cooper type of thing."

"How was it?"

She cocked her head. "Not half-bad. Richard had a way with the written word."

"And his associates?"

"They were horrified. 'Everything old is new again' became the new security dogma. The cloak-and-dagger game had gone full circle. We progressed from smuggling written notes, to hiding microfilm in pieces of art, to flash drives, to chips hidden in a watch, to cyberspace, firewalls, and the space force. Now we're back to papyrus. Anything the Russians or Chinese can't take out in a cyberattack. All our resources, all our guns, are trained in the wrong direction."

"Fighting yesterday's war."

A lost gull landed on the near side of the pond. He looked at us looking at it. I felt bad for not shooing it away. That's what Mac would have done.

She leveled her eyes on me. "They want to know exactly what he told you."

"What I told you was for your ears only."

"I've got to tell them something."

"He told me the bag of colored noses at fifty percent off was the doorbuster."

"I can't sit on it long."

"Give me a day or two."

"And the bookstore—novel something?"

"A Novel Experience."

"How genuine was their reaction?"

My eyes wandered out to the gull while I thought of Patti. "Pretty straight," I said. "But I'm not really good at those things."

"Better than you think."

I turned to Binelli. She was staring at me.

"I need the book Richard left with his ex-wife," she said. "I'll give it to my people. It won't go beyond my inner circle."

"It's a first edition," I said, but as I heard my words, I realized how foolish they sounded.

"You don't know that. Two readers. One reading a copy and the other following along on the book Richard gave you. Looking for changed words, addresses, anything. It's tedious work."

I should have turned the book over to Binelli earlier. She had the resources to scour it to see if it was an original or doctored copy, with a seemingly meaningless alteration of a word or two buried deep in the text, unveiled and understood only by a pair of human eyes. But what if it fell into the wrong hands? What if it was read by someone not interested in supporting Richard's turned agents?

"You trust your inner circle?" I asked.

"With my life."

"You'll let me know?"

"Sure," she retorted, her slumbering anger waking. "Just like you called me when a man you knew I was hunting bled out in your arms."

"Yet here we are."

"Here we are," she said, and maybe it was just in my head, but her words sounded like music.

"It's in my truck," I rushed out, for *here we are* had unspooled me. "Would you like a tour first?"

"Sure," she said, but the word was softer this time.

We did a quick walk-through of the house. She questioned me on our operation as we strolled from room to room. I introduced her to Domingo, and we made our way to the front. I got the copy of *Advise and Consent* that Richard—or a clown—had left at Elaine's house. As she reached for it, and with both our hands on opposite ends of the book, I said, "I should have told you, Natalie."

She took the book. "I told you some of the crew wanted to bring you in?" She said it as a question.

"I appreciate your persuasiveness in convincing them otherwise."

"I misled you—an unfortunate trait of yours that's rubbed off on me. The word came from the top—and I mean no questions allowed—to let you run."

She waited for a response, but I offered none.

"Know who your protector is?"

"No idea," I said, lying once again.

She gave an admonishing shake of her head, got in her car, and left me standing there, the sun searing my back.

30

The crackling hiss of fish fillets in a black iron skillet snapped my mind out of the fog where it had been mired in the image of Sundown's lips and the look in Natalie Binelli's eyes when I'd lied to her about not knowing who my "protector" was. I didn't think those two things were related, but apparently they were.

"Torches?" Morgan said, coming into the kitchen.

"I filled them yesterday."

He went out the screen door and lit the four torches, two on each side of the property. Rolling swells from a passing boat thundered like molten lead against the seawall. A great blue heron perched on Morgan's dock. The bird, nothing more than a round body stuck between twig legs and a curved straw neck, stood unfazed, its entire being dedicated to survival.

I grabbed three wineglasses and a bottle of red, and joined Kathleen on the screened porch.

"Aren't we skipping tonight?" she said. She'd recently sprung the hair-brained idea, again, to initiate one alcohol-free day a week, seeing as how we were incapable—some might argue desireless—of drinking less.

"We've got a good thing going on here." I poured her a modest drink. "Tomorrow, we'll get up and do it again."

She raised her glass. "To getting up and doing it again."

We clanked glasses, and I asked her about her day.

"It was delightful," she said. "Joy's trying to turn the pages of books. She gurgled, but it sounded a little Spanishy to me. I hope it's right—teaching her two languages."

"It's a free gift at her age."

"I suppose, but I had a dream about her being a teenager and yelling at me in a language I don't understand."

"No you didn't."

"Not yet, but I will."

"And the teaching thingy?"

"I took Joy to my class today. But I moved it outside under the big oak by the student center."

Kathleen believed that where you read enhanced the experience, and she had a favorite tree under which she conducted her classes. A breeze brought the salt air off the water and clogged my sinuses with a musty, tropical potion. I wondered if we'd be different people if we lived elsewhere, and how much of us was shaped and chiseled by our environment.

What she said finally registered. "You took Joy?"

"I did. I came home for lunch, and Bonita had talk radio on. I don't want my daughter listening to politics in Spanish when we have Fitzgerald in English."

"What happened to Southern gothic civil rights?" I said, abandoning my quest for what shaped me.

She sighed. "I ditched it for a day. I needed a hedonistic writer who stretched for pleasure instead of reason. Someone fixated on the mirror in front of their face instead of mirroring society."

"That's not the same?"

"Let's hope not."

"And the class?"

"They loved it."

"That's because you teach with your heart and your mind follows."

She gave me a quizzical glance. "Really?"

"Didn't know that about yourself, did you?"

"Not in those terms."

"Now we're even."

"Hmm. I don't know about that. Thanks for filling the torches. It's good to know that nagging is still an effective tool."

"You didn't nag," I said.

"It wasn't from lack of effort. Are we walking after dinner?"

"I have an activity planned."

"Oh?"

"Stay tuned."

We ate as dark cotton chunks of clouds, so heavy you could only wonder with childlike awe why they did not crash to the ground, flashed bolts of lightning like dueling spaceships. I would not have been surprised if a chariot-riding Zeus burst from one, which told me I had Elaine on my mind. The dinner-cruise boat snuck past the end of the dock, barely creating a ripple. But there were no dolphins that night.

After dinner, I went into my study and brought out the contents of Sundown's leather purse. I turned on the overhead light, but then dimmed it. Morgan, Kathleen, and I spread the contents over the glass table that held a single flickering candle. I poured us each two ounces of twenty-year port, dropped an album on the Magnavox, and settled in the chair next to Kathleen.

"What are we looking for again?" she said.

"What we don't see," I said.

I'd explained to them that Richard had visited Sundown and—per my new theory—left a trail, or copies of his knowledge of the Network, along with names of agents he'd turned. Maybe he told Sundown that if something happened to him, she should give whatever he gave her to a specific person. His son? The Gatekeeper? But the Gatekeeper would presumably have that information. Perhaps Callaghan was scrambling in his final days to spread his knowledge, to hedge his bets. And he might have run out of time—leaving us a puzzle with missing pieces, a most frustrating and useless predicament.

"I don't know." Morgan examined the ticket Sundown had saved from the football game. "It's a little hard to see this as anything other than what it is."

"And what is it?" Kathleen asked him.

"A souvenir from impressionable years. Maybe her first kiss."

"Too easy," Kathleen said. "A boy talked to her under the bleachers. A boy she'd been sharing glances with."

"There was a group of them," Morgan said, picking up the thread. His wet-sand-colored hair rested on his shoulders, not in his customary ponytail. The candle flicked shadows across his face. "But he kept his eyes on her."

"And she was conscious," Kathleen said, "of every word she spoke. Worried that she'd chosen the wrong outfit—her mind flashing to what she'd left hanging in her closet—but confident she looked good. She pledged her life to God, but he would save his eyes for her." She took the worn ticket from Morgan's hand and handed it to me. "That is what this represents. But there's no code here to track ransomware."

"'She pledged her life to God, but he would save his eyes for her,'" Morgan said. "Who is that?"

Kathleen crinkled her face. "I'm not sure. Maybe me."

"All right, Bobbsey Twins," I said. "One at a time."

And we did. The pictures. The empty envelope. We turned them over in our hands. We passed them back and forth as if by massaging the scraps of Sundown's life, time would bend to our wishes.

Kathleen studied the picture of Patti. "'Sundown, good luck

to a 'swell' girl and my best friend. RMA. Patti.' I dunno," she said, evoking old reliable. "Seems like standard fare."

"But what of this?" Morgan held up the page of class notes. "A random page of English lit notes?"

He handed it to Kathleen. It was a mimeographed sheet. Across the top it read, "Popular Spy Lit, Elective, Upper Class. Mr. Baxter."

Kathleen studied the list. "Smiley. Jackal. Holmes. C. Auguste Dupin—there's a name from the past. It certainly spans the years. Maybe she liked the class."

"Or the boy under the bleacher was in it," Morgan added.

"Or she had a crush on Mr. Baxter," I said. The sheet contained a numbered listing of books with the author and protagonist after each title.

"And this?" Kathleen said, picking up a page of math problems. "I know of no woman who saved high school math problems."

She handed me the sheet.

I know of no woman who saved high school math problems.

Across the top it read "Algebra II." There was no date or name. I compared the two sheets. They were of the same stock but didn't feel as worn as they should, considering their age.

I handed it to Morgan without studying it any further. "What do you think? Twenty-some-old paper or not?"

"I'm sure there are tests that can verify the age, but that's not what sticks out."

"Oh?"

"This is basic algebra, and the answers are wrong." He placed the sheet on the glass table in front of us. "Notice anything?"

I considered the paper. "The answers are latitudes and longitudes. Eleven problems and each answer is a coordinate."

"Not even close to algebra."

I picked up Mr. Baxter's upperclassman English lit syllabus.

There were eleven books. I glanced at the algebra sheet. Eleven problems. All with fake answers.

Morgan turned his phone to us. "Look at this."

"What are we looking at?" Kathleen asked.

"This one is MacDill Air Force Base. And this one"—he flipped to another picture—"is Langley, headquarters of the CIA."

"Do the rest," I said.

We calculated the other coordinates. Some were government buildings, others were universities, and still others just cities. San Diego. Seattle. Atlanta. Morgan wrote them down.

Kathleen said, "Whoever killed Sundown missed this."

"He likely dismissed it as meaningless memorabilia," I said. I recalled Richard Callaghan telling me that someone had taken what he left.

Was that someone me?

"I've got a theory," K said. "The protagonist is listed alongside the author. See?" She traced her finger over the sheet. "The Jackal goes with MacDill." She glanced at Morgan. "And George Smiley's in—what's this building?"

Morgan consulted his notepad. "Florida Department of State. The Division of Elections is headquartered there."

"So—a code name for each agent at a specific location?"

"Even so," I said. "There would have to be another piece of the puzzle to identify the agent's real name."

"It does get a little Bondish, doesn't it," she said.

"These coordinates are the middle of the Pacific Ocean," Morgan said, still calculating the numbers.

"Which number?" Kathleen asked.

"Eleven."

"Let's see." She studied her sheet. "James Grady's *Six Days of the Condor*."

"Condor lives on a boat," I said.

We tossed around a few more theories, but I had tuned out.

I knew what I had to do and was anxious to move forward. Morgan and I reviewed a few items about Harbor House before he crossed the dark lawn to his home. As Kathleen prepared for bed, I walked to the end of the dock, leaving the soft glow of my life behind me.

We possessed what whoever had killed Sundown and Richard was looking for. They would not stop. Richard Callaghan thought someone had stolen his secrets; he had no way of knowing it was me, and his presumption that it was someone else had likely cost him his life. You never know where you are in the game. Life is a clock with no hands. All you hear is the ticking.

I punched my phone.

"Talk to me," Garrett answered.

"It's time."

31

I sent the two sheets of paper to Binelli in an encrypted email, with the promise that she would retain control and not blindly pass them up the chain. She assured me that she was working within a small and secure group.

There was another reason I reversed my earlier decision and decided to confide in her. What if I lost? That information could not die with me. I'm far more interested in me, myself, and I than I am in God, country, and you—but I'm not without my moments.

"Any more thoughts on who Callaghan trusted with the information?" she asked me. She'd called to confirm that she'd received the email.

"None," I said.

"We might check out the bookstore."

"I'd rather you not."

"Care to give me a reason?"

"I can't."

"Won't or can't?" she asked.

I gave that a second.

"Go by yourself," I said.

There was a teaspoon of silence.

"I can do that," she said in a soft voice.

It hit me then—although it had nothing to do with our conversation, and God knows it took me long enough to figure out: Natalie Binelli was an almost lover. She would claw my emotions. Forever.

SHE RANG THE NEXT DAY AS I SAT IN A CAR OUTSIDE OF A Novel Experience. She'd been unexpectedly summoned back to DC before she'd gotten a chance to drop by A Novel Experience. I liked her there better. She informed me that the two sheets of paper, one with longitudes and latitudes and the other with fictitious names, were both printed within the last three years.

She had opened with a declaration that she'd kept the information within her group.

"Advise and Consent," I said.

"Fake."

"It said it was a first edition."

"Fake," she repeated.

"Any information to be gleaned from it?"

"We're not prepared to divulge that."

"We?"

"A tight group, remember? There's a growing consensus that something's rotten in Denmark."

"That was my theory."

"Yeah? Well, you admitted you stole it from me. One other thing."

"Shoot."

"There's no longer even a rumbling of bringing you in."

Silence.

Binelli said, "Do you work for the CIA?"

"Not that I'm aware of."

"You might want to reexamine the people in your life. You know, when you reverse *god* you get *dog*."

"Good to know."

She hung up on me.

Yankee Conrad's words when we'd met for lunch pierced my thoughts. *Recruitment is always a delicate operation.*

I reached for my thermos of coffee and took another lukewarm sip. I'd been observing Patti making her rounds: open the bookstore, scuttle over to the Pirates' Deck, grab a cup at Woodstock—she was in there longer than I would have thought, perhaps conversing with Calloway in his smooth apron and wrinkled face—and then back to the bookstore. A business owner in a small town. It looked pretty good to me. Maybe the brightest don't leave their nest. Maybe they stay, perfect what they do, and allow their roots to grow even deeper, while others go forth and have to start over again in rocky and untillable soil.

There was no white car today, just a policeman strolling the square. He likely did not notice the athletic Black man—or, unfortunately, perhaps he did—wearing a hoodie and having a cup of coffee at an outside table at Woodstock. Garrett had gotten in that morning. We'd driven separately and would rarely be together, preferring to save that element of surprise for the ending, for everything has an ending, and you want to bring more to it than the other guy does. Stonewall Jackson said, "Always mystify, mislead, and surprise the enemy." He also said, "Never fight against heavy odds." We operate by those dictums. There are countless memoirs on the art of conflict, but it is far better to be obsessed by a few principles than to engage in shifting and countless ideologies.

Keep your roots deep and your philosophy simple.

I climbed out of my truck, my gun in a holster under my jacket. The chimes above the door announced my arrival.

Patti looked up from her computer screen. "Someone else die?"

"Are those books on the table upstairs for sale yet?"

"Sure, let's skip 'good morning' and 'how are you.'"

"Just following your lead."

"I had good cause. No. They're not for sale."

"Mind if I take a look at them?"

She leaned back in her chair. Tippy let out a deep sigh and rolled over in his bed.

"Be my guest."

"Tell me again where you got them from?"

"You were here when they came in. The Garfield estate."

"You sticking to that story?"

"Like glue."

"Brandon brought them in, right?"

She shook her head and went back to her work.

I climbed the squeaky stairs, the temperature rising with each step. The scratched farmer's table sat in the middle of the room still supporting crooked stacks of books. I pulled out the copy of the sheet we'd found in Sundown's house and rummaged through the books, positioning off to the side ones that matched titles on the sheet.

The Day of the Jackal. Eye of The Needle. The Quiet American. Tinker Tailor Soldier Spy. From Russia with Love. The Human Factor. The Secret Agent. I checked my list; they all appeared to be there. Finally, the last one.

Six Days of the Condor.

All first editions. Excellent condition. Original covers. Not what you would expect from a rural-town bookstore. I stacked my books and flipped through other titles. They were mostly first editions from the 1940s and 50s, but no other spy novels. *The Robe. How Green Was My Valley. Mrs. Miniver. Atlas Shrugged. From Here to Eternity. On the Road. Exodus. The Catcher in the—*

"May I help you?"

Suzanne stood behind me. Never heard her coming—surprising—big woman, rickety-squeaky steps and all.

I patted my stack and said, "I was going to see if I could purchase these."

"They're not for sale."

"Everything's for sale."

I hoisted my tower of books and maneuvered around her to the steps, leaning them against my chest to keep them from tumbling out of my hands. I navigated the steps and plopped them on Patti's desk.

"You don't do gift wrapping, do you?"

Suzanne had scuttled down the stairs after me. Patti shot her a nervous look.

"I told you, they aren't for sale," Patti said. "Give me a few days, and I'll have the whole Garfield estate inventoried."

"What was his first name?"

"Who?"

"Garfield."

"Willard. Why?"

"Thought I'd check and see if these really did belong to him or if Brandon brought them from somewhere else."

Nervous eyes again to Suzanne. Did I have it wrong?

"A hundred dollars," I said. "For all the books."

Patti winced a smile. "They will go for a pretty penny more than that."

"Two hundred."

"I told—"

"Five hundred."

"Listen. I told—"

"Two thousand dollars."

Tippy let out a muffled "woof" in his sleep. Patti gave a nervous smile. "You're not going to pay two grand for those books."

I took out my wallet. "I will."

Patti's eyes flicked past mine toward Suzanne. "They're not for sale," Patti said, punching out each word.

"We both know Richard dropped these books off to you," I said. "Or someone instructed by Richard."

Patti coughed out a tense laugh. "I thought your purpose in life was to ascertain that Chris died years ago."

I leaned over the desk. "Sundown was strangled to death. Richard Callaghan died in my arms, a knife sticking out of his back. He told me his son was in danger. Do I have your attention?"

Patti swallowed and again stole another glance at Suzanne, who now stepped from behind me and planted herself next to Patti. She towered over her sitting friend.

"We have the situation under control," Suzanne said.

"What situation would that be?"

"We might be contacting you."

Suzanne talking. Taking control. Patti not cutting in. Relieved at not having to be the lead.

"You can trust me," I said to Suzanne. "But you know that, don't you?"

She gnawed her lower lip.

"Come with me," I said. "Both of you. Now."

Suzanne held my eyes with hers. But unlike Sundown's quiet eyes—eyes that had not looked away, nor tried to speak—Suzanne's eyes were screaming.

"Everything has risks," Suzanne said.

"What risk is worth dying for?" I asked.

She smiled at me.

Dolphins have two distinct parts to their minds. That is how they are capable of sleeping while still surfacing to breathe. One half sleeps while the other half keeps them alive. My dolphin brain was running wild—one side maintaining the conversation, the other half rearranging the pieces on a chessboard, back-playing the game, plotting ahead.

Suzanne shifted her weight. Patti studied her friend. I'd stumbled onto a topic of contention.

"I help manage a refugee house." I pressed my case. "We just added new bedrooms. We'd love to have you both as our inaugural guests." I flashed my eyes between the two of them. "You can even bring the books."

Patti said, "I think you've demonstrated that you're a day late when someone is threatened."

That stung a little, but I recovered.

"I'm trying to break that habit."

"We need to talk," Suzanne said.

"You know, I never got your last name," I said to Suzanne.

She brushed back her long hair, lifting and tilting her face at the same time. "Emerson. My name is Suzanne Emerson."

I said, "Tell your boss he's lost control of the game. The risks outweigh the rewards."

"Whomever are you talking about?" Suzanne said nervously.

I walked out the door, making a point to glance up at the chimes as I did so.

Thought so.

I should have called Binelli and urged her to send a team to collect the books. But I saw a dozen moves ahead and felt it could all work out as planned. After all, if I was the eye of the storm, then I mastered the hurricane.

32

Condor

No wizard ever held a wand as powerful as the pencil. Condor knew the best plan was the plan that could be easily erased. Effortlessly altered. A plan that by its very instrument exuded no sense of permanence. No chance of being picked up by some distant cell tower or orbiting satellite, or fossilized in cloud storage—whatever that was. A plan that the sun itself would eventually yellow and fade, for all is dust, and that was inherent in the instrument he used. No, it was hard to beat a pencil. To think that people were posting videos and digital messages that would follow them to the grave. Beyond the grave. *Dummkopfs!* What if they changed? After all, goals ebbed and flowed. There was no shame in that, no weakness, only survival. And there was nothing better than the pencil, with its trusty rear-end eraser to navigate shifting policies, opinions, and Teflon beliefs. Condor never allowed himself to get emotionally involved with his beliefs. Although he disagreed with the man's economic philosophy, he was fond of John Maynard Keynes's quip, "When the facts change, I change my mind."

On that hallelujah Florida morning, with the breeze on his face and the sun mocking the awning on the aft deck of his yacht, Condor felt the inexplicable urge to put to sea. For he acknowledged this: he was engaging an enemy he knew nothing of. Most educated and highly intelligent men would pay little attention to what they *felt*, but not Condor. He never permitted his gifted mind to condescend his senses, and that was the true gift of his mind. It listened to his instincts. For what constitutes facts? Is it the job of the heart or the mind? Condor believed in, and practiced, the democracy of the body.

Baptiste called. He explained that police patrolled the square all day and how they changed shifts. But that was not all.

"He was there as well," Baptiste said as Condor doodled on a sheet of notebook paper.

"He?" Condor asked this only for clarification.

"The man Callaghan talked to. Who I told clown jokes to. He was at the bookstore."

"The bookstore."

Pause.

"The one—"

"It wasn't a question. This other man—was the hippie with him again?"

"No."

"Alone, then?"

"Yes."

Condor steadied his pencil and drew lines, connecting names that he'd scribbled on the paper. Some names received no lines, and that disturbed him. The woman. The bookstore. The man. He could find no connection to Romeo and Juliet, other than one of them had been a schoolmate of Juliet's. He knew that, like him, Romeo preferred to keep things embarrassingly simple. Could this schoolmate be the one?

He circled Patti, for he had learned her name.

"You didn't take your time with Juliet," he said over the phone. Condor was a man who rarely revisited past failure, but he sensed that Baptiste had committed a costly blunder.

"She knew nothing," Baptiste said.

"They were lovers. It's not what she knew, but what she possessed."

"She possessed nothing of meaning," Baptiste said in a defensive tone. "What are my instructions?"

Maybe this is the last time for Baptiste. His attitude has gotten too casual.

Condor considered the names on the piece of paper. The man Romeo had talked to before he died—he bothered him. What did he know? Condor knew that Richard Callaghan had once lived in Sandy Springs, and that he had been employed at a government facility there. Had he buried his secrets in such a meaningless crossroads?

That is exactly what I would have done.

"The bookstore," Condor said, more to himself than to his phone. "This woman, Patti, works there?"

"Yes. She and another spend most of their time there, although Patti is in and out of other establishments as well."

"Bring both to me. I will question them this time. Have you learned anything else about the man Mr. Callaghan talked to before he died?"

"He and the hippie work at some type of retreat for immigrants. It's called Harbor House. There is nothing military about it."

"How do you know this?"

"I drove there. I walked the grounds."

"What if he spotted you previously?"

"He wasn't there. The only one who saw me was a skinny

old man who thought nothing of me. I'm also on my second car, not including the piano van."

"Piano van?"

"I was a piano tuner."

"The name again?"

"Harbor House."

Condor googled it. Certainly appeared harmless. Maybe he was being too paranoid, although he knew there was no such thing.

"Grab the women."

"If the man interferes? Or the hippie?"

"Clean the room if need be. We'll be departing with the women."

He disconnected and looked at his page. He had only used the top half of the page, and now his attention shifted to the bottom half. Condor was always fascinated by what he could not see. What are we missing in the blank pages of our lives? He erased the top portion of the page and then—and this was one of his favorite things to do—blew his words into the air.

It's hard to beat a pencil.

33

Domingo and I sat in rocking chairs on the back porch of Harbor House. He unsheathed Sundown's father's knife and peeled an orange as if he'd done it a thousand times.

I'd just received approval for the additional bathroom and Domingo, a man of incalculable gifts, had volunteered to do much of the work himself. I asked him how he was so comfortable with construction as, like Morgan, he'd spent the majority of his life on sailboats. I half listened, for my mind was preoccupied with my frustration with Patti and Suzanne.

"We would anchor in a harbor for months," he said, handing me an orange wedge. "My crew and I would help repair schools and medical clinics damaged by hurricanes. Storm insurance is difficult. The island governments have few resources. We spent five months on Saint Thomas after Maria hit. There were no plumbers. We did it all. Plumbing. Electrical. HVAC." He placed the knife back in its sheath. "It is a good utility knife. There is nothing it cannot do. It is difficult to throw, but I am learning. By the way, I placed a dead-end sign at the beginning of the drive. We have several cars a week turning around in our drive.

"One man got out of his car. He walked around. He said he was thinking of building. He wondered if we'd be open to selling a parcel of the land."

"You tell him no?"

"I did. But it meant nothing to him."

"I don't follow."

"He just shrugged. He thanked me for his time and left. He wasn't interested in building. He was not an honest man."

I tossed my orange peel at a trash can and missed.

"Did he have a gold earring by chance? Left ear?"

"He did."

"Drive a white car?"

"No. Blue. I've seen such condescending men," he said. "They do not seek permission or beg forgiveness. They are dangerous men."

I thanked Domingo and told him to call if anyone else aroused his suspicion. I called Patti, but it just went to voice mail. I bent over, picked up the orange peel, and dropped it into the trash.

34

The summer Florida air occupied the stools on either side of me, for the windows were open this time at Seabreeze. A sullen couple, both carrying an extra twenty pounds, came in and requested an outdoor table. The hostess plucked up two menus and instructed them to follow her.

I reached for my mug of coffee when my phone buzzed.

"This is Jake."

"It's me," Natalie Binelli said. "We got a break on Callaghan's killer. A woman walking her dog saw a car pull out from the Palladium around the time of the murder. No big deal, people were starting to leave. But she notices this car because a clown is driving it. Said that's not something she sees every day. But this clown was ripping off his fake nose, ears, the whole shebang fast as he could."

"Why did she come forth?"

"She didn't. Your buddy, Detective Rambler? He knocked on doors. Nothing beats feet on the ground."

"He didn't tell me."

"You were next on his list. I told him I'd pass it along. I gave him a little of our backstory. You need to trust him more."

"He tried to pin a murder on me years ago."

"You would have done the same in his shoes."

"What else?" I asked.

"A security camera caught the license. It was a rental to a man with an Italian passport. So far untraceable."

"It wasn't a white car with the first three letters JLV, was it?" Silence.

"Why do you ask?"

"Is that yes?"

"Why do you ask?" she repeated.

"I thought I might have been followed once. What was after JLV?"

"Eight, three, five."

"Got a visual?" I said.

"Baseball cap. Sunglasses. Your typical I-know-I'm-on-a-camera-so-you're-not-seeing-my-face."

"Earring?"

"Silver. Left lobe. Driver's side."

"Not gold?"

"Sorry. But you know why these guys never get tattoos, right? He might have five rings for that ear."

"You mentioned a button man. Baptiste with no last name."

"We couldn't make a positive ID." She skipped a beat and then added, "Have you called Garrett?"

When I'd first met Binelli, Garrett was in on the final bloody scene. The two had spoken few words to each other over the years, but that in no manner diminished their respect and awareness of each other. She was tepid around him, for Garrett operated in deep shadows where a bullet's path rarely sought legal reasoning. He was equally skeptical of her. She wore a badge.

"He's here," I said. "Do me a favor?"

"At your beck and call."

"Suzanne Emerson. She's a friend of Patti's. See what you can find on her."

"Looking for anything in particular?"

"I just want to know the players," I said, but wished I'd been more selective with my words.

"Why do you think she's a player?"

"I don't," I said, attempting to back off. "I'm just fishing for information." I thought of asking her to look into Brandon as well, but I didn't see it playing that way.

"A lot of Suzanne Emersons in the world."

I recalled when Patti had first mentioned Suzanne to me. "This one went to the University of Florida. Twenty-something years ago."

"I'll see what I come up with."

"One more thing," I said. "The clown driver—was he a smoker?"

"Hmm. I don't see that mentioned here. Why?"

"Nothing."

LATER THAT DAY, GARRETT AND I SAT IN THE SHADE ON the rooftop bar of Barkley House in Pass-a-Grille. Beneath us rows of crowded cottages hid under tropical foliage, and beyond them the incomprehensible expanse of water lay flat in the summer doldrums. Legend is that the French would grill their dinners on the southern tip of Long Key. *La passe aux grilleurs* translates to "passageway of the grillers." In 1841 the name Passe aux Grilleurs appeared on a map. After that it was anglicized to Pass-a-Grille. Its history as a beach resort predates the Civil War. If you're lucky enough to live on the west coast of Florida, on the "passageway of the grillers," you forfeit all claim that lady luck passed you by. You also get kitchen duty in heaven—for your heaven was on earth.

Garrett's skin melted into his black short-sleeve shirt that strained to contain his upper arms. He wore jeans and tennis shoes. Always. His bald head was interrupted only by his dark sunglasses. Although a corporate utility lawyer in Cleveland, Garrett never left the conditioning and training regime of the Rangers. I'd been surprised when he resigned from the army, but we'd walked in and out together. Same when I terminated our association with the colonel. If you have someone in your life who moves with you like that, you're one lucky person. And so sitting there that day, I was doubly blessed.

He'd grown antsy, though, since we disengaged. His law gig was nothing more than an effort to appease his mental capacity, to bide his time, until his mind and body could again mesh as one. He shared none of the self-doubt and guilt-wrecked dreams that accompanied me. He told me once that I had enough conscience for both of us, and he was happy for me to carry the double burden as it fit me better than him. That was an honest assessment of our relationship. A part of me wished I were more like him, and a part of him wished he were more like me. I suppose there is more to it than that, but I'm wary of digging any deeper. Like the thin antenna from Calloway's radio picking up electromagnetic radiation—something few of us comprehend—it is not necessary that we understand how friendship works. Just enjoy the music.

"You're down two bodies," he said. He took a drink of water. He never sought solace in alcohol. That was something I did for us both as well. "Whoever you're chasing has a lap on you. Maybe two."

We'd reviewed, for the second time, the events of the past week.

"Who sent him to you?"

It was a question I'd been wrestling with.

"I don't know."

"Guess."

"Pick 'em: Sundown? Patti? Suzanne?"

"Or?" he said.

"Yankee Conrad."

He grunted. "I had Mary Evelyn do a background check on him."

Mary Evelyn was Garrett's middle-aged never-married devout-Catholic secretary who rarely saw a reason to leave the east side of Cleveland, Ohio. She was perhaps the only person on the planet who reveled in Midwest winters. Garrett had confided our deeds to her years ago, and she supported us with unquestioning loyalty, functioning as a one-person research department.

"And?" I said.

"Nothing. The man doesn't exist. But you know that, don't you?"

"Suspected it."

"Are you digging your own grave?"

"Trying not to."

"There's no dishonesty in retreat, only another day."

"I've got this."

The edge of his lip curled up in silent approval. He leveled his sun-glass covered eyes on me. "Why the game?"

I shared my wild thoughts with him.

He took a sip of water. Our world darkened as a thunder-head blocked the sun. A great white egret rose in the wind, its body pure and clean against the menacing clouds.

"It might work to our advantage," he said with a slow nod of his head. "It never hurts to have friends in high places. Regular schedule?"

Regular schedule: Garrett bunked with Morgan, as he had the previous night, and took the graveyard shift. He'd sleep a few hours after I was up, and maybe grab thirty minutes later in the day. The man thrived on as little sleep as anyone I knew.

"Regular schedule," I confirmed.

We were quiet as a low-flying Coast Guard plane rumbled

the air where a moment ago the bird had been. I marveled at the noise man makes and wondered if we'd ever be able to fly as quiet as a bird.

"Murdered in Midnight Cove," he said with another curl of his lip.

"It's amazing what you can kill and still keep alive."

"Yes, it is."

Mystify, mislead, and surprise.

THE FOUR OF US HAD DINNER ON THE SCREENED PORCH AS the rising full moon scorched the bay like a Vegas runway. Morgan had brought over sea trout. I lightly floured it, added salt and pepper, placed the fillets in a black iron skillet for two minutes, flipped them, and then straight into the preheated oven. The pearl-white fish meat fell between the tines of the fork.

Morgan insisted on doing the dishes while Garrett took a run—after he'd eaten. He exercised at odd times of the day, the polar opposite of my regime. He felt it foolish to train his body to peak at a specific hour. I believe it a Greek tragedy to interfere with the hedonistic evening hours.

"You don't think you're a target, right?" Kathleen said. We'd been discussing the murders of Sundown and Richard Callaghan.

"No. But Patti, and perhaps Suzanne, might be in danger."

She was quiet for a moment, and I wondered if she thought I was to blame for placing them in harm's way. But her silence was not directed at me, for she did not use the absence of words as a weapon.

"Didn't you say the police are keeping an eye on Patti?"

"They'd be a minor inconvenience."

"Well"—she tapped my forearm with her finger—"no one will ever say that about you."

"Here you go," Morgan said, coming into the porch. I'd asked him to bring out the remnants of Sundown's purse. "But we've been over everything twice."

"Just one more thing," I said.

For the final time, Morgan and I spread the remnants of Sundown's life over the table while Kathleen moved the solitary candle that she lit every night. We touch the remains of a life, hoping to arch into another realm where those we knew still breathe. Or perhaps it's the other way around, and their spirit infuses us from beyond. My take on that changes with every sip of whiskey.

"What is it you're looking for?" Kathleen said.

"This," I said, picking up the picture of Chris Callaghan.

"He is devilishly good looking," she said, leaning over to view the picture. "What about him?"

"The anchor around his neck."

A gold chain, with an anchor barely visible, hung from his neck. I'd seen it before. The chimes above the front door of A Novel Experience.

I told them that.

"I dunno," K said, apparently having fallen in love with the phrase. "Gold anchors. Could be a zillion in the world. Or Chris made it and gave it to one of them before he died. We could 'or' all night."

She shifted her eyes to me. Her lipstick had faded and she looked pale and wanting in the dim light, and I thought of Sundown's unlipsticked lips and Elaine's promiscuous aura and it swirled all around me. *There is no sin.* Something about the anchor. I'd seen it someplace else. Someplace representing a different time. A wrong time. A time that wasn't supposed to exist.

Like a song in my head that I couldn't decide whether I'd heard before or not, I fought to make sense of it all. I thought I had it—a few chords, a familiar beat—but then it was gone.

35

There are normal things we measure our days by—I mentioned previously the sweet monotonies of life. But as the following days compressed and blended together, like the dolphins I did not see, they left me bewildered as to where they'd gone or how I'd failed to notice them.

And so we leave the colored sunrises, the crashing pelicans, the annoying crows, Orion sliding through the doomed night sky, the fornicating odor of low tide, the whiff of Kathleen as she brushes past me with a smile that shades the sun, and a touch of her finger that sparks the wind. It was all there; I am certain of that. But it would have to wait. I'll do my best to tell it straight, but when the stranger within, that bleached shadow, took over, it rushed by with an addictive thrill.

MY PHONE RANG AS I ENTERED MY HOUSE AFTER THE morning run. Patti.

"Joe's Grill," I answered. "Pickup or delivery?"

Pause.

"You deliver? Since when?"

Patti was fast. "Just started," I said.

"It's good to know," she said. "But in this case we're coming to you."

"Both of you?"

"Yes. Now."

"Good."

"Bring the books."

"Duh."

TWO HOURS LATER, AS I FRIED EGGS AT HARBOR HOUSE, A tentative, "Hello?" echoed from the front parlor.

"Follow your nose," I shouted.

First Patti, and then Suzanne strolled into the kitchen.

"Eggs?" I said.

"You must be Joe," Patti said. She seemed relaxed. Something had changed in her.

"One of many hats."

"We're good," Patti said.

"Speak for yourself, woman," Suzanne said. "A couple would be great."

"Fried or scrambled?" I asked Suzanne.

"Over medium."

Patti said, "A man who introduced himself as Domingo insisted on taking our luggage."

"He's the live-aboard help. Did you bring the books?"

"We decided not to," Suzanne said. "But we didn't leave them in the bookstore."

My hand tightened around the spatula. Must it always be so hard?

"Where are they?" I said, my voice unable to hide my frustration.

Suzanne patted me on the shoulder as she walked to the refrigerator. "How about those eggs, Joe?"

I fried eggs, bacon—no one passes on bacon—and prepared toast and fresh fruit. I used the mezzaluna knife that had come with the property to slice the fruit. Morgan came in, and I made introductions. He announced with boyish enthusiasm that they were the first guests to enjoy the room.

"What changed your mind?" I said to Patti as the three of us sat at the kitchen counter. Morgan had left to prepare for an ESL class starting in thirty minutes. Patti had just taken the last strip of bacon that I had my eye on. That was after she'd scarfed down a pair of eggs I'd added to the skillet to accommodate her change of opinion.

"We had a visitor," Suzanne said, even though my question had been directed to Patti.

"Oh?"

"Some FBI agent. White shirt. Tight skirt. Linda Ronstadt bangs. Know her?"

Binelli must have jetted down from DC.

"Sounds familiar."

"Said she knows you and was interested in our books."

"You can trust her."

"But not the people above her."

Suzanne and I are on the same page.

"Why do you say that?"

But she didn't get a chance to answer. My phone rang.

"Excuse me," I said. I went to the back porch to take the call.

"Me again," Binelli said. "Have you seen Patti or Suzanne? I was going to put a tail on them, but they vanished."

"I'm having breakfast with them now."

"Where?"

I remained silent.

"Oh for god's sake, Jake."

"Harbor House. How was your visit with them? You didn't tell me you were back in town."

"Let's take them one at a time. First, charming. Second, I

was unaware I was required to file a flight plan. Did they bring the books?"

"I told them to, but they didn't. Nor would they tell me where they stashed them. Just that they are out of the bookstore."

"What have you discussed with them?"

"Whether they wanted their eggs fried or scrambled."

"OK. Beyond that."

"They just walked through the front door. I fixed us all breakfast. Patti took the last piece of bacon, and that's something I'm going to have to deal with. Now, you're up to speed."

The voice at the other end of the plastic pressed against my ear chuckled.

"We all have our challenges," she said. "Still interested in Suzanne Emerson?"

"I am."

"So are we. Your nose didn't mislead you. She comes with a few discrepancies. For starters, she has a diploma from UF— University of Florida. Simple, right? But once you get past the diploma, there is no evidence that she ever took classes there. But social security number, driver's license—it all checks out. Employment history is nonexistent."

"Meaning?"

"We recognize our own work."

"Callaghan?"

"That's what we think. She could be a sleeper, an agent Callaghan turned into his prized recruit and gave a new identity to. Or someone he recruited without telling the agency. The same hook they're dangling in front of you now."

"No one's recruiting me."

"There's no place like home. There's no place like home."

"And Brandon?"

After I'd asked her to look into Suzanne, I'd called her back and requested the same treatment for Brandon Asher. I'd gotten his last name from Calloway. Word of that would make its way back to Patti, but that hardly mattered.

"Straight record. That doesn't mean anything, though. If he is Chris reincarnated, you'd expect a paper trail. Suzanne's a little more intriguing."

"Best guess on her?" I said.

"She was a friend of Sundown and Patti's who was looking to juice up her life. I asked how they initially got to know each other."

"And?"

"They offered me a free leather bookmark."

"Those women share secrets," I said.

"Who doesn't?"

We were silent a moment, and she said, "The books."

"Does Denmark still smell?" I said.

Binelli and I shared the fear that in the wrong hands—a leak in the CIA or another government agency—the books could do more damage than good, and possibly threaten both Patti and Suzanne.

"Rancid with rumors and innuendo," Binelli said. "You have no clue how hot the Network is right now. I stroll into Hoover with those books and they'll be snatched from me like a mother grabbing a gun from her child. I hate to admit it, but whatever game you're playing is the only way. What game are you playing?"

"I think Patti and Suzanne have the right to live the lives they choose."

"Okaaay. I'm not sure what you mean by that. But seeing as how I already admitted you had a nose for the business, we'll move on. You know a hired gun is after them, right?"

"I do."

"And he will likely follow them."

I didn't respond to her.

"I can't sit on this," she said.

"You can. That's why you called on a burner."

"My mother wanted me to be a teacher."

"When your house is clean, I'll give you what I know. One string attached. You can never reveal my source. The information? Yes. Identity? No. Deal?"

"We already suspect that Suzanne is Richard's recruit. Not much to hide there."

"Deal or not?"

"Deal."

We hung up.

When I returned inside, Domingo was conducting a brief tour of the property. Morgan's ESL class was gathering in the main room. It consisted mostly of women. The men were out cutting lawns, roofing homes, laying bricks, and performing manual labor under the merciless Florida sun, 27.69 degrees north of the equator.

I caught up with them in a hall that smelled like fresh drywall and paint.

"They suspect you," I said to Suzanne. She trailed Domingo and Patti.

"They?"

"FBI girl."

She stopped as Domingo and Patti kept walking down the hall. "What is it exactly that she suspects?"

"That Richard recruited you. That you're the Gatekeeper, or at least, have knowledge of the Network."

"My, the words you come up with. Gatekeeper? The Network? What's next, sorcerer? Prince of the underworld?"

"It was Callaghan's word. He was worried, wasn't he? Worried that someone in the agency was compromised."

Suzanne hesitated. Does she keep her front or drop it?

She dropped it.

"In the wrong hands, they could be disastrous."

"Who has the right hands?" I asked, for the question had been on my mind for some time.

"We need more time," she said. "The Network has sources in the government. If it lands in their lap, it gets buried. Worse yet, good people—people who have been loyal to us and trust us—will be jeopardized."

"Where are they? FBI? CIA?"

"If it were only that simple. They're being dealt with as we speak."

"How are you involved?" I said.

"I'm sorry. You have to trust me."

"How close are you to having the house cleaned?"

"Days."

"It's not only about the books, is it?" I said.

She skipped a beat. "Thanks for the eggs."

WE NEEDED TO BE ABLE TO MOVE BY BOTH LAND AND SEA. I went back to the house and lowered the lift. My thirty-foot Grady-White, *Impulse*, bounced a few times on the wood stringers, and then floated free. I backed it out, spun the wheel, slammed the throttle down, and curved a sprawling wake out of the mouth of the pass and south to Harbor House. I idled it through the narrow channel to the weathered dock half-tangled in naked mangrove roots, the hunter-green leaves of the trees streaked white with bird droppings.

We had utilized the property for a similar exercise a few years ago when a Russian mob paid us a social call. On that memorable occasion, I used the relic antiaircraft gun—Sallie-Mae—to scare them away. I had no such firepower up my sleeve this time.

There was no way of knowing if whoever had killed Sundown and Callaghan would take our bait. No one walks into a trap, but hopefully we were disguised enough to entice some action. We were, after all, a refugee house that took in battered women and taught ESL classes. On paper, hardly a threat, let alone a fortress.

"ANYTHING I CAN DO FOR YOU?" I ASKED PATTI LATER THAT evening. We stood on the threshold of their bedroom. Suzanne had gone to the kitchen to fetch two bottles of water.

"We're good." She planted her hands on her hips. "Are we worms at the end of a hook?"

"That's a little graphic."

"Are we?"

"It could be construed that way. But you're safe here."

"Convince me."

"We have cameras. You met Morgan and Domingo. My friend Garrett is here as well."

"Should I have brought Melinda?"

I hadn't thought of her daughter. Would Condor go after her?

"She'll be fine," I said, hopefully before Patti registered my hesitation. "She's removed from all of this. If you'd like, I can have someone watch her house, or bring her here."

"No. I thought of that. It would probably just scare her. I don't want her involved. You know I don't run this, right?"

"Do now."

We were quiet for a minute.

"Care to tell me more?" I said.

"Shame on you for asking."

I humped my shoulder. "Worth a try. Remember, if you hear any commotion tonight—"

She rolled her head. "I know, we've been over it. Lock the door and stay inside."

I picked up a framed picture she had placed on the rattan dresser.

"One of my favorites," she said. "Our day in the sun."

The picture was of her, Sundown, and Chris on a sandbar. The glinting waters of the Gulf of Mexico surrounded them. I'd seen it before, on her computer the first day I'd entered A Novel Experience. But it had only lingered for a fraction of time, and I hadn't gotten a good look at it.

"We asked some guy hiking the beach to take it. Good picture, right?" She spoke as if trying to rouse me, for I was lost in the photograph.

Sundown's dinghy, *Seashell*, was anchored on the sand behind the happy faces of three close friends. The gold chain with the anchor shimmered on Christopher Callaghan's neck. Then I heard it. The song I thought I knew but couldn't hold the tune. It came to me in all its stereophonic glory. But it left just as quickly as it had come. And in its absence I felt like Dustin Hoffman in *The Graduate*, screaming and pounding the glass in the church.

Elaine. Elaine. Elaine.

36

THEY CAME ONE NIGHT later at 4:06 a.m.

Garrett texted me.

Two. Walking.

I dispatched Domingo to the left. His responsibility was to report if they attempted an end around. Garrett would close in behind them.

Morgan had moved in with Kathleen and Joy. While I had shrugged off Patti's concern for her own daughter, I was taking no chance with my family. The hypocrisy bothered me, but that was attic material. K argued that it wasn't necessary, but I'd insisted. I didn't tell her that Rambler agreed to put an unmarked on the street for a few nights.

I'll skip the next sixty minutes—it was not our finest hour. Not that we didn't think so at the time.

When it was over, one intruder was wounded, courtesy of Garrett's gifted shooting—he had taught marksmanship in the Rangers. We propped the two men up, tended the wounds of the one man, and told them to start talking. But in the flood-lights of the back porch, we could see that neither man had a pierced ear, nor were they professionals. They were rent-a-thugs. A pair of desperados coaxed off a barstool by an inch of fifties. Likely scared, they had barely entered the property, keeping most of the action far from the house. I wondered if Patti and Suzanne had even heard anything.

Instead of answering a question, the injured one smiled at me.

They kept most of the action far from the house.

Was that by design?

The roar of outboard motors fractured the night. My panicked eyes locked on Garrett. We both knew. I didn't need to rush to Patti's and Suzanne's room to validate my fears, but I did. We thought we were good—that we hadn't missed a beat and all that—but we'd been played. Out-mystified, out-misled, and out-surprised. Think you're the only one who knows history?

I called Morgan. Everything was quiet, and the unmarked was still outside. There was no time for regrets, for what we should have done. You can ride that horse into the sea. But here's the sunny side: we had been the hunted, and now we were the hunters. That was a natural role for Garrett and me. Sad—but that's the best spin I could put on it.

The two men we'd captured had been paid a hefty sum to saunter down the driveway. "Be visible, but not too visible. Draw the action away from the house." Yes, the man who hired us had a pierced ear. No, we know nothing about him. No, we didn't know this was private property. Call the police? Yes, please do, we need a place to stay for the night. Chuckle, chuckle. Breakfast would be great. Maybe you can join us. We were just taking a walk, and you shot us. What do you think of that, gringo?

To amend my earlier statement: they were smart-aleck rent-a-thugs.

Time was acid on my soul. In twelve hours they could be a continent away. I called Rambler, and he dispatched a cruiser to pick up the two men. We didn't want them calling whoever had hired them. It wasn't that easy, of course. But the details aren't important. This is: I was creating a giant IOU to Detective Rambler.

"Let's think this through, seeing as how we just got played," Garrett advised me, like it was my fault, which it was. "We're not going to catch them with *Impulse*. They likely have a racer."

I reached for my phone to call Binelli but hesitated. Instead, I decided to call Yankee Conrad. Ever since I saw the picture in Patti's and Suzanne's bedroom, I knew it was all circling back to him. I wanted to kick myself for not being proactive, but her secret had to be protected, and that's what it was—and had always been—about.

But I didn't call him. He called me.

"Tell me," I answered.

"They're headed into Tampa Bay," he said in an eerily calm voice.

"She's got a tracker," I said.

"Yes."

"Suzanne."

"Yes."

I thought of throwing out another name, but there'd be a time and place for that later.

"You have a boat?" Yankee Conrad said, although his tone revealed that he knew the answer.

"I do. Do you have any resources?"

"That is what I hired you for," he said with a rare note of irritation.

"It was foolish of you to play it this close."

"Not now. I'd advise you to go by water in the event they avoid land and plan a rendezvous at sea. If you should need a car, I can arrange one. Have you called your FBI friend?"

"Getting ready to."

"Don't. We are within a day of complete victory. You must hold your end."

He disconnected.

You must hold your end.

We tied the two men, and Garrett and I sprinted to *Impulse.* As we pushed off, Domingo jumped aboard. It was low tide, and I had to idle her frustratingly slow out of the narrow and murky channel. Garrett retrieved the red spinnaker bag from the cuddy. We kept an assortment of firearms, currency, night goggles, passports, and satellite phones in Morgan's former sail bag. He offered a gun to Domingo, who shook his head and patted Sundown's Cattaraugus 225Q navy knife that had belonged to her father.

Free of the shallow water of the inlet, I shoved down the throttles and *Impulse* reared up before settling on a plane. I cut the running lights so that if we did sneak up on them, we would not announce our presence. Domingo rode in the bow, his hand on the stainless-steel bar, his head jutting forward like a warrior osprey. We ripped the darkness as if it weren't even there.

A text from Yankee Conrad.

Entering Vinoy Marina.

Binelli had told me that Condor lived on boats. Had he been under my nose the whole time? Did he, like his counterpart, Richard Callaghan, prefer hiding in plain sight?

Another text.

Reason to believe Condor on yacht *Sea Mistress.*

Yankee Conrad did have resources.

I checked my GPS and calculated that they had about ten minutes on us. I didn't think Condor would kill Suzanne or Patti, at least not until he got the information he wanted. I also doubted Condor would abide by the Geneva convention.

We passed the pier in downtown Saint Petersburg, and I eased back the throttle. The Vinoy Marina sat off Beach Drive,

A Different Way to Die

and even at 5:10 in the morning, streetlights and the marina's lampposts created a welcoming glow. Yachts and sailboats slept in their berths while high-rising condos and the Vinoy Hotel, a Roaring Twenties Mediterranean Revival masterpiece, sat unimpressed by our distressing situation.

With the twin engines not competing with us, Garrett and I tossed out half a dozen scenarios, depending on whether Suzanne's GPS tracked her to a car or to another boat. I'd instructed them both to be alert to a yacht christened *Sea Mistress*.

While we talked, Domingo, who had been staring into the marina, turned to us.

"It is her," he said.

"What is her?" I said.

He jutted his chin. "The big one in the back. It is the boat you seek. I recognize her lines. After Hurricane Maria, when we finished at Saint Thomas, I sailed to Saint Kitts. She was there when three medical students went missing."

"I've got it," Garrett said. The ATN night vision goggles were pressed to his eyes. "No name yet."

"The sea is full of dirty money," Domingo said. "You can tell by talking with the crews when they shop for supplies. You can hear it in their voices. See it their jittery eyes. The great yachts never sleep. There is always a guard." He swung toward the yacht. "She is your *Sea Mistress*."

Garrett lowered the binoculars. "Confirmed. There's muscle walking her deck."

I killed the engines. Garrett got the paddle out of the cuddy and stroked us beside a large cruiser where we were hidden from the yacht.

"Her rear platform has a boarding ladder," Domingo said. "It is used when people swim and do water sports. But we would be visible. We need to distract them."

Garrett looked at me. "Any ideas?"

I proposed an opening gambit that could not be ignored. We agreed to split as the advantages of operating independently outweighed the risks. At least it had worked that way in the past.

Garrett addressed Domingo. "Have you killed a man before?"

"Yes. But it is not something I am proud of."

"Could you do it again?"

"You will be better with me than without me."

Garrett nodded at a sailfish sailboat. "We'll paddle over in that, then climb aboard her aft platform. No speaking."

He turned to me. "We have dawn in thirty."

I'd just finished emptying my pockets and switched my shoes for a pair I kept in the red spinnaker bag.

"Give me ten minutes."

37

The eastern sky bled hues of pink and the promise of a new day. I hoped it kept that promise.

I marched to the pier that held *Sea Mistress*, hoisted myself over the locked gate at the entrance to the dock—that was a lot harder than I thought it would be—and bounded up the gangplank to *Sea Mistress*.

The man with the pierced ear stood waiting for me.

"Your hippie friend's not with you?" he said. His voice sounded vaguely familiar.

"He's got a pair of gunboats coming as we speak. Maybe a Huey as well."

"I think not."

"A caravan of Deadheads?"

"I do not know your humor."

Another man, dressed in beige slacks and a black shirt, came up behind him. His hair was in a tight ponytail.

"Mr. Travis, correct?"

"You have me at a disadvantage."

"My name is Murdoch. What brings you here?"

"My morning stroll."

"You're trespassing."

"Invite me to board."

"Leave or I'll call the police."

"And I'll dial the FBI. Tell them I've found who murdered three government agents in Saint Kitts."

His mouth twitched. "I haven't a clue what you're talking about."

"I'll also add that you are holding two women against their will."

He hesitated. "What is it you want?"

"I want to propose a trade with Condor."

He shifted his weight. "Who?"

"Your bird friend."

A muscled-veined stevedore came up behind him. He had cropped hair and a scar under his left eye that cut a thin purple ravine to the corner of his lips.

"Our guest needs assistance leaving the boat," Murdoch said, his eyes never dropping from mine.

He stepped aside, leaving me to face Scar. The man with the gold earring had never taken his eyes off me. His arms were loose at his sides, his feet apart, his body balanced. I believed him to be the man who killed both Sundown and Richard Callaghan.

And who had played me.

"I have the books," I blurted out.

Murdoch arched his eyebrows. "The books?"

"Richard Callaghan kept the Network in books. I, alone, know where those books are. The women are clueless."

"You're bluffing."

"I'm five seconds away from walking off this barge and calling the feds. Your call."

Murdoch skipped a beat and then turned to Scar. "Stay with Baptiste and me." He shifted his attention to me. "Follow me."

That made earring man Baptiste.

Sea Mistress might have been dirty money, but she was a clean yacht. Varnished mahogany handrails, planked flooring without a hint of sun or salt damage, and tinted, streakless glass windows. Murdoch led our small parade around the port side to the aft deck. Hopefully, enough time had passed. An expansive awning, permanently anchored for high winds, covered a sitting area that included couches and an Arthurian banquet table.

"Sit," Murdoch instructed me.

I took a seat on a cushioned chair. As the sun ascended the sky, the light worked its way down the Renaissance bell tower of the Vinoy Hotel. A delivery truck farted down Beach Drive, and the first joggers of the day huffed by in Straub Park. All in all, an acceptably civil setting.

"Could I have a menu, please?" I said.

He disappeared into the main stateroom, its heavily tinted windows blocking any view.

Scar posted behind me, and Baptiste took a seat in the shade. He pulled out a cigarette and took a leisurely draw on it, trailing the smoke out the right side of his mouth.

I'd seen that move before.

"Hey," I said. "Did you hear about the two cannibals who ate the clown?"

His dull eyes rested on mine. He took another drag from his death stick.

The door to the stateroom opened, and a thin man walked through. His steps were easy. His body relaxed, yet straight. A meditative man who refused to rush the world, he commanded all he saw, and all he saw served him. He had short hair, although curls nestled behind his ears. He took a seat on a couch across from me, crossed his pressed pants, and said, "Tell me why you are on my boat."

"Is this not the ferry to Tampa?"

"It's hard to believe we are losing to people like you."

"Are you the birdman?"

He eyed me as if I were a minor nuisance to his day, debating how much effort I was worth. The yacht hummed a low and sustained note. We started to creep out of the harbor.

Birdman lit a cigarette. A thin rope of smoke coiled out from his feminine pursed lips.

"If you insist on practicing poor humor," he said, "your chances of surviving this day will be quite small."

"Speaking of—you do know those things will kill you, right?"

"You're challenging my patience."

"And you kidnapped my friends."

"I don't know what you're talking about."

"I'll trade you."

"Oh?"

"My friends for the Network."

"Stand up, please."

"I prefer to sit."

"Must we?"

Scar moved to my side. Baptiste rose and drew back his jacket, revealing a gun in a shoulder holster.

I stood.

Scar patted me down. I had left everything on my boat. My shoes, which I'd switched out, had a small tracking device sewn into them. Hopefully they weren't going to lead someone to the bottom of the ocean.

"Clean," Scar said and took a step back.

I reclaimed my seat.

The thin man, presumably Condor, said, "What kind of man travels with no identification? Do you not want others to know who you are, or do you not know yourself?"

"I didn't catch your name," I said.

"Hank."

"Hank?"

"Yes. My name is Hank."

"Mind if I call you Condor?"

"Why would you call a man named Hank 'Condor'?"

"Do you not want others to know who you are, or do you not know yourself?"

He uncrossed his legs. "State what you want. If you're lucky, we'll toss you overboard where you still have a sporting chance of making shore."

"I want Patti and Suzanne."

"And what do I get?"

I was surprised he didn't contest that he had them.

"Agents in the Network."

"The Network. Tell me—it is Mr. Travis, correct? I admit, it wasn't until a few hours ago that we finally got a handle on you. Ex-military, lovely wife and child. One would think with so much to lose, one would be more selective in one's endeavors. Yet, here you sit. Tell me, Mr. Travis, just what you think this Network is and in what form you possess it."

"A list of Russian agents in the United States, some—the brighter ones—who are no longer loyal to your bloodied Stalinist nightmare."

His jaw tightened. He took his time but did not reach for his coffee or his cigarette smoldering in a gold ashtray. Condor was a man in control of his vices and not the other way around.

"Who do you work for?" he said.

"Disney."

His eyes brightened. "Disney?"

"We'd like to feature the KGB in our world showcase. It does, after all, celebrate human achievement."

"The KGB? You think it still exists?"

"Alive and kicking, or shall I say killing. You combined the SVR and the FSB into the Ministry of State Security, the exact name Stalin used when he launched his oppressive police force."

He considered me for a moment. "You were seen getting into a government car not far from here a few nights ago. Who were you talking with?"

"I don't recall."

"I can make you talk."

"I'm doing fine on my own, thank you."

"Killing you might be doing the world a favor."

"Who would feed my cat?"

"Enough."

"Do you want to play cards or not?"

"I *am* the Network," he spit out. "I created it. Why do I need to negotiate with you?"

He was probing me to reveal what I knew. I was only worth keeping alive if I had something of value to him.

"Some of the assets have been turned by Richard Callaghan." I jutted my chin at Baptiste. "The man killed by your clown. Killed so he can't warn them. He also killed a woman, Richard's lover, in a vain attempt to get his list. But your clown's a clown. He missed it. I have it."

He took a sip of coffee. "The women," he said. "They will tell me."

"They know nothing."

"Debatable. Go on."

"Callaghan disguised the list in reproduced first editions. Patti, one of the women who you kidnapped, owns a bookstore. But neither she nor her friend knows the importance or location of the books. They are not who Richard Callaghan entrusted with his secrets."

"And who might that be?"

"Me."

He massaged his chin, stood, and walked into the state-room. Guess we were done. A minute later Murdoch came out and planted himself in front of me.

"Hank," he said with a wisp of a smile, "asked me to inquire if you would like breakfast."

"I'd like to continue my conversation with him."

"That is not an option, but breakfast is."

"What's the plan?" I said. "Wait until we're in international waters before the fun begins?"

"Would you like breakfast or not?"

After eggs, poached salmon, buttered toast, coffee, and fresh fruit—really all first class—and just as I was wiping my mouth with a soft cloth napkin embroidered with *SM*, Scar came up beside me. As I placed my discarded napkin on the teak table, he reached around my head. I vaulted to my feet, but he leaned his five-ton frame over me, and the buffoon stuffed my mouth with a chloroform-soaked rag, and what I remember was that the sky was full of a thousand stars and they all scattered around me and I thought the end would be more meaningful, but that's all, folks.

38

"He doesn't know."

"I think he does."

"Why?"

"He saw the picture."

"He's not that bright. If he were, he wouldn't be stuck here with us."

"Hard to argue with that. I don't know, Pats, does it even matter now?"

"Don't say that, Suzie. If—well, well, well, what do we have here? Looks like someone's waking up."

PATTI AND SUZANNE WERE TALKING, BUT WHERE? I popped open one eye and then the other, although the second one—the right eye—was a tough little cuss. They towered over me, looking at me looking at them.

It was coming into focus, but what it was, I wasn't sure. Trout hissing on a black iron skillet? Kathleen—but why September? Something about Simon & Garfunkel. Take a breath. Try another.

Garrett. Domingo. *Sea Mistress.*

"Morning, girls," I said, thinking a few minutes to myself would be preferable.

"It's more like good evening," Patti said. "Suzie and I were just wondering; you didn't come to rescue us, did you?"

"Depends. How'd I do?" I said, sounding far more in control of my facilities than I felt.

"Please tell us you have a plan B," Suzanne said.

I sat up, took a moment to get my bearings, stood, and surveyed my surroundings. Small stateroom. Two beds. One dresser. A partially opened door that led to the head. A porthole with nothing but characterless ocean-green water rushing by.

"Where are we?" I asked whoever wished to field the question.

"At sea," Suzanne said in her throaty voice. "We've been heading south all day."

"Time?"

"Little before six. Cocktails are at six thirty, followed by dinner."

"You're joking?"

"The occasion hardly calls for it—or perhaps that's all we have left. Murdoch gave us the schedule."

I tried the door. Locked. I went into the bathroom and splashed water on my face. I assumed Garrett and Domingo were on board, although hiding in a yacht all day would have been challenging. I didn't want to confide in Patti or Suzanne. They could spill it under pressure, and the room was likely bugged, something I needed to convey to them sooner than later. I rummaged through the vanity drawers, found a new toothbrush, broke it free of its package, and stuck it in my pocket.

Suzanne stood by the window observing the endless rush of water. I walked up behind her. She turned. I kept walking until she took a step back, pressing herself against the wall. I leaned into her, my mouth grazing her ear. Her body stiffened, but she kept her arms at her side. She smelled like—honeysuckle. Honeysuckle in May in Tennessee. When you pluck the flower and place it on the tip of your tongue and you understand the flower's name. Not that it was in any manner important—it wasn't. The sense of smell will commandeer your thoughts and transmit you faster than any of the other senses. Likely the result of something long buried in our evolutionary journey.

"The room is bugged," I whispered into her honeysuckle ear.

She nodded, her warm breath fogging my neck.

"Tell Patti."

"Hey, what are you two up to?"

Suzanne and I disengaged, and she went to her friend. As Suzanne whispered in her ear, Patti's fearful eyes did not leave mine. I felt bad for bungling it and vowed to get them out—and me, too.

Suzanne came back to me and leaned in, her mouth on my ear, her hair tingling my lips. "Does Yankee know you're here?" she whispered.

Before I could answer, there was a knock on the door.

"Duck," I whispered, pulling her tight to me, for she had started to back away.

"What?"

"When the bullets fly, duck."

I let her go just as the door swung open. Murdoch, nauticaled out in white slacks and a blue long-sleeve shirt, stood with Scar behind him.

He hesitated, his eyes darting between Suzanne and me. "I see you've awakened from your nap. I am to escort you to the aft deck."

"Where are we?" I asked him.

"At sea."

"Where are we going?"

"Someplace."

"Should I inquire as to the time of arrival?"

"Follow me."

"Ladies." I extended my arm in a sweeping motion. Patti and Suzanne walked out the door. As I trailed them down the narrow hall—even yachts do not sacrifice space for halls—I turned to Scar, who was behind me.

"Perhaps you, me, and some of the crew would be up for a late game of poker."

No smile. He'd added a holstered badass gun to his dinner haute couture.

Poor guy. He had no clue that I had a toothbrush.

39

C ondor butted out his half-smoked cigarette as our procession arrived. He motioned to the couch across from him. "Please, have a seat."

The empty water held no hint of horizon, and Suzanne was right—we were heading south doing about fifteen knots. Patti and Suzanne each took a corner of the couch, and I selected the chair. Scar, again, took his post behind me. No sign of Baptiste. There we sat, all cozy except the man in charge would twist our teeth out with rusted pliers to extract the information he wanted and then feed us to the sharks. Condor was likely familiar with every form of iron-curtain torture to ever grace the cover of *Gulag Today* magazine.

"I trust you slept well this afternoon, Mr. Travis?"

"Like a drugged baby."

"It was easier to shut you up than to tolerate you during business hours."

"I don't suppose my Brahms 'Lullaby' time had anything to do with getting out of US waters and framing this conversation on the eve of darkness."

The left side of his lip curled up, revealing the soulless man he was. Condor would give no more thought to the taking of an innocent life than selecting dinner entrées.

A man dressed in a white server smock and with greased black hair walked out of the stateroom. He carried a wobbling silver tray that held a bottle of champagne and fluted glasses. His hands trembled as he placed the heavy tray on the teak table. He poured four glasses, positioned a napkin under each one, hesitated, and then passed out the glasses, serving his lord and master first.

Condor took a sip, held the glass under his nose, and then took another sip before placing the flute on a table.

"I want Richard Callaghan's books," he said. His eyes scanned first Patti, and then Suzanne. "He gave them to one of you." He shifted his gaze to me. "And, although I doubt it, perhaps even you. But you are not his type. He prefers rank amateurs, and you are just rank."

I tipped my glass. "I have feelings for you as well. Here's an issue for you, Hank."

He arched an eyebrow. "Yes?"

"Suppose we spill it all, tie it up with a bow. What do you envision for our future?"

"We dock in less than ten hours. If I ascertain that you are truthful with me, then you are free to disembark. I have no need for you."

I took a sip of bubbly and placed it back on my napkin that had a smudge on it. Disgraceful.

"I have a problem with that," I said.

"How so?"

"I like being needed. I find it keeps me alive."

He gave me a mocking smile. Little prick. We both knew I held zero cards. He could instruct Scar to pick Patti up by the ankles and hold her over the rail until someone talked. And after we did, he'd calmly order Scar to release his grip. It would be a swell time for Garrett to enter stage left. The plan had been for me to draw their attention when I climbed aboard and for Garrett and Domingo to sneak over the aft platform. It was my job to keep things breezy until the point of maximum surprise. I'd blown that when I'd allowed Scar to get the drop on me. Hopefully, it only delayed the kickoff.

"It was the Achilles' heel of Richard Callaghan's operation," Condor said, directing his comment to Patti and Suzanne. "Brilliant, really, his insistence on using paper, his allergic reaction to anything electronic. His apparent gift for turning agents and earning their loyalty. But there is yin and yang in all we do. His insistence on using untrained and unversed assets placed those he loved in the most uncompromising positions. He had too much self-confidence. 'Pride goeth before a fall.'"

"No," I said.

He looked at me. "Pardon?"

"'Pride goeth before destruction. A haughty spirit before a fall.'"

He tilted his head. "I stand corrected. Pity we don't have the luxury of debating the subtle difference." His smirk said he could misquote scripture all evening, and in the morning he'd be sipping coffee and I'd be at the bottom of the sea, so who gave a rat's ass about the translation of two-thousand-year-old scripture and the nearly indiscernible difference between pride and a haughty spirit?

I took another sip and placed the glass down. "9:30" was scrawled on the napkin. Garrett had likely bribed the jittery waiter. I took a deep breath, clasped and unclasped my hands. I just needed to keep us alive until the appointed hour. I didn't think Condor would toss us overboard before dark, but seeing as how I held a toothbrush and the man behind me a badass gun, clearly I'd been outmaneuvered.

The waiter came back and stopped in front of Patti.

"Would you like filet mignon or hogfish snapper for dinner?"

"Filet. Medium. And I don't mean medium-well."

It was good to know she had not lost her spunk. It might come in handy later.

He turned to Suzanne. "Ma'am?"

Suzanne cocked her head. "How is the hogfish snapper prepared?"

"Panfried and baked."

"That would be fine."

"Sir?"

"The same," I said. "Fresh fish for my final meal seems fitting."

He left without consulting the boss. I brought the flute to my lips along with the napkin. When I placed the flute back on the table, I kept the napkin and dabbed my mouth with it, soiling it so as to smear the ink. I slid it into my pocket. I didn't want Condor to see the writing on the napkin. A toothbrush and a dirty napkin. Look out, world.

Condor leaned back, tapping another cigarette from the package. "Who would like to start?"

"Can we shelve the talk until after dinner?" I chimed in.

"And why would that be?"

"Hogfish snapper is one of my favorite fishes, assuming your chef doesn't overcook it. Maintaining my value through dinner ensures that I enjoy it."

Condor dipped his head. "I accept your logic."

And so, after we resituated to the outdoor teak table, and over exquisitely presented hogfish snapper, we chatted about his yacht and his work. He gave far more information than he would to anyone he expected to survive the night. We discussed European cities. Paris. London. Rome. Berlin. He pondered the Japanese. "The politest race on earth, really. Above reproach. Such an about-face from the atrocities of the Second World War, there's something to learn there." And the Chinese. "Xi has absolute power; he will balance the state and harness the individual's lust for money to create a global monster that will dwarf the U.S." And, speaking of those thuggery capitalists, "America has no foundation. It shifts its bloating muscle in errant direction without thought or consideration."

"And Russia," I said, trying to keep him going while pretending to drink more wine than I was. "What delusions do you still cling to regarding your cartoonish suppressive regime?"

"You harbor the same simplistic view of all westerners," he said, unfazed by my words. He looked at Patti. "And you, my dear. You've hardly uttered a word during dinner. What are your thoughts on the human zoo?"

"You kidnapped me," Patti said. "Your barbaric act speaks for you and your wolf-den government."

His jaw tightened. He was not used to being put in his place by a woman.

"Your government's done far worse."

"Not to me."

He shifted his attention to Suzanne. "You are a beautiful woman," he said, as if appraising a racehorse. "Tall and statuesque. Eastern European, perhaps? Do you agree that you have been kidnapped?"

"I find your condescending and verbal sparring insulting."

While I admired Patti and Suzanne's attitude, I'd much rather engage in idle chat until dark. Nine thirty couldn't come fast enough.

He formed a pyramid with his hand and rolled his fingertips. "Let's end it then, shall we?"

He stood and strolled around the table behind us, speaking as he moved.

"Richard Callaghan discovered a list of our agents—the Network—working within the U.S. Mr. Callaghan was a formidable opponent, wise and patient. Instead of silencing those assets, he drugged them to be loyal to him.

"This tactic came with considerable risk—I know, for I have done the same in my country. There are those within Mr. Callaghan's own organization who doubt his effectiveness— feel, perhaps, that he compromised himself in his loyalties. That there is no place in the world for sentimental spies with conflicted loyalties. They wanted to shut him down, tell the men and women he turned that they are on their own. How do you say it? Good luck and good riddance. Are you with me?"

No one answered.

"We believed he maneuvered to protect them until a regime change—what you impressionable Americans refer to as an election—might look upon his life's work with more appreciative eyes."

Condor had moved to the rail where the black and red sunset stained the western sky. His comments revealed that he had a source in the FBI, CIA, or both. Richard Callaghan had been wise not to reveal the list.

"He gave one of you the names. The agents he turned. And, perhaps even more threatening to us, those he was aware of but who he chose not to turn. Instead, he fed them a steady diet of false information. I know he was partial to books—indeed, I've studied his methods. All you need to do in order to see the sun rise is tell me what you know. It does me no good to have blood on my hands. Nor is it necessary." He paused and then added, "It's amazing, really, what rational people will divulge when properly pressured."

I stood. Scar took a step toward me, but Condor waved him off. "They're in books," I said. "The second floor of A Novel Experience bookstore. First edition spy novels. You may even find yourself in one of them. Patti and Suzanne know nothing of this. They were used."

I put my hand in my pocket and curled my fingers around the toothbrush. To be honest, it failed to provide a rush of confidence. The sun had vanished into the Gulf of Mexico, revealing the darkness of the universe. A poem from my youth flashed in my mind: Oh hurry the dark and blot the sky, for we crave the night, although we know not why.

Condor took a step toward me. "I don't think so."

He shot a glance at Patti and Suzanne. "There is a Gate-keeper—yes, I know the word he was fond of. A *Torhüter*. A *portière*. *Privratnik*. Understand? Richard Callaghan would never leave it to chance." He walked behind Patti and Suzanne. "That person, who he trusted explicitly, would know where other books are and how to interpret them. We thought it was his lover, but we were wrong. It would not"—he shot me a glance—"be someone he did not know." He placed a hand on Patti's shoulder. "You knew the man from decades ago, although you were quite young when you met." He placed his other hand on Suzanne's shoulder. "And you, we know virtually nothing of. A dark horse, although I hesitate to call such a beautiful woman such an innapropriate name."

Baptiste came out of the stateroom. I hadn't seen Condor summon him and wondered if Condor, like me, was waiting for the moment. Another man, tall with sinewy muscles snaking out of his T-shirt, followed Baptiste and stood off to the side across from Scar. Two men behind me, one in front. They'd done this maneuver before.

"Please," Condor said, deliberately placing his hand to the back of Patti's chair. "Let us move over to the couches."

No one moved.

"Stand," he barked. "Now."

Both Patti and Suzanne sprang up. Baptiste drew his gun and nailed his eyes on me. Scar stepped into Patti. He slapped her across the cheek, sending her crumbling to the ground. She cried out. Suzanne dashed to her, kneeling by her side. By placing his hand on the back of Patti's chair, Condor had signaled which woman to strike.

Scar kicked Suzanne, rolling her on the deck. Her breath

left her with a "humph." Patti scrambled to her feet, taking a step back from Scar.

In a quiet voice, Condor said, "Now that we understand each other, will someone kindly tell me who the Gatekeeper is? It would be tiresome to continue with such primitive acts."

"I told you. I am."

I never saw Baptiste move. A crushing blow slammed the back of my head. I stumbled forward and caught the back of a chair with my left hand. I slid my right hand around the toothbrush.

"You lie," he said. He looked at Scar. "The shorter woman."

Scar lifted Patti and draped her over his shoulder.

"By the ankles," Condor said, surrendering all false propriety.

Patti kicked and shrieked. Suzanne scrambled to her feet and ran to her friend's side. Scar tried to backhand her. But Suzanne dropped to her knees, and Scar's hand swatted air. She wrapped her arms around his ankles and drove the big man down. Patti toppled off his back, breaking the fall with her hands. Scar bolted up to his feet. Suzanne stood and took a step back from him.

"Stop," Condor shouted.

Scar froze. Suzanne's chest rose and fell as if steeling herself for a fight.

Condor looked at me.

"You did not move."

I remained silent while noting the position of the five men: Condor, Scar, Baptiste, Murdoch, and Sinewy Man.

"You did not move," Condor repeated. "Murdoch?"

"Yes?"

"The man who served us drinks, he is new, correct?"

"He's been with us for a month," Murdoch said.

"He was nervous when he brought the champagne. Bring him to me."

Murdoch left. "It would be unfortunate," Condor said, "if you were foolish enough to smuggle your hippie friend on board."

I wanted to volley a sharp remark back but thought it wise to keep my mouth shut. Murdoch came back with the man who had served us.

Condor faced him.

"Angelo, correct?"

"Yes, sir."

"Do you like working on the boat?"

"Yes, sir."

"Do you like living?"

"Yes, sir."

"Angelo, do you know of anyone who is on this boat who should not be?"

Angelo hesitated. Poor Angelo. Poor, poor Angelo.

IT WOULD HAVE BEEN LIGHTS OUT FOR ANGELO HAD HE befriended anyone besides Garrett Demarcus. But Garrett is a fierce protector of those who help. Darkness had taken the day. The stage was ours.

40

Unless you've been at sea at night, you do not know true darkness.

It is not a city darkness with streetlights pinholing the black. It is not a suburban darkness with garage lights and lampposts emitting welcoming glows. It is not a northern front yard in June with fireflies sparkling the fresh-cut grass, and it's certainly not the darkness of a full moon brightening a field of Vermont snow. It envelops you. Swallows you. You cease to exist. You understand a little about yourself, but this is not the time or place for that.

The lights went out.

A shot split the night. Then another.

Sinewy Man went down.

I spun around just as Scar was drawing his gun. I was on him with one step. I jabbed the toothbrush into his neck. He reached for the toothbrush. I reached for his gun. I shot him twice.

Another shot cracked the dark. I pivoted to see where the others were. Condor. Baptiste. Murdoch. All gone. The man with the sinewy muscles was dead on the deck, as was Scar.

"Stay down," I yelled at Patti and Suzanne, but they were already under the teak table.

Bullets ricocheted off the deck.

I dove under the table and joined them.

"You have friends on board?" Suzanne whispered in a coarse voice.

"I do."

"Are they better than you?"

"I thought we were doing all right here."

"You killed that man," Patti said.

"They would kill us all," I said. "Still might."

"You killed him," Patti said again. "You didn't even hesitate."

"Take a deep breath." I looked at Suzanne. "Can you take care of her?"

She nodded.

"Here." I handed Suzanne Scar's gun. "They come for you? Shoot. Aim at the chest. Do you understand?"

Another nod. "You don't need it?"

"Garrett's on board, remember him? Black. Tall. Do not shoot him. Also Domingo. They—"

"How did they board?"

"You shot a man."

"Take deep breaths, Patti," I coached her, and then turned my attention to Suzanne. "They snuck aboard while I made a fool of myself. Anyone else you see is not friendly. Understand?"

"OK."

"Angelo. The waiter? Don't shoot him."

"OK."

I sprinted low to the ground. It was a big boat, and my adversary had the advantage of knowing the layout. The boat's generators were below deck and the pilothouse two floors above and forward—that was standard on all yachts. I took outside metal steps up to the next level. Bullets pinged off the guardrail to my right, and I hit the deck.

"Clear," Garrett yelled from above me. I vaulted the steps three at a time to the upper deck. Garrett crouched next to a door leading into the main lounge. His rifle with a night-vision scope rested in his hands.

"Nice of you to show," I said.

"Nice of you to drop out during the day," he said, staring down at the aft deck. "We spent twelve hours cramped in a guest closet, taking turns to see when you decided to make an appearance."

I'd never heard the man utter a complaint in his life. It must have been torturous.

"Chloroform," I said.

He flicked his eyes to me. "You let someone rag you?"

"Can we move on?"

"Twelve hours," he said, as if he still couldn't comprehend what he'd endured.

"Domingo?" I said.

"We split. No idea where he is. Did you get my message?"

"Nine thirty?"

"We told him he could live to see tomorrow or die with the crew. Name's Angelo. Know who I'm talking about?"

"Slick hair."

"Honor our word," Garrett said. "Also a short Frenchman, dressed like a chef."

"Why?"

"Why what?"

"Why's he dressed like a chef?"

"He's the chef. We moved to the galley instead of dying in the closet. Traded lives for cooperation."

"You try the hogfish?" I said.

"Wasn't bad."

"The captain?"

"No intel," Garrett said. "He's my next stop."

"We got two down. Condor, Murdoch, and Baptiste are still loose. Baptiste is the hitter who took out Sundown and Callaghan. But Murdoch looked just as capable. Cell reception?"

"Nothing."

The yacht had ceased its forward motion and sat dead in the water. The lights came back on but at a reduced wattage, as if a backup generator had kicked in. The only sound was the sea lapping against the hull.

"How were you able to kill the power?" I asked.

"A man in the engine room."

"How many mice on this hunk of cheese?"

"That's it. You need to get back to Patti and Suzanne," Garrett said. "We don't want a hostage situation."

"I left them a gun."

Garrett looked at me—he'd been peering into the forward deck. "Think they can use it?"

A shot rang out behind us, followed by another. It sounded like Scar's gun.

"I'm going to find out."

He gave me a handgun and we split. I flew down the metal stairs and rounded the corner. Suzanne stood holding the gun in both hands. Baptiste stood in front of her, with his back to me. I crouched behind a deck chair. Suzanne, intent upon Baptiste, didn't see me, or if she had, she exercised uncanny calmness in choosing not to acknowledge my presence. Baptiste had his gun drawn.

"Stay away," Suzanne said in a jittery voice.

Baptiste took a step toward her. "Put the gun down. We don't want to hurt you."

"Stay away," Suzanne repeated. She took a step back to compensate for the step Baptiste had taken. Patti hovered next to Suzanne, touching her shoulder as if to grant her support. I didn't know if Suzanne could shoot a man in cold blood.

Baptiste took another step forward.

"We can't tell you anything if we're dead," Suzanne said.

"I'm not here to hurt you."

"You're here to torture me."

"Suzanne, right? I won't hurt you or Patti. That was never our intention. I'm sorry if we scared you."

I drew my gun and stood.

"Hey, clown face."

Baptiste started to swing his head but stopped.

"You shoot me," he said, his back to me, "and in my final act I kill the woman."

And that's how we stood: Patti cowering behind Suzanne, Suzanne holding the gun I'd given her with both hands, Baptiste pointing his gun at Suzanne, and me pointing my gun at Baptiste's back. Such predicaments have a short life, and this scene changed dramatically when the hard barrel of a gun pressed against my head.

"Drop it," Murdoch said.

I lowered my gun.

"I said drop it."

I dropped it.

Suzanne's eyes darted between Baptiste and me. Murdoch walked around so that he was beside me. Five, maybe six feet. About the right distance.

Baptiste, trying to appear less threatening, partially lowered his gun. A costly error he would never make again.

"Please, your gun," he said to Suzanne. "Or Murdoch will kill your friend."

"Suzanne?" I said.

She glanced at me.

My voice was so calm it spooked even me. "He killed Richard Callaghan. Shoot him. Now."

Suzanne shot Baptiste twice in the chest.

I moved with the flinch of her finger. A perfectly executed vertical roundhouse kick that nearly took Murdoch's head off. My punching bag would have been proud.

Murdoch was out cold. But he'd gotten a shot off, and a streak of pain pierced my upper shoulder.

"Oh my god!" Suzanne said. "You're shot."

"It's not bad."

"I tried to warn him, to scare him off," Suzanne said, staring at Baptiste's body. "I shot twice in the air, but he just kept coming."

"You did great, Suzanne."

"Did he really kill Richard?"

"He did."

She bobbed her head a few times and then shifted her attention to Murdoch. "Is he dead?"

"No. I'll need to tie him." I glanced at Patti, who stood like stone.

"Patti, are you OK?"

"Oh, sure. I'm fine." She knotted her hands together. "No problems here. No siree."

I ripped several pieces from the edge of a black decorative curtain. I bound Murdoch's hands behind him, tied his ankles, and stuffed his mouth. I took part of the curtain and wrapped my shoulder and upper arm.

"Where's Condor?" Suzanne said.

"He's still at large." I struggled with the curtain. "I need to get back to Garrett."

"Let me help." Suzanne tied the shredded curtain tightly around my shoulder. The wound was more of a nuisance than anything else. "I'm going with you."

"You're better here with Patti. You did well. Don't be afraid to use your gun again."

But like Baptiste, I'd made a costly error.

41

G arrett was in the pilothouse with the captain, a man in a white short-sleeve shirt, a dark tie, a trimmed beard and an attitude that needed a little work.

"He says we're heading to the Caymans," Garrett said. "But when I came in, he tried to pull this on me." He held up a small pistol.

"Think he has another one?" I said.

"How about it, Captain?" Garrett said.

The man clenched his jaw and kept his stoic face on the dark windshield. I slapped him on the back of the head.

"What about it, Nemo?" I said. "You packing anything else?"

"No."

"We're in charge now. You understand?"

"Yes."

"Like you mean it."

"Yes, sir."

I turned to Garrett. "Baptiste's dead. Murdoch, Condor's assistant, is tied up. Domingo?"

"Still no sign of him. I'd rather him take this post than either of us."

"I'm going to do a walk-through. See if I can flush out our bird friend."

"Bring Patti and Suzanne up here," Garrett said. "I can watch them while I babysit. We're vulnerable if Condor gets to them."

I hustled back to Patti and Suzanne, thinking I should have thought of that.

I was feeling jovial about the evening—thanks to my narrow escape with death when Suzanne bailed me out—when, for the final time, I approached the aft deck of *Sea Mistress*.

"Lower your weapon. Slowly."

Condor was behind me, but at a safe distance. I'd purposely hugged the wall. To this day, I have no idea what crevice the little screwball stepped out of.

"Is that you, Hank?"

"Your weapon."

"I'd rather not."

"One, two . . ."

I lowered my weapon.

"Now, open your hand and let the gun drop."

I did as instructed.

"Move."

I moved. He did not, letting the space grow between us.

We rounded the corner. Suzanne and Patti were waiting for us. Suzanne held her gun with both hands. She pointed it at Condor.

Condor was about ten feet behind me. He kept his back against the entry to the stateroom so as not to be exposed. He looked at Suzanne, aimed his gun at Patti, and said, "Toss it or I'll shoot her." The calmness of his voice conveyed the simple honesty of his statement.

Suzanne pulled the trigger twice.

Click. Click.

Then I did the math. Two shots I put in Scar, two I heard before I'd previously rushed to the aft deck, and two shots at Baptiste.

Six.

Is there anything hard about that? The thrill of executing a perfect vertical roundhouse kick was obliterated by my abject failure to perform basic math while in the arena of conflict. I could have easily switched out another gun for Suzanne.

Suzanne gave me a quizzical and disappointed look. She dropped the gun.

I turned to Condor and said, "Your lucky day, Hank."

"Inside." He motioned with his gun to the open doors of the lower stateroom. He wanted off the aft deck. I was still ticked that he'd gotten the jump on me, but I wasn't going to compound my error by haranguing myself.

Patti, Suzanne, and I marched into the stateroom, a spacious cabin with a large glass table in the middle supported by a gargoyleian piece of driftwood.

"You do know," I said, "that we control the pilothouse."

"She's all yours. I've arranged transportation off the boat. One woman will accompany me."

"One?"

He glanced at Patti and Suzanne. "Two would be preferable, but I'm assuming one of you will try something stupid, and to earn your cooperation it will be necessary to eliminate one. Do you understand?"

Kathleen's creation, Alida with two hearts, dropped into my head.

"What if you kill the wrong one?" I said. "The surviving one will be useless to you."

"You will talk," he said, although it was unclear whom he was addressing. He'd positioned himself in front of us, his back against a solid wall. He waved his gun between Patti and

259

Suzanne. "Which one of you did Richard Callaghan confide in?"

"I am the Gatekeeper," Suzanne said.

"I am the Gatekeeper," Patti chimed in.

I said to Condor, "Did you ever watch *To Tell the Truth*?"

Condor's eyes danced between the two women. "If you insist on these games, there will be great suffering. Do you understand?"

Suzanne took a step forward. "It is me."

"What proof can you offer?" Condor sneered.

"What will you accept?"

"Agents. Locations. Code names."

"I don't have that in my head."

"Then you are bluffing."

"I have something better," Suzanne said with a baffling smile.

Condor leveled his gun at Patti. She bit her lip, whimpered, and took a step back.

"Tell me, or she dies now," Condor growled.

"You're a one-nut wonder," Suzanne said. "You were born with one testicle."

A smile spread across Condor's face, but it was nothing you would want your child to see.

"Yes," he gushed. "Yes. It is you." He took a step back and nodded toward Patti and me. "And now you two are expendable. Ladies first, so you will witness this worthless man stand idly by while you die."

Worthless man had been working hard to keep his face stone. For the entire time we were in the stateroom, Domingo had been squatting behind the couch against the far wall. I didn't want to give him away and doubted that either Patti or Suzanne had noticed him.

Domingo leaped from his position and landed with his feet evenly apart. Sensing the threat from behind, Condor spun, his gun leading the way. But by the time he accomplished his pivot, the Cattaraugus 225Q knife was curving in a downward trajectory. It planted itself in Condor's neck, just below his jaw, the heavy blade burying itself in the defenseless tissue. Condor's eyes popped open and his hand fell to his side, dropping the gun. He tumbled to the teak floor. His flailing hands struck a side table where they knocked off a menagerie of glass flowers and an aqua glass basket. They shattered on the floor.

"It is a heavy knife. I had to compensate for that," said the thin man who spoke in short sentences and carried a long knife. "It is good that I've been living with it. I know it well."

"You've been here all evening?" I asked him.

"No one expects a man who does not exist."

I looked at Suzanne. *How right you are.*

Condor wasn't dead yet, although nothing could be done for him. He fumbled with the knife, his throat gurgling blood and spurting wasted air.

Suzanne strode over to him. She lowered herself to her knees, bent over, and pressed her lips to his ears, her hair blanketing Condor's face. She whispered something. Not just a word, maybe a few sentences. She stood back up. Her lips spread into a thin smile, but it did not match the look in her eyes.

Condor stared at her in disbelief. Then he, too, formed a faint smile, followed by what I believe was a congratulatory nod of his head.

Chris Callaghan picked up Condor's gun and ended Condor's life.

42

The chimes announced my final arrival at A Novel Experience. I'd called earlier to let them know I was coming. Tippy perked up his ears when I came in, and Patti glanced up from her desk. Snatches of music came from her computer.

"How's Tippy?"

"Doing great."

"And business in a small town?"

"I don't think I'll ever gripe over a busted freezer again."

"You will."

She gave me a crooked smile. "Damn right, and it will feel good. Your FBI friend—Bangs Girl—was by the other day to collect the books. I told her they were all hers."

"She took them?"

"She and a couple of guys. Cleared them out. She asked if you came by."

"What did you say?"

"Told her the truth. That I hadn't seen you. Think she'll be back when she finds they're fake—you know, ordinary books that Suzanne switched out?"

"No."

"Why not?"

"She knows—or at least suspects."

"What makes you so certain?"

I popped open my hands, palms outward.

Patti tilted her head. "You two got history, don't you?"

"Suzanne here?"

She let that linger and then jutted her chin toward the steps. "Upstairs. Ask you something?"

"Shoot."

"When did you know?"

"I think I should talk to her first."

"I respect that. Hey, I got something for you."

She reached into a drawer and took out a copy of *The Quiet American*. She handed it to me. "We got this in a few days ago. First edition, great shape. I thought you might like it. You don't already have it, do you? Because that would suck."

"I do not. I have *The Ugly American*."

"Are they related?"

"In a roundabout way."

"Like a lot of things."

"Like a lot of things."

We were silent for a moment.

"I'm sorry it was so close," I said. "I never should have allowed that."

She covered her mouth with her hand, leaning in on the desk. "I miss Sundown." She raked her hand through her hair. "Jesus, I miss her so much. You need to help Suzanne. She blames herself—for everything. She and Sundown were always close because of—you know. I don't want to lose her." I thought she was going to say something else, but she just waved her hand. "She's expecting you. Go."

I again took the narrow steps to the second floor, where the boards creaked under my feet and the walls caved in with the weight of the books of yesterday and the air was thick with the odor of aged paper and time stood still. Time is always moving, but when you are in a used bookstore it does not move, and you can smell time—and that's what I was trying to explain the first time I fumbled telling you about how Elaine's house had trapped time layered on its walls, and about my first trip to the second floor of A Novel Experience. I couldn't find the words. I looked too hard for them. All I had to do was breathe. Like a low tide, time has its own identifying odor.

Suzanne had her back to me. She turned as I hit the last step.

"Well, if it isn't Errol Flynn," she said in her nightclub voice.

She wore jeans and a tucked-in white shirt. That tucked-in shirt was unbuttoned for the first four inches, revealing the missing tarnished-copper Saint Christina medallion. I'd long ago decided that Yankee Conrad had a good reason to gift the rare female saint of mariners to his nephew.

"Buy you lunch?" I said.

"When we were hiding under the table? I thought, screw it. If we get out alive, I'm dedicating my life to raising my cholesterol."

"May I be of assistance?"

"Absolutely."

WHEN I STEPPED ON JCPENNEY AND OPENED THE DOOR AT the Pirates' Deck, Suzanne said, "Don't worry, Melinda knows."

She ordered a cheeseburger, and we made it a pair. Mine came with iced tea and hers with a glass of chardonnay. We shared an order of fries. She liked ketchup with hers, while I favored vinegar, a culinary accompaniment she claimed to have never paired with fries. It's a complicated world. People are different in a lot of ways.

"The stage is yours," I said. "And the theater is empty."

"I always liked that," she said.

"So I was told. Do you harbor any guilt?"

"For killing the man who killed Richard? And then Richard's nemesis?"

I nodded, thinking she certainly knew my question cut deeper.

"None. It was a banner day."

"And the other?"

She blew out her breath, her sad eyes resting on mine "No. But I'm constantly reinforcing that. Tell me, when did the picture come into focus?"

"There's more to a picture than meets the eye."

"That keeps with the metaphor, but it hardly breaks new ground."

"Patti brought a picture with her to Harbor House. Chris— you—her, and Sundown standing in front of Sundown's dinghy, *Seashell*."

"And?" she challenged me.

"Sundown told me that the name of her dinghy was *Little Sea* and that she didn't change it to *Seashell* until a few months after your death. In that picture—in which you are supposed to be dead—you're wearing the gold anchor that is part of the chimes above the front door of the bookstore."

"Which means . . ."

"Precisely."

She plucked a fry from the plate. "Well, we screwed up there, didn't we? All those years, it was in plain sight for everyone to see. But you certainly had further suspicions."

"I met a crab trapper. He said Sundown's boat was at your boat, the *Ms. Buckeye,* nearly every morning. He added that Sundown's boat, *Seaduction*, stayed in Midnight Cove after the fire, but Sundown told me she moved out." I shrugged. "When I first met you, you tilted your head and ran your fingers up your neck. Your mother has a similar move."

"Like this?" she said. She cocked her head and raked her hand along her neck and into her hair.

"Like that."

"And that struck a match?"

"You were a guy once."

"No, I wasn't. That's the point. But I understand what you're saying."

We were quiet as Melinda passed by on the other side of the counter to serve a couple who had taken stools at the end of the bar.

"Does Patti know that you worked for your father?" I asked.

"Does now. But in the spirit of your question—no. I only told her right before we went to Harbor House. I should have told her earlier, of course, but there it is."

"She fiercely protected your identity."

She twiddled her hair. "As I asked her to. I'm afraid I have some fence-mending to do."

"Sundown."

"She knew everything."

"So Patti—"

"Odd woman out. For her good, but like I said, I've got work to do."

Her comment validated Patti's sincere ignorance in my earlier questioning. Patti had also seemed more relaxed at Harbor House. She certainly must have entertained her own suspicions and was likely pleased to have that tension lifted from her and Suzanne's relationship.

"Was he in from the beginning?" I said.

She interlocked her fingers. "Richard?"

"Your father."

"I've always been more comfortable calling him by his name."

"Was he?"

"What do you think?" she said.

"I think he helped you escape a complicated relationship with your mother, become the beautiful woman you are, create a new life, and that you have worked for him ever since."

"My," she gave me a coy smile. "Yankee was right about you. I don't think Sundown expected you to be so diligent."

"But Yankee Conrad hired me to be so."

She bobbed her head a few times. "No argument here. He—we—certainly took advantage of you, but for a good reason."

"I can hardly wait."

She eyed me for a beat. "It would be easier if you said some of this, so I can claim I didn't tell you."

And this is what I told her: that Yankee Conrad was a powerful figure in the CIA, more so due to his secrecy. His picture would never grace the organization's website. He would attend no picnics, no retirement parties. He was as involved in running the double agents in the Network as Richard Callaghan was. When he received the medallion demanding ransom, he had no idea where it came from but couldn't take the chance. And once Sundown was murdered, there was no backing out. The agency had an informer—a defector—and if the books got in the wrong hands, it would mean death to those agents who had been recruited by Callaghan. I was winging the latter part of my speech but felt rock solid on the first part.

"Impressive," she said after I'd finished. "I'm not sure I'd go with him being in the employ of the CIA—not that he didn't spend decades there. He's more like an operator who has carte blanche to intervene in multiple theaters. Did you see last week where the secretary to the CIA's head of counterintelligence died in a boating accident?"

"Swept overboard, although it was a calm sea."

"Richard had been trying to expose him for years," she said. "Later this week, there will be shuffling at the FBI's Joint Terrorism Task Force. Your girlfriend, Binelli, might be moving up."

"She's not my girlfriend."

"I bet you say that a lot."

I ignored her quip.

"After Sundown's murder," I said, "my job was to protect your identity and—as a bonus for everyone—take out Condor."

"You mean we used you."

"I'm being kind."

"One could hardly blame you if you forgo politeness," she said in an airy voice. "I was outvoted, not that I'm trolling for any forgiveness. The time you came in the bookstore after you told Patti about Sundown? When I said 'Hey?' I almost spilled it then."

I recalled the moment but didn't berate myself for not reading more into her monosyllable comment at the time.

"But you didn't," I pointed out.

"No. I didn't." She leveled her eyes on mine. "Thank you. With both my hearts."

"My pleasure. The books?"

"I think you know."

I pictured Yankee Conrad's massive bookshelves.

"He has them, doesn't he? It's been him all along."

She dragged a french fry through a pool of vinegar on the plate and stuck it in her mouth. "You might be onto something here."

I mulled over how I'd been more lucky than good on board *Sea Mistress* that night. It had been bothering me. I had to get my head in the game.

"You handled yourself well that night on the boat," I said, my thoughts seeping out of me.

"Richard insisted I know my way around firearms from an early age. 'Death is a hesitant finger,' he told me." She swayed her head. "Other fathers attended school plays. I got 'Death is a hesitant finger.'"

"Good advice comes back around."

"And don't you think I know it."

"One-nut wonder?"

She laughed. "Richard gifted me that singular trait about Condor. I'm not sure where he unearthed it, but it wasn't something one forgets."

"Tell me about the night you murdered yourself in Midnight Cove."

She adjusted her weight on the stool and ran her hand down her neck, fondling the medallion.

"First of all, you got it right. Suicide is when you kill yourself. Murder is when you kill someone else. I'm a woman who was born into a man's body. We don't pick our gender, right? I mean you grow up worshipping whatever god your parents bow to, speak whatever language is babbled around you—all of that comes after birth. But you're given your sex, and sometimes nature gets it wrong. My whole life, before the change, I felt like music struggling to be free. That there was a stranger within, and that stranger was me."

She shook her head, smiling at a ghost of a memory. "Sundown actually moved in for a while. She gave me girl lessons. That was a time of my life when I was free to be who I was. Living on the *Ms. Buckeye*? There was no one to judge me. No one I had to pretend around. I became who I am. The surgeries and name changes, all the"—she gave me a flirtatious glance, arching her eyebrows—"details came later."

She shrugged. "I torched her. Slipped overboard and Richard picked me up. Sundown knew it was going down that night. We wanted her on her boat so her story was authentic. We picked a night with a strong outgoing tide. We knew there'd be no murder scene to investigate."

"Richard," I said, envisioning him standing on the sand waiting for his son to swim to shore and emerge as a daughter.

"You know he and Sundown were in love, right?"

"I do."

"She was the bridge, the go-between, when we conceived our plan. But we couldn't do it without Richard's contacts. His savvy."

I nodded. "His initial response?"

"He, Sundown, and I were having dinner at the Vinoy. Richard traveled extensively and stayed there when he was in town. Sundown had warned him. Greased the skids. But she'd pulled up short of announcing my intentions. He deserved to hear it from me. I'll never forget his reaction. He looked at me, his empty fork stuck in midair, and said, 'And so the impossible moves instantly to the inevitable.' It was one of his favorite phrases. He seemed pleased to be able to call upon it that evening. He took a sip of wine, said he always wanted a daughter and told me he thought it was a good move. He asked me if I'd picked out a name. I said I always liked Jennifer. He floated Suzanne. I admitted I liked that as well."

"When did he recruit you?"

"Over dessert. When the appetizers came, I was his unemployed son, Chris Callaghan. By the time dessert was cleared, we'd hatched a plan to make me his daughter, Suzanne, and a prized recruit to his department—counterintelligence."

"Big dinner."

"None bigger."

"How was the transition from a man—as the world saw you —to a woman?" I asked.

She raised her eyebrows. "It was a novel experience."

"Do tell."

"Patti couldn't resist naming her bookstore in honor of what we'd all been through. A best friend changes sexes. Another falls madly in love with her friend's father. The death of one daughter creates the blessed life of another."

She looked at me, and her eyes were no longer sad but were bright and open. I wondered if the transition was my imagination or if they slid effortlessly from one to the other as she had slid from man to woman. For if you really looked into Suzanne Emerson's eyes, the genderless soul within us all stared back at you.

"I think," she said, deliberately pronouncing her words, "that Richard—my loving father—also acted in self-interest. He saw what a great agent I'd make."

"And did you?"

"Heavens no." She laughed. "In the end, he trusted me with his life's work, but I wasn't worth a damn. I teach art classes. That's my passion. He'd occasionally toss me an assignment, but nothing borderline dangerous."

We were quiet for a moment as four older men shuffled through the front door. They took a table with a reserved sign on it under a window. Melinda fixed a tray of drinks and delivered them to the table, serving smack talk with the drinks. One of the men reached down and unplugged a blinking beer sign in the window.

"Elaine," I said.

She took a sip of chardonnay, keeping her hand on the glass after she placed it back on the counter.

"Elaine." She stretched out the name, as if an army of words could not match its power. "We had a . . . thorny relationship." She paused. "It seems so long ago I wonder if it's the same life."

I didn't want to be rude, or pry, but I wanted to know. I deserved to know.

"Thorny?" I said.

She humped a shoulder. "Literally. Figuratively. Whateverly. Think *The Thorn Birds*. Something so beautiful, you can't help but touch it and by doing so you destroy yourself. My mother observes no boundaries to pleasure. I'm not condemning or condoning, you understand?"

"I do," I said, but I didn't.

As if reading my mind, she said, "It was one night. I was

confused, to say the least. I was born a woman in a man's body. What the *hell* do you do with that?"

"You did—"

She raised her hand, cutting me off. "It's not a question with an answer. We went to Maine every September. After that last trip, I had to get out. I loved my mother, but it became apparent that to survive, I had to die. It was the only way to undarken my heart. My mother would never have understood."

We were quiet. A song I'd not heard in a long time played over the speakers. I signaled for Melinda and asked for a beer.

"Wondered how long you would hold out," she said, handing me a frosty one before again respecting our space.

"She was your mother," I said. I could not look at Suzanne, for her act seemed cruel and massively self-centered. "You just admitted you loved her."

"You think I haven't had second thoughts?" she said with bite, her eyes drilling mine. "Suffered sleepless nights? Not to mention a phone book of shrinks—you should have seen how they looked at me, like I was some reincarnation from a medieval witch hunt. I came close to killing myself for a second time after my boat went down and my selfish act registered.

"I can probably thank the limitations of my character for my survival. I'm not cut to lead the archetypal guilt-ridden life. That's not saying it's easy. I get up every day. I look in the mirror. My decision stares back at me. I take a step. I take another step. Thinking is my enemy."

"I didn't mean to be—"

"It's not you." Her chest heaved and fell again. "Am I some monster with no second thoughts? Maybe, but consider my parents."

She went into herself as her eyes locked onto her wineglass, her mind wrestling with a question, a decision that would track her to her grave.

"I don't talk about this much, understand?" She flashed her

eyes to me. "It rattles around inside, but outside of Patti and Sundown, I haven't heard my voice say these words unless I paid someone to hear them. I've rationalized myself to hell and back a million times.

"If Chris lived, he could never see his mother again. I thought death would be kinder to her. Now? Every day is a deeper well of what I don't know. We only know the path we take."

She kept talking, although I think it was for her benefit more so than mine.

"My mother was never well—and I cast a wide net of acceptance. I made my decision. I could not go on how it was. That was all I knew. I had a choice that night in Midnight Cove: either commit suicide or murder. I chose murder." She humped her shoulders. "I chose a different way to die."

I wondered if her act of killing Elaine's son, of cutting Elaine so deeply, was as much about retribution as it was about sexual identity. It was a thought I'd been struggling with. But what do I know of such things? Yet, I am not without a morsel of common sense. Here's the best I could do: Both mother and child needed mercy more than anything. They'd hurt the one they loved.

I had a lineup of questions but decided to skip the ones that might put her in a compromising situation. I had, after all, one more stop to make.

"There were two bouquets on Finegan's Ridge," I said.

"The second flowers were for Chris."

I raised my mug in a toast. "To Chris," I said.

She raised her glass. We were silent for a stanza, and then I said, "I see you're wearing your medallion."

"Yankee sent it."

"It all seems overly complicated."

"Welcome to the agency."

"I don't work for the agency."

"Oh, babe," she said. "Richard said the good ones never fill out a job application. I'm afraid you passed with flying colors."

I rubbed my chin.

Oh, babe.

I wondered where I'd lost control of my life but then thought my good friend Marcus Aurelius. "For nowhere either with more quiet or more freedom from trouble does a man retire than into his own soul . . . constantly then give to yourself this retreat." I'd become comfortable in my retreat. Free, without guilt, to live the life I had caged within me. My mind finally stripped of the agonizing self-doubt and cancerous irresolution that had burdened my steps.

"You need to see her again," I said, because our lives are a circle. And if you are wise, you figure that out before the clock with no hands stops ticking.

"Yankee and I are taking her to church this Sunday. That woman used to walk into a church like a nude descending a staircase. I doubt she has changed."

"Will she know you?"

"We don't think so."

I pondered her disingenuous comment in silence.

"Call me," I said. "Let me know how that goes."

But she never did. I hope she forgave herself for the murder she committed in Midnight Cove, but I don't think it works that way.

43

A large box rested on the edge of Snarly secretary's desk, crowding her space. I'd not seen her since I was at Yankee Conrad's office at the conclusion of the Elizabeth Walker affair.

"Good to see you, Mr. Travis," she said. Her thick, silvery hair with streaks of black in it was sweetly disordered. "I understand you did an exemplary job for us."

"Wouldn't want to let the team down, would I?"

"No, we would not. He's expecting you."

My last conversation with Yankee Conrad had been the brief phone call the night we boarded *Sea Mistress* when he had exhorted me to hold my end. I entered his office. The desk, bookcases, and flooring had all been ripped out of the captain's quarters of his grandfather's freighter. Yankee Conrad, sitting behind his desk and peering through a magnifying glass at a stamp, looked up as I approached.

"You're a philatelist?" I said.

"I use them as currency. This particular one is an Inverted Jenny. You are familiar with it?"

I told him I was. An Inverted Jenny is a 1918 release of a

275

twenty-four-cent airmail stamp in which one of the hundred blocks was printed with an upside-down Curtiss JN-4 airplane. Single stamps are worth over a million dollars.

"They are perhaps the lightest and smallest form of international currency," he said. "The easiest manner to facilitate untraceable payment."

I was in no mood to discuss Inverted Jennies.

"You sent me into a gunfight with a toothbrush."

He put down the magnifying glass and stood. "It is the man that counts, not the instrument he carries."

"I'll do us a favor and let that ridiculous statement go."

He sucked in his cheeks. "I understand. We rode the edge much closer than we desired. But, as I believe Suzanne told you, it was a delicate assignment considering we had a mole in the agency and I dearly wanted to protect Suzanne's identity. I saw no other way of accomplishing that." He hesitated and then added, "You may think I overestimated your capabilities, or perhaps relied too heavily on luck, but here we stand. Suzanne's life is her own, and tomorrow she and Elaine will walk together."

"All those years she mourned."

"Decisions were made. I could argue that Elaine's life, given the unique challenges her body and mind created for her, was much better with her son deceased." He reached to his desk, picked up an envelope, and extended it to me. "Your pay. You'll find working for the agency can be quite rewarding."

"I don't work for any agency."

"None of us do. You earned a clearance level that will shock you."

"There's a man who guards the shuttered government facility in Sandy Springs. Facility 4A281."

"What about him?"

"His name is Joe. He needs a new truck. Fast."

He placed the envelope back on the desk. "I'll see to it."

"How long have you been in the business?" I asked. My inquest was driven by instinct, for I could not intellectualize any reason for the question.

"I interned for a local law firm decades ago." He paused, although he did not drop eye contact. "One of the partners recruited me while I was dating his daughter."

"Mac?"

He nodded.

Walter "Mac" MacDonald: the man with the antiaircraft gun. Who had gifted Harbor House and belonged to the OSS, the precursor to the CIA. Our lives had barely overlapped, but he was one of the most fascinating people I'd ever had the pleasure of encountering. And, apparently, one of the more influential persons in my circular life.

My memory of Mac seemed off—something Yankee Conrad had just said—but I dismissed it. I said, "When you called me to your office over a year ago regarding the letter from Elizabeth Walker, you already knew of me."

"Mac spoke well of you."

"Little slow, aren't I?"

"To the contrary. Until we were committed to you, we kept it as opaque as possible."

"You do opaque well."

"You know what they say about practice."

"A lot of my initial information came from an FBI agent. I passed information to her. Names. Locations. But you knew that as well. My connection to her makes me more valuable. Is that how this works?"

"Your relationship with Agent Binelli was a wild card. A risk —and a reward—we were willing to explore. The various agencies do not always communicate as they should. Perhaps in the future you could introduce her to me."

I had more questions—like what he wanted from me the day he visited Harbor House—but it was coming to me. I was a big boy. I'd figure it out. I'd already decided that Harlan saw something at Sundown's that made him suspicious that Chris was not dead. His extortion attempt was not without reason.

I wandered over to the bookshelves.

"What is really in these books?" I said.

Yankee Conrad shrugged. "Like any book, whatever you bring is all you will find."

I turned to leave.

"I'd like to ask you a favor," he said from behind me.

"Yes?"

"There is a box of books on Constance's desk. Would you mind keeping them at Harbor House? Not in the box, of course. It's not good for them. Perhaps behind the hidden panel in the loft. Are you familiar with it?"

"I am. It's empty except for a magazine."

His eyes brightened. "Yes. *Look*, if my memory serves me correctly. That was all before my active employment. It's of no use now. I believe Mac kept it to commemorate an event. You haven't tossed it, have you? Not that it matters."

"No. Constance is your secretary?"

He chuckled. "Secretary? I suppose one could say that. Although it is such an antiquated word."

Richard had spoken of a Gatekeeper before he died. While I'd grown to believe that more than one person would hold the identities of the sleeper agents, ingeniously disguised in books, I couldn't shake his strong reference to a single person. *There is a master list,* he'd said, moments before he died in my arms. *The Gatekeeper has it—there is one.*

"Richard Callaghan mentioned a Gatekeeper," I said. "I inferred he was alluding to a single person."

"Gatekeeper—another antiquated word, I'm afraid. Oh, it may have started in such a fashion, but we've sensibly spread our risk. A single spoke cannot support a wheel. One more item, Mr. Travis. Your friend—Garrett Demarcus. I believe you two are close."

I didn't buy his answer, but I let it slide. Whoever the Gatekeeper was, it was not for me to know.

"Your point?"

"We like him."

"He'll never take a penny from you."

"Even better. But he'll work alongside you?"

"I'd advise you to be careful what you wish for."

"Yes. Yes, indeed. I think we'll get along just fine."

I took my leave and went to the reception room. Snarly secretary, Constance, stood and strolled over to me. She extended her hand as if we were meeting for the first time. Her wild hair draped over her shoulders, and her blue eyes held mine. She reminded me of Barbara Stanwyck, or maybe Suzanne's comment about *The Thorn Birds* was still riding my mind for it had disturbed me in many ways.

"Constance," she said as we shook hands. "It's a pleasure to have you on board."

"I'm not sure what frigate I'm on," I said.

"Now, Mr. Travis," she said, still holding my hand. "You will find it to be a lovely cruise."

"Tell me, Constance, what recruiting pool did Yankee Conrad fish you out of?"

"Is that what you think?"

I was going to retort that I assumed as much, but I pulled up short. Instead, I opted for, "I'm certainly open to your version."

She gave a slight tilt of her head. "You know that 'Truth is stranger than fiction.'"

"So I've heard."

"'But it is because fiction is obliged to stick to possibilities; Truth isn't.'"

"Oscar Wilde?"

"Mark Twain."

"Of course," I said, ticked that I'd muffed a quotation I knew.

"Has it occurred to you that you're looking at it from the wrong end?" she said.

No, Constance, it had not. But with that comment, I certainly did. I tossed out the old assumptions and started clean. Binelli's quip rolling in my head: God. Dog. Dog. God.

The woman in front of me stood straight. Confident. As if she expected me to know her. Her enticing hair waterfalling over thin shoulders. Her eyes twinkled with wisdom. They held my eyes firmer than her cool fingers that were still wrapped around my hand.

I've seen those eyes before.

I wondered if the life of every eye that had been pecked out of a dying sailor's head had been gifted to him—and his daughter. I thought of Yankee Conrad's comment that he had dated Mac's daughter, and how his statement had tripped my rusty memory. No longer. Mac had told me he and his wife were unable to have children. "It wasn't to be," he had said. Yet the inescapable truth was that I was looking at Walter MacDonald's daughter.

"It is you," I said, unconsciously squeezing her hand, for I saw the Madonna in the painting, and the world swirled around her. "You *are* Mac's daughter. He didn't tell me about you because your identity is never to be known. Or at least not to someone whom he had just met and was still evaluating. You're the Gatekeeper."

"Such an unflattering phrase." She released our hands, for like an electrical conduit, they had accomplished their task, having sparked and welded our lives together. "It is their word, not mine."

"Richard copied the trick with his son," I said. "I should have seen it—seen him in you—earlier."

"There was no way for you to have known. That was by design. Besides, it's a sexist world, no one suspects a woman."

"'The truth is rarely pure and never simple,'" I said.

"Mark Twain?"

"Oscar Wilde."

"Of course. It's good to have a new sparring partner. My father was an amazing man," she said with pride. Her comment endeared me to her and made me regret ever thinking of her as snarly. Erase that comment from all references.

"Why didn't Mac leave his property to you?"

"That would have been far too high a profile for my role, which I am quite comfortable in. I wholly supported his decision."

"You and Yankee are—"

"I was doubtful about you at first. Your attitude lacks refinement, a most underappreciated attribute. But Yankee and my father both insisted that was all stucco. They were right—that's between you and me, of course. I understand you found the magazine."

She must have the ability to listen to conversations in Yankee's—her husband's—office. I had an avalanche of questions but was oddly indifferent to them.

"Tell me about the magazine," I said.

"It is from the year of my birth. My father wanted to name me after Candice Bergen—she is on the cover. But my mother wouldn't hear of it. Constance was as close as she would allow."

"I'm sorry about your mother. I understand cancer took her at an early age."

"They had a beautiful marriage, cut cruelly short by her disease."

"Your father once told me, 'You only love once and just pretend to do it again.'"

She smiled, the memory of her father animating her face.

"His tidbits were always personalized to the person he was speaking to. What else did he impart on you?"

I recalled something else Mac had told me that had been of immense help. "'A man should never be afraid of his next step, or he will surely falter.'"

"And what is your next step, Mr. Travis?"

"I believe you want me to take the box."

"It is what you want that counts."

"It would be my pleasure."

"And your regret someday. For pleasure and regret are rarely out of sight of each other."

"I like my chances."

"As do we. Allow me to get the door for you."

I put the box in the back seat of the truck. As I drove away, it was either the beginning or the end, and I didn't know which and didn't care much.

ABOUT THE AUTHOR

 Robert Lane is the author of the Jake Travis stand-alone novels. *Florida Weekly* calls Jake Travis a "richly textured creation; one of the best leading men to take the thriller fiction stage in years." Lane's debut novel, *The Second Letter*, won the Gold Medal in the Independent Book Publishers Association's (IBPA's) 2015 Benjamin Franklin Awards for Best New Voice: Fiction. Lane resides on the west coast of Florida. Learn more at Robertlanebooks.com.

Receive a free copy of the Jake Travis series prequel, *Midnight on the Water*.

As much mystery as love story, *Midnight on the Water* is the saga of how Jake and Kathleen met, tumbled into love, and the drastic measures Jake, Morgan, and Garrett took to save Kathleen's life—and grant her a new identity. *Midnight on the Water* is available only to those on Robert Lane's mailing list. The newsletter contains book reviews across a wide range of genres, both fiction and nonfiction. It also includes updates and excerpts from the next Jake Travis novel.

Enjoy *Midnight on the Water.*

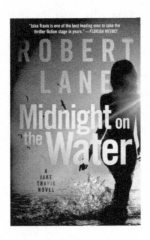

Also be sure to read these other stand-alone Jake Travis novels:

The Second Letter

Cooler Than Blood

The Cardinal's Sin

The Gail Force

Naked We Came

A Beautiful Voice

The Elizabeth Walker Affair

Visit Robert Lane's author page on Amazon.com:

Follow Robert Lane on: https://www.amazon.com/Robert-Lane/e/B00HZ2254A/

Facebook: https://www.facebook.com/RobertLaneBooks

Goodreads: https://www.goodreads.com/author/show/7790754.Robert_Lane

BookBub: https://www.bookbub.com/profile/robert-lane?list=about

Learn more and receive your free copy of *Midnight on the Water* at http://robertlanebooks.com

Made in the USA
Las Vegas, NV
04 February 2022

43136342R00173